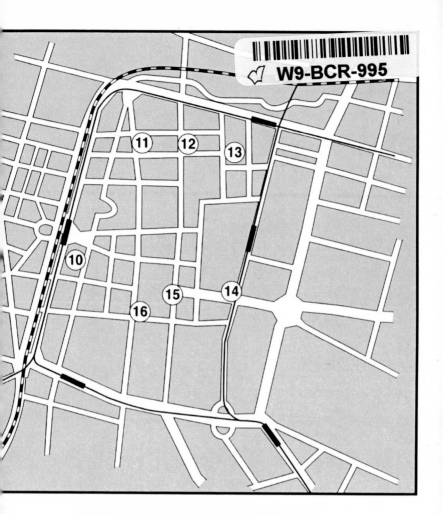

TAIPEI

THE OLD CAPITAL

Modern Chinese Literature from Taiwan

The Old Capital

A NOVEL OF TAIPEI

Chu T'ien-hsin

Translated from the Chinese
by Howard Goldblatt

COLUMBIA UNIVERSITY PRESS   NEW YORK

Columbia University Press wishes to express its appreciation for
assistance given by the Chiang Ching-kuo Foundation for International Scholarly Exchange and Council for Cultural Affairs in the
preparation of the translation and in the publication of this series.

Thanks to Tsai Chien-hsin for extensive research and translation
assistance in the preparation of the map.

COLUMBIA UNIVERSITY PRESS

Publishers Since 1893

New York   Chichester, West Sussex

Translation copyright © 2007 Columbia University Press

All rights reserved

Library of Congress Cataloging-in-Publication Data
Zhu, Tianxin.
[Gu du. English]
The old capital : a novel of Taipei / Chu T'ien-hsin ; translated
from the Chinese by Howard Goldblatt.
    p.   cm. — (Modern Chinese literature from Taiwan)
ISBN-13: 978-0-231-14112-3 (cloth : alk. paper)
ISBN-10: 0-231-14112-2 (cloth : alk. paper)
ISBN-13: 978-0-231-51181-0 (electronic)
ISBN-10: 0-231-51181-7 (electronic)
1. Zhu, Tianxin—Translations into English. I. Goldblatt, Howard.
II. Title. III. Series.
PL2852.T47G8213 2007
895.1'352—dc22
                                        2006027861

Columbia University Press books are printed on permanent and
durable acid-free paper.

This book was printed on paper with recycled content.
Printed in the United States of America

c 10 9 8 7 6 5 4 3

CONTENTS

Taiwan is like no other place in the world. One of a handful of countries shunned by the United Nations (the others are tyrannical pariahs), it is a democracy, the first in the history of Chinese society, a place where a lively, pluralistic, rich, and unrestrained culture flourishes and the standard of living is among the highest anywhere. And yet Taiwan (officially, the Republic of China) has no international standing. Its citizens live under the constant threat of invasion by China, which, like much of the rest of the world, considers it a "renegade province" that will invite military devastation if its government one day succumbs to the desires of most of its people by declaring independence. And, as in so many other developed countries, technological innovations, scientific advances, and rampant "globalization" outstrip the ability of the populace to comfortably deal with a rapidly changing national and social landscape.

Colonized by the Japanese for the first half of the twentieth century, Taiwan then sustained four decades of martial law during the regimes of the defeated Chinese general Chiang Kai-shek and his son, Chiang Ching-kuo. Linguistically, Taiwan functions, somewhat uncomfortably, with two mutually incomprehensible languages—Mandarin and Taiwanese—along with the widespread use of English and a smattering of other dialects and tribal languages. Since the late 1980s, writers, intellectuals, and artists have eagerly dug into the island's past, ancient and recent, in large part, as our author has written, in a "search for one's own country."

Chu T'ien-hsin, whose father fled to Taiwan from China with Chiang Kai-shek in 1949, sees two separate Taiwans, two distinct nations: one nationalistic, maintaining a closed-door policy in relation to the outside world; the other decidedly lyrical, cultural, philosophical. She proudly asserts that her work belongs to the second, that her writing comes closer (than politics) to revealing the true Taiwan. In truth, she writes not so much about Taiwan, with its 20-some-odd million inhabitants and half a dozen large cities, but about the northern city of Taipei—the capital, the base of the once dominant Kuomintang, and the center of commerce. Residents of central and southern Taiwan might wonder if the true division of the country is Taipei and everywhere else.

In the four stories that lead off this collection, three of which take their titles and, to a large extent, their thematic focus from movies and/or novels, Chu explores aspects of life in late twentieth-century Taiwan that will resonate with readers elsewhere, if not in their particularities, then certainly in their universal applications in modern life—philosophically, artistically, psychologically, and practically. The varied narrators share sensibilities, in spite of shifting gender and occupation, and reveal a sensual environment made compelling by detailed descriptions, with occasional tie-ins to the outside world of Marx, de Beers, and Adam Smith.

But it is the novella "The Old Capital," a deeply layered, intertextual masterpiece, that both mystifies and gratifies the attentive reader. The narrator's reflections "repeatedly return to the contrast between a serenely perennial Kyoto and a catastrophic Taipei rendered uninhabitable by amnesiac modernization and persistent cultural impoverishment." On the surface it is a simple story: the narrator travels to Kyoto to meet a friend who doesn't show, then returns to Taipei, where she is mistaken for a Japanese tourist and revisits the sites of her youth with the help of a Japanese map of the city. Memory—lost, recaptured, imperfect, imagined—and nostalgia are at the heart of the tale, which is carried along by the shifting use of Chinese and Japanese place names and inhabited by portions of other works—Yasunari Kawabata's 1962 novel *Koto* (*The Old Capital*), the fifth-century fable "Peach Blossom Spring" by Tao Yuanming, and *A Comprehensive History of Taiwan*. The past, distant and near, informs a growing angst, as the narrator, like many of her real-life contemporaries in Taiwan, seeks a personal and, by extension, national identity.

A liberal use of English and the Chinese phonetic alphabet in the Chinese original has not been carried over in any fashion in this translation. The integrated outside texts are denoted by asterisks or italics (no distinction is made in the Chinese original). The translator has been notably aided in his task by the financial support of the Chiang Ching-kuo Foundation for International Scholarly Communication, by the author's responses to the most opaque references and usages, by two extremely helpful and encouraging anonymous readers, and, most importantly, by the sharp eye, creative artistry, and smiling countenance (as she wielded her red pen) of Sylvia Li-chun Lin.

THE OLD CAPITAL

DEATH IN VENICE

Hey—don't worry, nobody dies and nothing happens.

No Thomas Mann, no Visconti, not even a formal link to the real Venice.

Why do I say "the real Venice"?

Known to us all, the real Venice is a water-bound city in the northeast corner of Italy that happens to be slowly sinking into the sea. A few years back, thanks to a generous literary prize that markedly improved my financial situation, I signed on to a fourteen-day best-of-Europe tour with my aged father and mother, and duly tramped along. I use the word "tramped" rather than "roamed" or "traveled" because, first, in regard to the word "roam," a fellow writer and her imitators have used it to death, and second, I lingered there for one measly day, didn't even spend the night, and in the four or five hours that remained after subtracting the tedious business of eating, I entrusted my father and mother to the tour guide and, map in hand, took in every bridge, every lane in the city, never resting and not leaving any time to visit a single shop to admire the traditional glassblowing arts of elderly craftsmen; didn't even surrender to the temptation to sit at one of the sidewalk cafés, each lovelier than the next. I actually forced myself to race through a marketplace teeming with strange flowers and unusual fruits, with women shouting to me to buy their offerings, like a de Sica movie, and I was relieved to learn that St. Mark's Basilica, which every tourist is obliged to visit, was undergoing one of those renovations that come along every few decades, which allowed me to pass it by with no feelings of unease and, in the process, squeeze out another precious hour.

At dusk, feeling confused and harried, I paced up and down a ferry landing from where the Bridge of Sighs was well within sight, incapable of generating any sympathy for condemned prisoners of an earlier age who had to cross the bridge on their way to the execution ground. Enrapt, I gazed out at the Adriatic, rippling in the dying rays of sunlight, and at the spot where the sky met the water, tiny Lido Island—where the annual Venice Film Festival is held, a sacred place for me, someone who grew up infatuated with master filmmakers—which at that moment sent its light to me from afar. At no other moment on this earth had so little distance separated us, and I dejectedly calculated the time once more, concluding that unless I left the tour altogether or some frenzied confusion broke out, there would not be enough time to get there and back.

And so, shuffling my frustrated feet along, I walked across the Bridge of Sighs like one of those condemned prisoners, without neglecting the practical obligation of buying five cheap plaster imitations of ancient wood carvings as gifts for the editorial girl whose job it was to pressure me for manuscripts.

Would you consider something like that worthy of the term "travel"?

I realize that opting for the word "tramped" to describe my experience might actually be a bit elegant, since I covered most of Venice as if I were on a forced march, just so I could say—to whom, I have no idea—I tramp, therefore I am, something as laughably foolish as the dog piss and cat turds you can find on any street corner.

That, then, is the sum total of my connection to the real Venice.

Does it then follow that there is another Venice?

Yes.

But that is a long story.

And it all begins with my return to Taipei.

Two years before returning, I took the prize money I'd won in a novella contest sponsored by a major newspaper and the paltry few thousand NT in my bank account and went to a spot on the eastern seaboard to live for two years. The place—nope, that's wrong!—was neither Yanliao, where the reclusive naturalist Meng Dongli lived, nor the Yilan town of Zhang Guixing, but a place between the two, a tiny spot on the Northern Rail Line, in a house a friend lent me without charge. During boom times you might call it a summer cottage, but now it was little more than a dilapidated beach house, like all the virtually identical neighboring structures, seldom if ever visited by their owners, the state of disrepair on a par with that of houses gutted in fires or blown apart in explosions.

I was ready to pack up and go home six months after moving in, a betrayal of the vow I'd taken before setting out, which was to live out my life there as a hermit, maybe even marry a mountain girl, and no, I hadn't run out of money, it wasn't my old bugaboo, finances, that caused it, nor that I'd reached sudden enlightenment or, even less grandiose, that I was suffering unbearable loneliness, nothing like that . . . I just didn't know how to pass the time.

I must have lacked my predecessor Meng Dongli's philosophy of life and did not possess the plans, the necessary survival skills, or the temperament for living a self-sustaining life in humble surroundings; neither was I invested with the depth of interest of Thoreau when he was observing the ecology of Walden Pond. I didn't even feel like opening the books or magazines I'd brought along or that my friends constantly sent from Taipei. I just let them pile up. They were no good as pillows or kindling, and my feeling toward them was that, at a time like this, having so many passionate or thoughtful or contentious words around was the act of an animal called imbecile.

As a result, I had too much time on my hands.

Most of the time, I just sat in the doorway all morning, soaking up the sun and laboriously picking the remains of breakfast from my teeth, like a cow chewing her cud, then minutely and gently cleaning my ears, picking my nose, and then moving on to my other orifices and crevices; on more than one occasion I had to stop myself from licking my paws after hallucinating that I was a big, lazy cat. . . . Sometime before noon the morning express train announced its speedy arrival, the whistle bringing an increasing sense of joy, much like that of bygone residents of little towns who waved and shouted innocently and good-naturedly at the daily train that never deigned to stop at their out-of-the-way spot.

During my last six months there, the magnitude of my frenzy grew increasingly absurd (viewed in retrospect). There were nights when typhoons knocked out the power and, since I couldn't sleep, I sat by a lit candle and reacted to every strange sound as if a malign ghost or someone who had sneaked into Taiwan from the mainland was coming for me, and as a result I actually wrote a story a là Stephen King. In the tranquil days that followed, I heard that a mountain torrent had swept down, carrying traces of gold, half a mile from where I was staying, at a spot where the river met the sea. Many amateur prospectors (including some from western Taiwan) came, and you can imagine what it was like having hundreds, maybe thousands of people converging on a riverside sandbar normally inhabited only by sandpipers and twisted driftwood, plus the occasional plastic soft-drink bottle thrown from a passing train (it all bore a striking resemblance to mediocre installation art). A true postmodern moment.

But rather than mock the scene, I inserted myself in it, pretending to be obsessed with finding gold while actually spying on these humanoids, who uttered human language, barely resisting the impulse to attack them when they weren't expecting it. By "attack" I mean jumping onto their backs as they bent over and, gaining the upper hand, quickly wrestling them to the ground, like during winters in primary school, when we'd wrestle each other after class, a foolish but eminently enjoyable way to pass the time while soaking up sun in the hallway.

The gold-digging frenzy lasted about a week. The prospectors took all the twisted driftwood away with them, and I was left with a sandbar deserted but for the sandpipers; so I sat there, as if sketching a still life, and in half a day, wrote a story. That story would be selected as a finalist in a short-story contest, and during the deliberations, Mr. A, a judge who favored it, would call it "a successful satirical allegory on money games in contemporary Taiwan." Mr. B, who disagreed with him, pointed out that it was cribbed from Nobel laureate Gabriel García Márquez's magic realism, pointing out that the river in the story was none other than the nameless river, with all its prehistoric boulders, that ran outside the town of Macondo in *One Hundred Years of Solitude*. Ms. C, another judge, insisted that the great river was not necessarily a real river at all, could in fact be the source of dreams running through people's lives, a river of faith. Mr. D did not vote for any of the finalists; instead he railed against the Taiwan he'd been away from for a dozen years or so as vulgar and corrupt, and incredibly degenerate. Mr. E, a good friend of mine, found quibbling faults with every story and, if my understanding of him is correct, read only the first and last pages of each; but in the end he voted for my story, which proves that he hadn't spotted it as one of mine.

The story did not win a prize, but my publisher submitted a collection of my stories, *Notes from a Melon Patch*, for that year's annual best fiction award, and it received the Jury Prize (which paid for the trip to Europe with my aged parents); all the judges either expressed or affirmed or admired or yearned for the contemporary significance of my hermitlike coastal stay.

I'm not sure what role this affirmation of my literary accomplishments played in the awarding of the prize, but it certainly delayed my plans to return to Taipei. You know, people started coming all the way from Taipei to see me, including old friends, strangers, college students, newspaper and magazine reporters, environmentalists, as well as a bunch of lunatics who don't fit into any category. Most of the time I sent them home satisfied by describing for them my daily routine, including the early morning strolls through the watermelon patch; by showing them the spot at the mouth of the river where the gold-prospecting frenzy had taken place; by taking them bird-watching; and, finally, by helping them carry pieces of twisted driftwood they'd collected to the train.

In some respects I'm an old-fashioned person. If someone wants to give me a prize for my lifestyle (as my fellow writer, the German Günter Grass, said, "What they want is gods, or heroes, and what I write about is people"), I cannot immediately or publicly destroy their myth.

Ultimately, I did return to Taipei. For reasons I've already given, plus the fact that my younger brothers and sisters had all married and moved away, leaving me the only sibling without a mate or a place of my own, I could find no excuse not to move back in with my aged parents, so we could all look after one another.

In the days that followed, I chose to live a cloistered

urban life. Even though the editor of a newspaper literary supplement whose stockholders could not decide whether to pull their money out or put more in and a publishing house with annual sales in the range of a hundred million NT both offered me jobs, I made the easy decision to try my luck as a full-time writer. Undeniably, the fact that my parents, who lived on pensions, made sure I always had a place to call home and didn't have to worry about going hungry figured significantly, but more important, since quitting my last regular job several years before, I believe that a writer is in the prime of his professional life between the ages of thirty-five and forty-five, and even though it had been really, really hard, I'd managed to reach that point in my life, so how could I hand the essence of my prime years over to someone else and earn a living by working for others?

Do you think I'm superstitious, that I'm spouting nonsense?

There are grounds for my belief. Based upon the results of my own small-scale survey, important works by important writers have, throughout the history of literature, been completed when the authors were between the ages of thirty-five and forty-five; not only that, in the years that followed, whether the writers threw themselves into their work or simply took it easy, the difference in the quality of their writing was minuscule. Take, for example, García Márquez, whose work I was accused of cribbing. His *One Hundred Years of Solitude* was written when he was thirty-six and thirty-seven years old. After that, I heard that he never rested on his laurels or was self-satisfied; no, he kept writing and, along the way, won the Nobel Prize, and yet, eighteen years later, his novel *Love in the Time of Cholera* shocked readers, who wondered why his writing hadn't improved or, more surprising, hadn't worsened.

Honestly speaking, that's depressing.

But that, after all, doesn't happen until after middle age.

The sort of conclusion I normally favor is this: from the time they leave school until they reach the age of thirty-five, the writers are out having a good time, involved in trivial jobs like bookstore clerk, telegraph operator, small local newspaper reporter . . . from time to time producing immature writing, avoiding the sorts of things that occupy other people of the same age, such as marriage. Americans hang out in Paris or enjoy themselves in the Far East; Europeans trot off to the Soviet Union or Africa; Latin Americans hoof it over Spain; Spanish make their way to Mexico. . . .

Keeping this in mind, are you still surprised to learn that, at an age when most people are hard at work, I just took it easy and had a good time? Of course, compared to the lives of great masters before they became great masters, mine might seem excessively moral and overly cautious. You know, I'm a lot like many creative artists, in that I strongly believe (and put the belief into practice) that moral decadence is often a breeding ground for great literature.

But in any case, that was my attitude when I returned to Taipei.

After being away from my fellow writers for two years, I discovered that half of them were studying Buddhist meditation, while the remainder were in either real estate or the stock market, and in contrast with the complex and diverse motivations of the former, those of the latter were remarkably simple. After making a hundred million or so in the market, one of them, a woman some years older than I, discovered what it was like to live in the lap of luxury and move in new social circles, raw material for a series of novels in which she attacked Taiwanese capitalists for knowing only how to make money, not how to respect culture (like spending hundreds of thousands on an antique from an ancient dynasty, only to learn that it's a fake; or being ignorant of British high tea—the tea service, the accompanying snacks, and the proper etiquette;

or making spectacles of themselves through hideous buying sprees in New York and Paris, yet being unwilling to buy pieds-à-terre in which to spend their holidays so they can enjoy leisurely visits to museums and be entertained by street artists and performers . . .).

There were, of course, people outside these two categories, writers whose situation and lifestyle were similar to mine, but they were viewed as short-circuited rarities.

I cannot say why those writers did not take up Buddhism or join the money game, but I had parents who were honest public servants of an earlier generation and who had missed out on a previous redistribution of wealth when the economy took off, while I spent two years living in a melon field, and thereby lost a golden opportunity during Taiwan's gigantic—and most likely last—millionaires' game; as Marx wrote, "We have nothing to lose but our chains." In my case, rising up in revolution would have been easier than making some real money, and far more likely to succeed.

Buddhist meditation? That was simple, since I felt I didn't "have" enough, so far from enough, in fact, that it took a lot for me to give up anything, whether it was money, knowledge, wisdom, or worries.

Who was it who said, "Thank God I'm an atheist"?

And then, slowly but surely, I began to enjoy the fruits of a period of peak production.

In the manner of so many writers, ancient and modern, Chinese and foreign, I was in the habit of writing in coffee shops. I'm not sure why that is the case with other writers, nor do I necessarily approve; one of the reasons I heard involved a woman who complained that there were too many snacking opportunities at home, too soft a bed, and too many fun-loving kids. Others took the high road, saying that being away from home and alone kept them from calling upon their illustrious predecessors, whose works filled their bookshelves, when words simply wouldn't come. A reason with even more positive significance was that a coffee shop is a microcosm of society at large, and offers the writer a platform from which to observe and eavesdrop on people. There were even some whose sole motivation was to emulate Balzac, who claimed that the muse came to him only after he'd finished off ten or more cups of coffee. . . .

My reason was simplicity itself: I went to a coffee shop and wrote from nine to five each day to spare my aged mother, who had never accepted my career choice, from having to explain to neighbors what it was I did for a living.

During this period I completed several pieces, just as I'd hoped, and the reviews that followed publication of the collection were pretty good; while not all the critics agreed in every respect, they were positive, even going so far as to praise my subject matter as rich and diverse.

To be honest, that upset me, since none of the stories developed or concluded in line with my original conception, and even the so-called messages were lost. Here, in simplest terms, is how my writing style developed and took form: a coffee shop atmosphere dictated the style of each story. Thus I could only blame the fact that I hadn't found the right coffee shop.

How's that? you ask. ·

I'll give you an example: my revered elder, Meng Dong-li, was the inspiration for one of the stories, in which I'd planned to exploit the rare opportunity of spending two years on the coast to describe the soul-searching and thoughts of a committed environmentalist about present-day Taiwan.

That should not have been difficult, at least not from my standpoint and with the materials at my disposal. The problem—can you believe this?—is that I walked into the wrong coffee shop!

I walked into the wrong coffee shop (obviously, I only realized this afterward), although, as coffee shops go, it wasn't bad, one that appealed to popular tastes, a place where the servers were trained in the Japanese attitude of treating customers like royalty, where the prices were reasonable, and where you got unlimited refills, which meant you could work there all day if you felt like it. . . . So what was the problem?

At first, it was the endless howls from cell phones, I think. That has pretty much been the case the past couple of years, hasn't it? It used to be pagers; now it's mobile phones, whose owners are invariably men who can't even drink a cup of coffee without trying to look incredibly busy, heavy key rings hanging from their belts, like prison guards. From the start, my protagonist was unwilling to follow my design, choosing instead to leave his hometown and move to Taipei, insisting upon becoming a media correspondent.

And then, well, I don't want to place all the blame on the coffee shop, but with so many lovely Taipei girls—so enchanting, so fashionable—entering and leaving the place, I just had to find my protagonist a fetching companion, in line with the biblical saying that God would not want him to live alone. My protagonist enthusiastically accepted his companion without a murmur, even made eager advances in an inappropriate place. That's the sort of person he was, to my surprise, which made it necessary to stop work for two days in order to cool down their ardor and, at the same time, figure out what to do with his female companion, whether or not to let her play an introspective role so as to make him a stronger character; and if not, wouldn't I be abandoning my original idea for the story?

On the day I got back to work, all they played in the coffee shop all day long were songs by Elvis, who'd been dead nearly fifteen years (most likely the music choice was prompted by the box office success of several recent movies set in the 1960s, and the nostalgic feelings they evoked); as a result, my protagonist dragged my spotty knowledge of the '60s into the story, like a pile of garbage: he earned a degree from Berkeley, after which he and his girlfriend had sex anywhere they pleased, like a couple of potheads, imagining themselves "flower children" of that earlier time, and, owing to a sense of melancholy over the constant rupture between reality and ideals, he dragged out Karl Popper, Herbert Marcuse, and some other scholars I neither knew well nor particularly liked (which cost me two days, as I leafed through reference books and did some research to seek help from and create a dialogue with them).

Once the piece was finished (that is, when I'd written 11,900 words, in line with the editor's demand that I was not to exceed that length, so he could publish it in two installments in the literary supplement), he fawningly repeated to college students who were listening to him lecture, "Never, ever trust anyone over thirty!" It would have been easy to describe the students' reaction, but I laid down my pen and brooded, sensing that I'd been the target of his rebuke, that in his eyes I was a worthless old papa-san.

I could trot out more examples like this. For instance, I later moved to another coffee shop, one done up in standard British style, with floors, chairs, and tables made of heavy coffee-colored sandalwood and covered with Belgian lace tablecloths; wallpaper with an intricate rosebush design; and framed antique botanical drawings that looked as if they'd been cut out of Carl von Linné's illustrated book of plants. British bone china and handblown, colored, Mediterranean-style drinking glasses were laid out, and in one corner stood a large temperate-zone plant in a green ceramic vase; lush English ivy climbed the outside of the greenhouse windows, capturing the feel of the house where Shakespeare lived. . . .

So elegant, so Victorian a coffee shop that I finished a story without a hitch (the high prices made it necessary to shorten my workday), one that surprised even me. In it I described the homoerotic feelings of two men, with veiled refinement, in stark contrast to the naked descriptions of the same material by my fellow writers. Not long after that a liberal arts student innocently revealed in an interview that my story reminded her of E. M. Forster's *A Room with a View* and *Maurice*. I immediately knew why.

After that I frequented a coffee shop with decades of history, run by an old Shanghai fellow, and I was surprised to find it crowded with immaculately decked-out elderly patrons with fancy canes, who conversed in loud Shanghainese when they weren't reading a newspaper. After a couple of days, I knew how to say "money" and "me" in Shanghainese, just like a native. But what really caught my attention were their refined table manners and the liberal way they spent money. Some of the regulars treated the place as if it were their own drawing room. Throughout the afternoon they'd entertain guests, not at all like most conservative, frugal retirees.

Slowly I picked up some threads of conversation—at first I didn't try, feeling it was immoral to eavesdrop on neighboring tables while writing in a coffee shop, and maybe the reason they were nearly shouting was that they were hard of hearing—learning that their children and grandchildren all seemed to be involved in prostitution or gambling, or shady business deals, and that was all they could talk about, no matter how sad or how angry it made them, or whether they were talking to each other or to grandchildren who had returned from America or Canada and could only speak English, or to their middle-aged housekeepers. . . .

Before long, I learned that the unworthy sons and grandsons they spoke about were Lee Teng-hui, James Soong, Hau Po-tsun, and other leading comrades of the KMT, and I wondered what gave these old folks the right to talk about national affairs as if they were family matters and treat senior officials as if they were their own sons and grandsons, until it became clear that they were elderly national representatives who would be forced into retirement at year's end.

You can probably guess what happened next: my story, the progress of which had been taken out of my hands, was hijacked by those men and became a stage on which they could act out their absurd dramas.

Are you still surprised that critics applauded this story as a successful parody of Pai Hsien-yung's melancholy classic tales of survivors of a bygone era?

At this juncture, I must unambiguously state that I have no desire to mock conscientious readers or critics of fiction, but I feel obliged to point out that the coming together of what a reader believes is a well-knit or self-ordained structure is in fact completely open, unknowable, infinitely variable, and filled with risks; most of the time, it doesn't follow the person's (author's) will. Naturally, I still believe there are plenty of authors who can efficiently create works in which their will penetrates every page.

Take us—okay, me—for instance (I prefer not to impinge upon the rights of others to explain the act of creation): when I'm writing, the tiniest factor can enter the process and cause a dramatic shift, such as the need for the hero and heroine of my story to take a trip, and I considered sending them—it seemed perfectly natural to me—to Kending Park or Yilan's Dongshan River; of course, the potential for development in the latter spot was much greater, but just then, a naïve, idiotic campus song I loathed started playing in the coffee shop, and, regrettably, unleashed a flood of memories of traveling on the highway during my army days in a gypsy bus, my ears assaulted by "Say, girl, why are you crying, is it something unpleasant you're hiding?" and of the day I took off from work to wander alone in Qijin instead of returning to Taipei, after breaking up with the disconsolate girl, so my hero and heroine did not go to the Dongshan River and definitely did not go to Kending, but went to Qijin instead!

From there I adroitly let them take in the sights of Qijin in roughly 3,000 words, until another challenge surfaced: I didn't know if they should break up or keep on as they were or maybe even get married (unlike so many of my fellow writers, I take no pleasure in manipulating my characters' fate).

So I put the story aside for several days, during which I attended a symposium sponsored by a consumer rights group, discussed career planning for teenagers with the host of a certain TV show, took my nephew to the Mucha Zoo to see the butterfly collection and nocturnal animal exhibit, and, most important, read *Norwegian Woods*, a so-so novel by the Japanese writer Murakami Haruki. That night, I couldn't resist the singular impulse to work at home. My hero and heroine made mad passionate love, her boldness leaving me speechless. You know, they were in such good physical condition they went at it all night long, without letup, and it took more than 2,000 words to describe every detail of their lovemaking, including how their genitals looked and performed.

Just because I've volunteered all this information doesn't mean I'm trying to make the case that creative writing is unscientific, irrational, perhaps even somewhat idiotic, although, in the eyes of some people (Freud, for one), writers and the mentally ill fall into the same category.

I believe that creativity is a riddle far more mysterious and difficult to understand than any mental illness. One moment, the power of creation takes hold of you like a tropical fever; the next, it abandons you for no good reason and vanishes without a trace, refusing to return, even in the face of diligence or anticipation. Look through art yearbooks. How many writers, artists, or dramatists who were considered that year's most important produced nothing more, not even garbage, over the next two or three years, or, for some, the next few decades?

If we calmly accept this fact, then maybe Jung's comment won't be so hard to understand: "Faust was not created by Goethe, Goethe was created by Faust."

Jung, a proponent of the so-called collective unconscious, considered writers' invented fantasies to be not a substitute for reality, but a sort of primordial human experience born in antiquity. All other people either avoid it out of fear or protect themselves with the shield of science or the armor of reason, while writers explore it, confront it, convert it into a kind of living experience of reality. He who can transform it into the consciousness of his age can then lead and shape the subconscious spiritual life of all humanity.

No wonder William Blake said, "Every poet takes part in the Devil's party."

Are we then to be shocked by Rilke, who suffered great spiritual pain and underwent a period of psychotherapy, when he said, "If my demons were to leave me, I'm afraid my angels too would fly away"?

And as Picasso said, "All creations are, at first, destructions."

And Degas said, "The feelings of a painter, when he is painting, are the same as a sinner, when he is sinning."

The comments by the latter two are relatively easy to comprehend, for they both held the view, independently, that all creation implies the imminent destruction of the old order.

While I'm not ashamed to be seen as being on a par with the mentally ill (some people believe that artists and the mentally ill are humanity's spiritual radar stations, that, because of their elusive primal vitality, they have a keener sense than normal people of the imminent unraveling and collapse of the existing social order), I'm willing to accept psychologist Rollo May's distinction, when he says that artistic creations are like a river, with primal vitality as its water, and consciousness the banks that guide it in a certain direction. The riverbanks of consciousness help artists direct primal vitality to territories in need of development by using special "forms" (such as the sonnet, seven-character regulated poetry, a lengthy novel, or a quarto canvas); the mentally ill, on the other hand, are "rivers without banks" whose barriers of consciousness have disintegrated. Their primal vitality or subconscious flows irretrievably in all directions and becomes an "unending dream."

André Gide held a similar view, contending that a masterpiece originates from madness and ends with rationality.

I guess I ought to put it in my own words.

I believe that artists conquer primal vitality and the mentally ill succumb to it. It's as simple as that, and as merciless.

And so, I cannot avoid being weighed down by an anxiety, a fear that I'm swimming in a river without banks, asleep in an unending dream.

Distracted, I'm forced to confront my sonnet, my quatrain, a piece of canvas, and a lump of potter's clay. . . .

I spent most of my time searching for a suitable coffee shop, in the grip of a superstitious belief that a coffee shop with a distinctive style would seize and determine the style of my story or my book. You know, in recent years, there's been an explosion of coffee shops in Taipei's streets and lanes. To be competitive, they strive to create a unique image, through décor, menu, and background music. I once sat in a little shop, surrounded by rag dolls, while the owner, Mama X, in a white apron, baked gingerbread and almond cookies. I looked down at the milky white pottery cups and plates on a tablecloth with cats and dogs and little bears, trying hard not to imitate a friend and fellow writer who had turned to writing fairy tales in his forties.

Sometimes I feel like I'm in a greenhouse, trapped beneath a pair of lush Sichuan plane trees. A profusion of dry flowers and leaves hangs from the windowless walls, emitting the smell of mummies, and I'm forced to drink an alpine herbal tea recommended by the owner's daughter, who is made up like a witch, and I discover that what I really wanted to write has already been written by a fellow writer, a woman. Have you read it? Hotly debated last year in literary circles, it's about a reclusive twenty-five-year-old woman, haggard as an old nun, who lives in a little penthouse apartment that has the feel of this particular coffee shop. All day long she dries medicinal herbs, makes strange tea, and gazes at the sunsets and the city skyline. It's the most terrifying story I've read in recent years.

I also haunted a postmodern coffee shop, made frigid by air conditioning, the exposed pipes and wires along the ceiling looking like a mass of internal organs, where the servers' faces and actions were cold and robotic. I made absolutely no progress and felt as if I were engaged in an inappropriate and utterly pathetic endeavor.

Things dragged on like that until the end of summer, when I'd fallen seriously behind, already six months past the deadline for submission of the manuscript I'd promised a certain publisher. I tried writing in one particular coffee shop, and it went well. Not at all distinctive, the shop was located in a third-floor corner of a popular department store, and only someone looking for the toilet or a public telephone would likely discover it (I stumbled upon it during a family banquet on the fourth floor, when I took my nephew downstairs to the toilet). There was no music. One of the walls was made of cold stainless steel that glinted like a knife blade; two others were of colorless, transparent, frameless, floor-to-ceiling glass—I guess no one with acrophobia would dare sit next to one of those—and the last was white plaster decorated with wheat stalks, like those you see in southern Europe. The floor was oak, simple, unspectacular, the same material as the simple chairs. The whole place, you could say, was a hodgepodge.

There were only seven or eight tables, and except for mealtimes, I had the place pretty much to myself, which is why I never felt uneasy about sitting there a long time. Another attraction was that the cold windows drained warmth from the hardwood floor, and the stainless steel crushed the wheat stalk–enhanced white plaster wall, imbued with the mythical aura of ancient Greece and Rome. At last I'd found a spot free of disturbances from my surroundings.

Most important of all, the shop's name—Venice—made it easy to find a title for my story: "Death in Venice" (I frequently have trouble naming my stories, even after they're finished, and a couple of times I had to ask the literary page editor to give me a title, unprofessional as that sounds).

"Death in Venice." . . . Now what to write about?

Neither Visconti's film nor Thomas Mann's novella offered even the tiniest element.

Element?

Want to know the professional secret of my creations?

With some of my fellow writers, the beginning of creation is a bit like putting predetermined material onto an assembly line, and at the end of a quality-controlled production process, what comes out is precisely what was expected—no worse, but no better. For some, that apparatus is like a printing press for cash, the envy of many. But for me, literary creation is increasingly analogous to a chemistry experiment. I dump in all the elements my intuition tells me are necessary, but what sort of chemical reaction, what product will result (gold or shit), I neither know nor wish to control. And even the danger I occasionally sense is not something I try to avoid. That's because it is the unpredictable, the unknowable that I find particularly intriguing.

The elements themselves are even harder to explain. Why, for instance, choose A and discard B? Why take pains to search for C? Why should D, a jewel in the eyes of others (maybe a conclusion born of professional knowledge, or a rare and peculiar life experience, or uniquely insightful observations) become utterly useless? Why spend ten years, or twenty, or even a lifetime waiting for E to appear, as if its absence makes progress impossible? There are times when you've prepared the necessary elements and lack only a flash, a spark, the simplest action, a nice day, a special mood, a scent (just think about rich memories of burning coal or Star Cologne) . . . maybe it's what people who have had no creative experience call "inspiration."

It's been my experience that while the experiment (writing) requires anywhere from a couple of days to half a month, the selection of elements may require nothing more than looking up a word in a dictionary or, as I said earlier, may take ten years, even a lifetime. Most of the time, I feel like a scavenger— Let me interrupt myself here. Have you read the first chapter of García Márquez's *One Hundred Years of Solitude*? A gypsy magician sells the protagonist two magnetized ingots, claiming that if he walks over a spot where gold or treasures are hidden, they will draw the items out. The master walks down the street with them and, as promised, the ingots draw out pieces of scrap metal, including a sixteenth-century suit of armor.

That's it! Writers who create the way we do are just like that, always thinking, always searching as we drag a magnet behind us, walking alone through cities and the wilderness, down every block and around every corner of a long life.

And usually the treasures we seek and find are trash in the eyes of others. Given that the things we care about are so different, is it any wonder that we are unproductive, that making a living isn't as important to us as it is to most people?

With "Death in Venice" I began another seemingly endless dream.

I decided to engage an earlier me in a dialogue. The story would be in the form of correspondence between two old friends (one in Taipei, the other traveling in Venice), both nearing middle age. It would be built around a dialogue in letters, some light and airy, some serious, between the me of today and the me who, several years before, had spent all of one day tramping through Venice.

The writing progressed smoothly (though I only wrote a thousand words a day, slower than my normal pace), but there was no ending in sight. You know, sometimes you can finish a story in four or five days, yet you never feel it's going the way you want it to, which was the opposite of what I felt with this one.

Before long, I discovered that that was what I had in mind. At first I really enjoyed this particular coffee shop, since it didn't influence me one way or the other, good or bad, and I was perfectly satisfied with the shop's one daytime waitress, who dressed like a Japanese office lady and courteously and ceremoniously supplied me with tea, but otherwise left me alone (in more prosperous times I might have asked her to marry me). Most important, however, I got caught up in the correspondence between the two old friends, and in the second letter, a good friend from my youth, whom I hadn't thought of for years, not only popped up in my draft but actually snatched away the character traveling in Venice (let's call him A). Because his sometimes absurd, sometimes melancholy tone fit my plans perfectly, I gave him free rein and concentrated on the thoughts of the narrator, B. As the novel progressed, I began to care a great deal about and look forward to A's letters from Venice.

Normally, my working hours are limited and ordered. I spend more than half the time reading newspapers and magazines I've brought along, occasionally, and reluctantly, agreeing to an interview or two, and sometimes embarrassingly lost in a fog. On any given day, I probably devote no more than a couple of hours to the actual writing; when I sense that it's time to quit, I go to the department store supermarket, buy some fruit and milk, and take it home, where I effortlessly put my writing aside. And I rest both days of the weekend, even if I've stopped at a climactic moment in the story's progress, never curious about what the next hundred words or a sudden and dramatic turn of events will bring.

But the expectation of receiving letters from A broke a writing practice I'd formed over many years. I wrote from autumn into winter, the season that frightened me the most. Dressing in heavy winter clothes, I reported to Venice early each morning and didn't go home until late in the evening. I even wrote on New Year's Eve until asked to leave so they could close up early, at six o'clock.

Winter was on its way out, and there were no signs of an ending to the story. I loved the back-and-forth conversation between these two old friends, loved and envied it, and I could find no reason to bring it to a close. Besides, I treasured, however vicariously, the opportunity to reconnect with my youthful friend, particularly since he spoke to me honestly in the story (though we'd both lived in Taipei for years, we managed to see each other no more than once or twice a year, and chatted about nothing special when we did, since I wasn't interested in his circle of friends, nor he in mine). Truth is, I was shocked to discover his feelings and lifestyle during all the years we'd been living separate lives, and I read with great seriousness what, in the role of the fictional character A, he said he'd seen and heard in his travels in Venice. His curious and idiosyncratic view of things brought me enjoyment, even a sense . . . a sense of . . . well-being.

I couldn't bear to bring that to an end.

And so I dreamed up an odd assortment of obstacles for myself. For instance, cracks began to show in the life and mood of B, a busy and successful old yuppie, as a result of A's letters. He lost interest in everything; after a stressful lunch date, without telling anyone where he was going, he took off to a small coffee shop, where business was slow, and just sat there, waiting for another letter from his friend A in Venice.

I described the coffee shop in a few hundred words, using Venice as the model, but leaving out the incongruous stainless steel wall and the two walls with tall windows that faced the street. Then I hit a snag. I needed to select a painting to hang on the southern European-style plaster wall with the wheat stalks. Maybe this was to be the element I referred to earlier, the catalyst that could initiate a brilliant and dramatic experimental process and outcome, even if, in the eyes of the reader, it lasted only a second, perhaps a single sentence.

One by Paul Klee seemed most appropriate, since I'd seen his paintings in plenty of coffee shops and hotel rooms abroad. But . . . too ordinary for my purposes, not significant enough. How about Van Gogh? In the wake of the centennial anniversary of his death a couple of years earlier, he'd become too popular, too commonplace. So how about Dali? Sorry, I couldn't come up with a lengthy, rich, and interesting description of his *Persistance de la Mémoire* or his views on excrement. Klimt? His works fit the *fin-de-siècle* decadence I was looking for, but they were too precise, short on nuance. So what about Renoir's *Ball at the Moulin de la Galette*? I'd seen it in other coffee shops, and the joyous ambience it conveyed contrasted well with B's despondence, but the thought of how this so closely followed the ABCs of writing made me take it down.

Why not simply go with the eighteenth-century *Venetian Lagoon* by Guardi that hung amid the wheat stalks on the wall of my Venice coffee shop? Often it's the simplest and most common object that contains the deepest significance.

Then, while I was agonizing over the choice of a painting, without my permission, A took a few days out of his schedule to visit Fellini's birthplace of Rimini, and as a result, I dug out some Fellini movies and watched them again in order to understand the letters he sent from Rimini. I was frantic that, on an impulse, he'd visit nearby Ravenna, because then I supposed I'd have to dig out

Dante's *Divine Comedy*, which I hadn't read since college, to refresh my memory.

He went to Florence!

Reluctantly, I started gathering up Renaissance histories, art books, works on architecture and gardens, religion, and so on. I was poring over a history of the Medicis with mounting interest and excitement when, after only two days in Florence, A was on the move again, without writing about painting (just think, Michelangelo and Da Vinci, and Titian); without mentioning the statue of David, with its coat of pigeon droppings; without visiting St. Florence's Basilica, which is on everyone's itinerary (I'd planned to talk about the building's architect, Brunelleschi); he didn't even go to the Arno River, outside the city, which served as a backdrop for *A Room with a View*, which would have given him something to write about. He went only to the old marketplace, lingering there a good part of the day and buying a handcrafted leather backpack. Other than that, all he did was complain about the Florentines, who seem so sophisticated and worldly but are actually quite pretentious, like the people of Kyoto.

I was speechless when I read his letter, fearing he'd get the bug to visit the island of Sicily or Pisa or the little town of Urbino, where Raphael was born. . . . I couldn't figure out why A was always so incurably despondent.

By now my story had far exceeded the length prescribed by the editor who'd commissioned the piece. And still I didn't know how to end it, until A returned to Venice and mailed a letter in which he said, "When I started out on my travels I imagined myself to be one of those argonauts on their dangerous and difficult quest for the golden fleece. . . ." In those two lines I sensed his profound sorrow, but could do nothing to change or stop it—for the first time, the very first time as a writer, not only was I unafraid, I wanted never to awaken from this dream. By the end of the letter, A's narrative tone was warm again, and he begged me, no, he begged the character B, begged us to plant the flower seeds he'd picked up in his travels and described in detail where they'd all come from. . . .

At that point, I knew without question what A was planning to do.

So I didn't go to the Venice coffee shop for several days, preferring to stay home and polish some of what I saw now were no longer important sections of the story; for instance, I hung Picasso's simple drawing of Don Quixote on the southern European-style wall with the wheat stalks, and I changed the order of one or two of the letters. . . . I was bored to death, like a soldier cleaning his rifle as he awaits an attack at dawn.

I did not want to face that last day.

. . .

That last day, summer had arrived.

Mulberry bushes lining the sidewalk outside the coffee shop were laden with fruit as red as bayberries, attracting treefuls of happily chirping silver-eyes. Yet these elements were of no use to me now.

The next shock was that the Venice coffee shop had changed! The person who greeted me wasn't the girl I'd all but proposed to, but a young man in a white shirt and tight-fitting black slacks, his hair cut in the style of a KTV waiter (I instinctively knew he'd come to Taipei to avoid military service). He handed me a brand new menu; flustered, I ordered something and took a look around. The walls, the floor, the tables and chairs, they were all the same, including the copy of *Venetian Lagoon* hanging on one of the walls.

I regained my composure as the waiter laid out a set of plastic utensils. Unable to believe my eyes, I called him over and asked if the place had changed ownership. He nodded yes, but said nothing.

After finishing eating, I realized how much I missed the white china, the ashtrays, and the beautiful crystal water glasses I'd gotten used to. Without waiting for him to clear the table and bring the coffee I'd ordered with my meal, I took out my notebook and effortlessly carried out A's plan: he shot himself in Venice.

Something I'd put off for days took five minutes, 300 words to finish.

After hearing the news, B sat in the small, never busy coffee shop, where Picasso's *Don Quixote* hung on a southern European-style wheat stalk–enhanced plaster wall, waiting for night to fall outside, waiting for winter to pass, waiting for the last (if there was one) letter from his friend A in Venice.

And with that I deserted B as he sat waiting. Put an end to him.

I walked down the sidewalk lined with red fruit–laden mulberry bushes, my arms and legs trembling, not knowing why in the world I was so heartbroken.

Was it A's suicide?

Or was it because I'd lost the familiar coffee shop that had been so conducive to my work?

Or was it that I'd discovered that it wasn't really A I'd finished off, but a good friend I'd known in real life as a youth? "Dying is better than living," after all. In my story, A was dead and could have no further contact with B, while in real life, I had long since fallen out of touch with my good friend, who, like me, lived a good life in the same city, and that was the same as being separated by death.

As I walked down the sidewalk lined with red fruit–laden mulberry bushes on an unbearably sultry afternoon in May, before the early summer rains came, groups of middle school girls passed me coming in the opposite direction, having just gotten out of school, full of vigor and smelling of sweat, and I imagined that one of them might one day be my wife, because I was alone and oh, so lonely.

July 1992

MAN OF LA MANCHA

Strictly speaking, that was the day I began thinking about making preparations for my own death.

I should probably start from the night before.

Because a short essay of absolutely no importance was due the following noon, my brain, as usual, defied orders and turned itself on, ignoring the lure of the dream world and causing me to stay awake till dawn.

A few hours later, barely making it there before breakfast hours ended, I set to work in a Japanese-style chain coffee shop, effortlessly finishing that short, unimportant essay. It was then that I had the leisure to notice that, in order to fortify myself against the cold blasts from the air conditioner, I'd already downed five or six scalding refills of coffee, which had turned my fingers and toes numb, as if I'd been poisoned. I quietly stretched in my cramped seat, only to discover that my lips were so numb I couldn't open them to yawn. Even more strange was that my internal organs, whose existence had pretty much gone unnoticed over the three decades or so they'd been with me, were now frozen and shrunken, like little clenched fists, hanging tightly in their places inside me. I looked up at the girl who, in her clean, crisply pressed, nurselike uniform and apron, diligently refilled my cup over and over, and just about called out to her for help.

I was anxiously pondering the language to use in seeking help from a stranger—even though this stranger was all smiles and would never refuse requests such as "Please give me another pat of butter," "Let me have another look at the menu," "Where can I make a phone call?" etc. But, "Help me?" "Please call me an ambulance?" "Please help me stand up?" . . .

Yet for someone else, obviously, it was too late. The noontime headline news over the coffee shop radio announced that a certain second-generation descendant of the *ancien régime* had been discovered early that morning dead in a hospital examination room, still in the prime of his youth, cause of death unknown, a peaceful look on his face. Which meant he hadn't even had time to struggle or call out for help.

That was all I needed: picking up my essay and bag, I paid and left.

I refused to pass out during the few minutes I spent waiting for a bus or a taxi (whichever came first), but if I'd wanted to, I could have slumped to the pavement and plunged into a deep slumber. Then a series of screams would have erupted around me, mixed with whisperings, and many heads, framed in the light behind them, would have bent down and appeared on the retina of my enlarged iris, as in the camera shot used in all movies for such scenes.

No matter how you looked at it, it would have been a pretty loutish way to go, so I refused to fall or even to rest, though by then the chill from my internal organs was spreading out to my flesh and skin. I forced myself to head toward an old and small nearby clinic. My mind was a blank; I have no idea how long it took me to get there. "I'm going to faint, please help me," I said to the work-study student nurse, who was about the same age as the coffee shop girl who'd served me.

When I came to, I was lying on a narrow examination bed; the gray-haired old doctor, mixing Mandarin and Taiwanese, answered the puzzled look and questions brimming in my eyes with a voice that seemed very loud, very far away, and very slow: "Not enough oxygen to your heart. We're giving you an IV. Lie here a while before you leave. The nurse can help you phone your family, if you want. Don't stay up too late or eat anything that might upset you. Arrhythmia is a serious matter."

With that warning, he went off to see the next patient.

So concise, so precise, he'd pinpointed my problems: insomnia, too much coffee, and arrhythmia. Strange, why was a very, very cold tear hanging in the corner of each of my eyes?

I still felt cold, but it was only the chill of the old Japanese-style clinic, no longer the deadly silent, numbing cold from the gradual loss of vital signs I'd experienced a few minutes earlier. But I hesitated, like a spirit floating in the air, as if I could choose not to return to my body. I missed the body that had nearly slumped to the pavement a few minutes before. The site of the near fall was the bus stop in front of McDonald's, so there would have been young mothers with their children and old men with grandchildren waiting for the bus. The sharp-eyed youngsters would be the first to spot it, then the mothers would vigilantly pull them away or draw them under their wings for protection, instinctively believing that it must be a beggar, a vagrant, or a mental patient, or maybe someone suffering from the effects of the plague, cholera, or epilepsy. But some of the grandpas who'd seen more of the world would come up to check and then, judging from my more or less respectable attire, take me off the list of the aforementioned suspects and decide to save me.

Looking into my wide-open but enlarged irises, they'd shout, "Who are you? Who should we call? What's the number?" They'd also order one of the gawking young women, "Go call an ambulance."

Who am I? Who should I call? What number?

I'd think back to how, on busy mornings, my significant other would lay out his schedule for the day, and I'd promptly forget; it would go something like this: "At ten-thirty I'm going to X's office; at noon I have to be at XX Bank as a guarantor. Do we have bills to pay? In the afternoon I'll go. . . . Want me to get you. . . . Or page me when you decide. . . ."

So I'd give up searching for and trying to recall his whereabouts.

Grandpa would say, "We have no choice, we have to go through his bag."

And, under watchful eyes, so as to avoid suspicion, he'd open my bag. Let's see, plenty of money—coins and bills—some ATM receipts, one or two unused lengths of dental floss, a claim ticket for film developing and a coupon for a free enlargement from the same photo studio; here, here's a business card . . . given to me yesterday by a friend, for a super-cheap London B&B (16 pounds a night), at 45 Lupton Street, phone and fax (071) 4854075. Even though it would have an address and a phone number, it would of course provide no clue to my identity. So Grandpa would have to check my pockets; in one he'd find a small packet of facial tissues, in the other, after ordering the onlookers to help turn me over, a small stack of napkins with the name of the Japanese coffee shop I'd just visited printed in the corner. Different from the plain, unprinted McDonald's napkins in their pockets.

Then someone would take out that short, insignificant essay and start to read, but be unable to retrieve, from my insignificant pen name, any information to decipher my identity.

Finally a tender-hearted, timid young mother would cover her sobbing face and cry out, "Please, someone hurry, send him to the hospital."

That's what scared me most. Just like that, I could become a nameless vegetable lying in a hospital for who knows how long; of course, even more likely, I'd become an anonymous corpse picked up on a sidewalk and lie for years in cold storage at the city morgue.

Could all this really result from an absence of identifiable items?

From that moment on, from that very moment on, I began to think about making preparations for my own death—or should I say, it occurred to me that I ought to prepare for unpredictable, unpreventable circumstances surrounding my death?

Maybe you'll say nothing could be easier; all I had to do was start carrying a picture ID or a business card, like someone with a heart condition who's never without a note that says: whoever finds this please send the bearer to a certain hospital, phone the following family members, in the order their numbers appear here, and, most important, take a glycerin pill out of the little bottle in my pocket and place it under my tongue. But no, that's not what I meant. Maybe I should say that was the genesis of my worries but, as my thoughts unfolded, they went far beyond that.

Let me cite a couple of examples by way of explanation.

Not long ago I found a wallet in a phone booth. It was a poor-quality knock-off of a name-brand item. So I opened it without much curiosity, with the simple intention of finding the owner's address in order to, as my good deed for the day, mail it back to him or her—before opening it, I couldn't get a sense of the owner's gender, given its unisex look.

The wallet was quite thick, even though the money inside amounted to a meager 400 NT. In addition to a color photo of Amy Lau, it was all puffed up with over a dozen cards: a phone card, a KTV member discount card, a student card from a chain hair salon, a point-collecting card from a bakery, a raffle ticket stub, a membership exchange card for a TV video game club, an iced tea shop manager's business card, an honor card for nonsmokers, etc.

I probably didn't look beyond the third card before I was confident I could describe the wallet's owner: a sixteen- or seventeen-year-old insipid (in my view) female student. That, in fact, turned out to be the case; my assumption was corroborated by a swimming pool membership card, which included her school and grade, so I could return the wallet to her when I found the time.

Here's another example. I don't know if you've read the autobiography of the Spanish director, Luis Buñuel, but I recall that he said he stopped going on long trips after turning sixty because he was afraid of dying in a foreign land, afraid of the movielike scene of opened suitcases and documents strewn all over the ground, ambulance sirens and flashing police lights, hotel owners, local policemen, small-town reporters, gawkers, total chaos, awkward and embarrassing. Most important, he was probably afraid that, lacking the ability to defend himself, he'd be identified and labeled, whether or not he'd led a life that was serious, complex, worthy.

Here's another related example, although it doesn't concern death, taken from a certain short story that nicely describes the extramarital affair of a graceful and refined lady. When, by chance, she encounters her lover, and sex is on the agenda, she changes her mind. What stops her is surely not morality, nor her loving husband, who treats her just fine, nor the enjoyment-killing idea that there's no time for birth control measures. Rather, it's that she left home that day on the spur of the moment to take a stroll and do some shopping during a time when everything was scarce, and she was wearing ordinary cotton undergarments that were tattered from too many washings.

What would you have done?

Let me put it this way: these examples quickly convinced me that, if death came suddenly and without warning, who could manage to follow the intention of "a dying tiger leaves its skin intact"?

And that's why I envy chronically ill patients and old folks nearing the end of their lives, like Buñuel, for they have adequate time to make their preparations, since death is anticipated. I don't mean just writing a will or making their own funeral arrangements, stuff like that. What I'm saying is: they have enough time to decide what to burn and destroy and what to leave behind—the diaries, correspondence, photographs, and curious objects from idiosyncratic collecting habits they've treasured and kept throughout their lives.

For example, I was once asked by the heartbroken wife of a teacher who had died unexpectedly to go through the effects in his office. Among the mountains of research material on the Zhou dynasty city-state, I found a notebook recording the dates of conjugal bliss with his wife over the thirty years of their marriage. The dates were accompanied by complicated notations that were clearly secret codes, perhaps to describe the degree of satisfaction he'd achieved. I couldn't decide whether to burn it to protect the old man or treat it as a rare treasure and turn it over to his wife.

Actually, in addition to destroying things, I should also fabricate or arrange things in such a way that people would think what I wanted them to think about me. A minor ruse might be to obtain some receipts for charitable donations or copy down some occasional, personal notes that are more or less readable and might even be self-published by the surviving family. Even more delicate was a case I once read about in the health and medical section of the newspaper: a gramps in his seventies who had a penile implant wrote to ask if he should have it removed before emigrating to mainland China, for he was afraid that, after he died and was cremated, his children and grandchildren would discover his secret from the curious object that neither burned nor melted.

So you need to understand that the advance preparations I'm talking about go far beyond passive procedures to prevent becoming a nameless vegetable or an anonymous corpse; in fact, they have developed into an exquisite, highly proactive state.

I decided to begin by attending to my wallet.

The first thing I threw away was the sloppy-looking dental floss; then I tossed some business cards I'd taken out of politeness from people whose names I could no longer remember, a few baffling but colorful paper clips, a soft drink pull-tab to exchange for a free can, a book coupon, etc. In sum, a bunch of junk whose only significance was to show how shabby I was.

What then are the things that are both meaningful and fully explanatory, and are reasonably found in a wallet?

First of all, my career does not require business cards, and I had no employee ID card or work permit. I didn't have a driver's license and hadn't joined any serious organization or recreational club, so I had no membership cards. I didn't even have a credit card!

—Speaking of credit cards, they create a mystery that causes considerable consternation. I'm sure you've experienced this: you're in a department store or a large shop or a restaurant, and the cashier asks, "Cash or charge?"

Based on my observations, even though the cashier's tone is usually neutral and quite proper, those who pay cash stammer their response, while those who pay with a credit card answer loud and clear. Isn't that weird? Aren't the credit card users, simply put, debtors? The implication, at least, is: I have the money to pay you, but for now, or for the next few weeks, the credit guarantee system of my bank lets me owe you without having to settle up.

But what about those who pay cash? They are able to hand over the money with one hand and take possession of the goods with the other, with neither party owing the other a thing. Why then should they be so diffident? And what makes those paying with a credit card so self-assured?

Could it be that the latter, after a credit check to prove that they are now and in the future will continue to be productive, can enter the system and be completely trusted? And the former, those who owe nothing to anyone, why are they so irretrievably timid? Is it possible they cannot be incorporated into the control system of an industrial, commercial society because their mode of production or their productivity is regarded as somehow uncivilized, unscientific, and unpredictable, the equivalent of an agricultural-age barter system? Simply put, when you are not a cog with a clearly defined purpose and prerequisite in the system, their trust in you is based on what they can see, and that must be a one-time exchange of money and goods, since there is no guarantee of exchange credit for the next time, or the time after that. You are neither trusted nor accepted by a gigantic, intimidating system, and that is why you are diffident, timid, even though you could well be able and diligent, and are not necessarily poor, at least not a beggar or a homeless person who pays no taxes.

By contrast, those whose wallets are choked with cards of every kind are trusted by organizations, big and small, which vie to admit them and consider them indispensable. They are so complacent, so confident, and all because: "I have credit, therefore I am."

Can a person living in this world be without a name, or a dwelling place?

My wallet was empty, with nothing to fill it up and no way to disguise that, but I didn't want the person who opened it to see at first glance that it belonged to one of life's losers. So I put in a few thousand-NT bills, which I wouldn't use for so long they'd begin to look as if they were part of the wallet itself.

The wallet may have been empty, but since it wouldn't hold a passport, I debated whether to include my ID card to establish my identity—when 20 million ID cards are attached to 20 million people, you see, the meaning is nullified—and I could not follow your suggestion to, in a feigned casual manner, insert a small note with my name and phone number on it. Which meant that putting aside the issue of becoming a nameless vegetable or an anonymous corpse on the sidewalk, this anonymous wallet would, sooner or later, become nonreturnable, even if found by a Samaritan.

Ah! A savorless, flavorless, colorless, odorless wallet. Sometimes I pretended to be a stranger, examining and fondling it, speculating how the Samaritan who found it would sigh emotionally: "What an uninteresting and unimportant person your owner must be!"

After I lost interest in the disguise and the construction of my wallet, for a while I turned my attention to my clothes. Especially my underwear. To be ready for an unexpected sexual encounter—no, I mean for the unannounced visit of death.

Underwear is very important, and it's not enough just to keep it from becoming tattered or turning yellow. On psychological, social, even political levels, it describes its owner more vividly than many other things. Didn't Bill Clinton respond shyly that his underpants weren't those trendy plaid boxers, but were skin-hugging briefs?

And just look at his foreign policy!

Still, I gave serious consideration to changing and washing my underwear religiously, and to the purchase of new sets. For starters, I tossed my black and purple sets, along with my Clinton-style briefs, all of which might have caused undue speculation. After mulling over the replacements, I decided to go to the open-rack garment section of Watson's, where no salesperson would bother me, and picked out several pairs of white Calvin Klein 100 percent cotton underpants, though their yuppie style didn't quite match my antisocial tendencies. My significant other was all but convinced I had a new love interest, and we had a big fight over that. But I didn't reveal the truth. If one day I happened to depart this world before him, then my clear, white underwear would remind that grief-stricken man of what I looked like after my shower on so many nights. Those sweet memories might comfort him, at least a little.

But my preparatory work didn't end there.

On some days, when I had to go to work, I passed the site where I'd nearly fallen, knowing full well that the strength that had sustained me and would not let me fall came from the thought: "I'll not be randomly discovered and identified like this."

Randomly discovered. In addition to the state I was in, the wallet, my clothes, there was also location.

That's right, location. I thought back carefully to the routes I took when I went out and realized that, even though I was in the habit of roaming a bit, there was a definite sense of order and, in the end, it would be easy for a secret agent, even a neophyte P.I., to follow me. Even so, I strove to simplify my routes, avoiding places that would be hard to explain, even if I was just passing by.

Let me put it this way. An upright, simple, extremely religious, and highly disciplined college classmate of mine died in a fire at a well-known sex sauna last year. The firefighters found him, neatly dressed, dead of asphyxiation, in the hallway. We went to give our condolences to his wife, also a college classmate, and as we warmly recalled all the good deeds he'd performed when alive and said he'd definitely be ushered into heaven, we couldn't completely shake the subtle sense of embarrassment—what exactly was the good fellow, our classmate, doing there?

We could not ask, and she could not answer.

So I was determined to avoid vulgar, tasteless little local temples, shrouded in incense smoke; I didn't want to die in front of a spirit altar, giving my significant other the impression I'd changed religions.

And I didn't want to go to the Ximen-ding area, which I'd pretty much avoided since graduating from college, afraid I'd end up dead in an area honeycombed with dilapidated sex-trade alleys, fall under suspicion, like that good classmate of mine, and be unable to defend myself.

From then on, I quickened my steps whenever I walked by some of my favorite deep-green alleys, with their Japanese-style houses, where time seemed to stand still. I no longer stopped or strolled there, afraid that my significant other would suspect I'd hidden away an illegitimate child or was having a secret rendezvous with an old flame.

I even stopped roaming wherever my feet took me, as I'd done when I was younger, just so I wouldn't be found dead on a beach where people came to watch the sunset. Otherwise, my credit card–carrying significant other would be embroiled in a lifelong puzzle and be mired in deep grief.

After all, death only visits us once in our lifetime, so we should make advance preparations for its arrival.

> Hundreds of years ago, the Man of La Mancha
>   howled at the sky—
> A windblown quest
> Seeking love in steel and rocks
> Using manners with savages

And me, afraid that the handwriting would be eaten away by mites and no longer legible, I wrote this down.

September 1994

BREAKFAST AT TIFFANY'S

During the spring of the sixth year of professional base-ball in Taiwan and my ninth in my profession, the urge to buy a diamond crept into my head for the first time, and it had to be a solitaire diamond ring from Tiffany's—not from another company or from some local jewelry store, and not a ring with colored diamond chips . . . it had to be a classic round, brilliant cut Tiffany diamond ring in a platinum setting with six prongs.

Why?

Why Tiffany's? Why . . . a diamond?

Common sense tells us that all the diamonds on the rings of all the people in the world total at least half a billion carats, and that if one day De Beers Consolidated Mines Ltd., which controls 80 percent of the world's production and trade in raw diamonds, were to lose that control or collapse (a remote possibility at best), and could no longer dominate the extant rich diamond mines in countries like Australia, Russia, Zaire, and Botswana, then the value of the less-than-one-carat diamond someone as strapped as

I could afford would be little different from that of a fresh rose or a lovely cobblestone lying in the road, just waiting to be picked up.

So investment wasn't the answer.

It was my misfortune to have placed the highest bid for this month's accumulation of the office banking cooperative, which put me in possession of seventy or eighty thousand in spare cash. I couldn't finance a trip abroad, since I'd used up all my vacation time, and I wasn't dumb enough to buy a CD at the bank for the interest and then watch it be gobbled up by inflation. I didn't even know anyone who needed a no-risk, low-interest loan. There wasn't enough to buy a house or a decent car, but I had hopes that my future spouse would already have one or both of these, or that, at the very least, our love, like a magic potion, would supply the motivation to work hard together to get them.

But it wasn't just the fact that I'd come into possession of this spare cash that spawned my desire to buy a diamond ring. In the past, whenever my bid won the bank or I got my share of the money at the end of the period, I never hesitated to use it to go abroad or invest it efficiently and rationally, such as handing over a deposit and the first year's rent on an illegal add-on attic suite in a lane in my favorite district in the city. Once I put it all into the annual reinvestment campaign of a magazine where I'd once worked; another time I gave it to my father to help some of his relatives on the mainland set up a local business, with no expectation I'd ever get any of it back.

Diamonds were first discovered several centuries before the common era, in India. People believed they protected wearers from snakebite, burns, poisons, acute illness, the plundering of their wealth, and curses.

The Greeks called diamonds *adamas*, which means indestructible. The Romans used them to cut metal. The Chinese used them as carving tools.

So what, besides a diamond, is better suited to memorializing an eternal vow?

> Sparkling diamond, a sign of love,
> Love that will never die,
> A diamond is forever,
> With you till the end of time.

That's what the ad says, and it sends shivers down my spine. Of course it isn't really about true love or all eternity or genuine feelings, things like immortality or permanence; stop and think for a minute—when something you possess will outlive you, maybe even last forever, it does not cease to exist just because you, its owner, cease to exist. A good illustration would be the 44.5-carat blue Hope Diamond, which you highly value in spite of its legendary history of misfortunes; is named for its first buyer after being cut, Henry Philip Hope; and now, after bringing calamities to several of its owners, resides in the Smithsonian in Washington, D.C.

The Florentine Diamond, an exquisite golden yellow stone weighing 137.27 carats, cut in a double rosette pattern with 126 facets, was Italy's most famous precious gem, and was said to have first been owned by a French nobleman, and then, after changing owners many times, fell into the hands of the King of Austria; it was, however, lost forever in the destruction of the Austro-Hungarian Empire.

Needless to say, it probably resembled the eye of a heathen idol and still emits a cold glare as it rests amid the scattered bones of a member of the royal family.

Slightly unfair, and somewhat frightening . . . why? Why would you want to own something that will not rot or decay after you die?

Not long before New Year's, by acting on impulse I succeeded in securing an appointment with someone who, it was rumored, had not sat down for a media interview for a very long time. How to define her? She straddled two or three realms, first gaining prominence through environmental protection–like essays. I say I succeeded by acting on impulse because I could see in my colleagues' faces, no matter how much they tried to hide it, that I had hit the jackpot.

Xiaohui, who was a bit more willing to reveal a weakness around me, said that the others lacked the nerve to go looking for that writer, to whom I'll refer as A from here on. In recent years, A had let it be known that she would not agree to a media interview even if you put a gun to her head; if you somehow ferreted out her phone number, a closely guarded secret, in that brief moment before the fax machine squeal or the answering machine kicked in, she'd come on the line and immediately turn you down in a severe and cold voice, and she would demand to know how you'd managed to get her number in a tone that left no doubt that she was determined to identify the guilty party, one way or another.

I thought back to how I'd managed to get A to agree to an interview, with little hesitation on her part. I think I blurted out, without so much as a nod to etiquette, that I'd been a fan of hers since high school, and wanted to know how life had been treating her in recent years, and wondered what she'd been doing, since she'd been out of the news for some time and had published nothing.

As a matter of fact, I'd been working for the specialty magazine for less than a year, and hadn't yet grasped the conventions regarding who were the big shots and who weren't, who required a joint interview and who was difficult to handle, so I had no preconceived stance, which made me seem as innocent and earnest as a newborn calf, someone you couldn't bear to turn down—at least this was how Xiaohui saw it.

The long and the short of it were, A and I met, at a time

and place of my choosing. Our company's year-end dinner presented an obstacle, requiring a change of date and time, though that was her call, since she said she had no commitments, and that we could meet when I was free and at any place I preferred—my co-workers' faces actually twitched when they heard that.

It had probably been nearly a decade since I'd last seen A, and on that occasion we'd been separated by a crowd of people. She'd come with some activists to lend support in the third day of a hunger strike as we sat at the base of the campus clock tower. I informed her of that in order to substantiate my next comment: "You haven't changed a bit."

A didn't respond with a self-effacing reply, nor did she show any sign of wanting to reminisce, and gave mostly irrelevant answers to my questions. Although the magazine I worked for differed from periodicals that were heavily into advertising, I still found it hard to work A's reclusive, simple philosophy of life into the story I'd planned to write, so we quickly agreed to bring the interview to a close and become normal people again.

Here's something interesting. In my experience, interviews are a sort of performance. The interviewer pretends she's the soul of ignorance, while the interviewee assumes the role of someone in command of all heavenly and earthly knowledge and a bellyful of unique views concerning the affairs of the world, which is why I particularly like the moment when the interview ends; it is as if a demonic curse has been lifted, and both parties are back to being human again. My interviewees are often out of touch with everything, from such unimportant concerns as the history and renown of the restaurant where our meeting takes place all the way up to hot topics in the realms of contemporary politics and economics, media, or the performing arts.

Now that we were back to being normal human beings, we ordered drinks, and while we waited for my jasmine tea and her coffee, she told me, rather apologetically, that she'd agreed to the interview mainly so she could chat with me.

With me?

She quickly added that no people my age, members of the so-called "new human" generation, had entered her circle of friends in a very long time, so for her this was a perfect and quite normal opportunity, and she hoped I wouldn't mind.

Not venturing a response, I was reminded of how our national leader had recently instructed relevant government organizations to study the "new humans," our Gen-Xers; his self-confident, explicit use of the term convinced me that a new generation of humans had, it seemed, been discovered, and that scientific methods, including basic rules of anatomy and biological characteristics, could be employed to classify them accurately, as if each pair of chromosomes were thus and so, and the front lobe of the left side of your brain was one thing or another.

In A's eyes—no, ears, since we were talking on the phone when she agreed to the interview—was I one of those new humans? I recalled from the material about her that she was ten years older than I, at most, but I felt that I was ten times wearier, far more burned out than she (it made no difference if, as she said, she did in fact lead a simple life), and that my life was ten times tougher than the simple life (let's say she was being honest) she led.

In the midst of my tactful silence (she was so considerate she mistakenly took my silence for anger), I spotted a brilliant diamond ring on the middle finger of her left hand, in a six-pronged, platinum Tiffany setting, one I hadn't taken note of in an ad I'd seen. Maybe her finger was so thin that the ring twisted easily back and forth, and during our interview "performance," it must have been turned into her palm and escaped my attention. But now it rested calmly on the back of her finger, a tiny diamond, no more than half a carat, a very, very ordinary diamond ring.

> The idols of the heathen are silver and gold,
>> the work of men's hands.
> They have mouths but they speak not; eyes
>> have they, but they see not.
> They have ears but they hear not; neither is
>> there any breath in their mouths.
> They that make them are like unto them: so is
>> every one that trusteth in them.
>
> Psalms 135

I was reminded of a romantic writer I'd once been fond of; he had described how, when he was traveling in Japan, he'd seen Japanese office ladies on streetcars choose not to sit down, even when there were empty seats, preferring to stare out the window, neither talking nor smiling, and that reminded him of the story of Wei Sheng's promise in the *Zhuangzi*: Wei Sheng had agreed to meet a girl under a bridge. The girl did not come, but the water did and he did not leave, so Wei Sheng died with his arms around a pillar.

Afterward, I read somewhere in a lifestyle piece that when Japanese office ladies, who had spent the day smiling at customers or male co-workers or bosses, got off work, they would rather stare at a wall and let their faces show the annoyance and exhaustion they felt than sit down and face someone across the way, even a stranger, and be required to once again wear the mask of modesty and poise.

In the post–economic bubble era—I mean, in Japan— exhausted office ladies who could not afford to buy a house or an apartment often used money they received beyond their salary, such as year-end bonuses, to buy a one-carat diamond ring to reward or console themselves for a year of hard work, and thus we have the so-called one-carat ladies. Of course it's been nearly two years since I read this report, and it's possible they've become two-carat ladies by now.

Had I decided to buy an ordinary diamond ring like the one A was wearing in order to reward or console myself for my hard work?

Star of the South, 128.8 carats, was found by a Brazilian slave in a diamond mine quite by accident. Needless to say, this happy discovery bought her her freedom.

According to Constantin Pecqueur's *A New Theory of Social and Political Economics: A Study of the Organization of Societies,* putting your labor up for hire constitutes the beginning of your life as a slave—well, I'd been a slave for nine years already!

I needed a diamond ring in order to regain my freedom.

At about this time, a building that workers been hammering away at and decorating for at least a year finally opened for business near where I waited for the bus to go home; it was a high-end department store. One day, when I was more presentable than usual, I went in for a quick look. It was like strolling through a modern museum, and there wasn't a single item I could afford; the business likely relied on the patronage of the wives of government ministers or entertainment industry godfathers or major players in the stock market, people who lived in the apartment building behind the store. "The production of too many useful things produces too large a useless population"—or so it says in *Economic and Philosophical Manuscripts of 1844.* But did this "useless population" refer to me or to the wives of high officials and moguls who kept this department store in business?

I was forced to wait at that bus stop every day, and on cold, rainy days the wait was longer than usual; but even on those days, and even if I'd forgotten to bring an umbrella, I was unwilling to wait inside, in spite of the fact that the building's main floor provided handsome, comfortable sofas and chairs, the kind you'd find in a five-star hotel lobby.

They were putting the finishing touches on a roadside display window of the modern museum, keeping what was inside hidden behind a curtain. I often stood in front of it, in an almost trancelike state, assuming the pose of Wei Sheng's promise, in order not to have to confront A, B, or C, who had become familiar faces, since they waited for the same bus every day. Gradually, this became the only time in my day when I was free and in tune with myself. I even gave up my habit of reading the evening paper with a thirty-five-NT cup of coffee to escape rush hour traffic.

"In the Middle Ages a social estate was emancipated as soon as it was allowed to carry the sword."

"Among nomadic peoples it is the horse that makes a free man and a participant in the life of the community."

How could I have believed that a diamond could set me free in that cold, damp moment as I waited to return to my lair?

Naturally, my thoughts turned to Xiao Ma, whose standard comment was, "That is a false need created under the control of an impulse of commodity aesthetics . . . ," but my God, a diamond, isn't that the standard symbol of commodity fetishism? Think about it: even more transnational than AT&T and Nissan, De Beers quietly but ingeniously controls the world's production and supply of diamonds, and at the same time promotes diamonds by advertising in all media, stressing the vital association between diamonds and romance. You don't believe me? Many of my co-workers who were in romantic relationships believed that love cannot exist without diamonds; there are even more men who actually believe that they cannot find love without diamonds.

Xiao Ma and I never, of course, celebrated each other's birthday or were together on Christmas or Valentine's Day or its Chinese equivalent, any of those holidays for which businesses mobilize in a big way. Naturally, back then, Valentine's Day was not taken as seriously as it is now.

These days, the push for Valentine's Day starts when the New Year's holiday ends, and the atmosphere in offices everywhere is no less charged than when people begin guessing how big their annual bonuses are going to be. This tense atmosphere reaches its peak a couple of days before Valentine's Day, and when a flower delivery girl walks in the door with a big bouquet, the feigned indifference on everyone's face resembles nothing so much as the breathless wait prior to an announcement of personnel changes.

But the results are almost always unanticipated. For instance, four or five bunches of roses and a box of chocolates appear on the desk of X, whom no one thought had a boyfriend; or there is only one bunch of roses on the desk of Y, who goes out nearly every night, and we assume that they must have come from a factory owner, who has bouquets delivered on Valentine's Day to just about everyone, except his wife . . . in the main, no one's desk is left out, although I must admit that over those few days, as my desk remained unadorned, I could barely resist the temptation to order a bouquet and write on the card that it was a gift from a secret admirer.

If Xiao Ma had been there, I wonder if he'd have felt an obligation to ritually give me something or send his current girlfriend flowers or some other gift.

Not long ago, I was flipping through a recent issue of a political magazine while I was taking my afternoon tea, and Xiao Ma was a former student activist interviewed for a sort of "where are they now?" piece.

In response to the reporter's inquiry about his plans for the future, Xiao Ma, who must have been in his seventh year abroad, said that after getting a Ph.D. in a year or two, he'd return to the island to continue his participation in opposition movements, that he'd never leave the opposition camp, which, of course, meant the Democratic People's Party. On that he was emphatic.

Xiao Ma, a poli-sci major, could not have predicted that within a month of that interview, the opposition party he'd sworn to support forever would hold the reins of power in the nation's capital, and could never have imagined that the comrades with whom we'd participated in a hunger strike at the foot of the campus bell tower now held regular suit-and-tie jobs or that many of them had the power to do things that directly affected people's lives. Xiao Ma, who had left the country before the lifting of martial law, likely viewed Taiwan through the eyes of someone still living under martial law, and it stands to reason that only *that* Taiwan, only *those* Taiwanese could get his juices flowing; they were the ones he wanted to protect, the ones he wanted to save, I guess.

In this respect, Xiao Ma and A are a lot alike, or so it seemed to me. For them "the people" are an abstraction, not real at all, and it is these unreal people to whom they feel especially close; the mere mention of those two words bring tears and a warm light to their eyes, as if such decent, oppressed, wholly virtuous people, who await protection and salvation, really do exist.

Why do I call them "unreal people"? Because if "the people" were to rest on the shoulders of those associates of mine, or on mine—the current me—for that matter, whether we'd need to protect and save them would be of secondary concern. Most importantly, it's absurd to believe that there are actually so many "people" in need of protection and salvation!

That is probably why such people so desperately miss the martial law era, for only in that aesthetic climate is there both the room and a need for them to exist.

Now I finally understand the inexplicable agitation I felt toward A that day, even though, when she asked a question, whatever it might have been, it was accompanied by pronounced solicitude and a caution born of breeding unique to people of her generation. When she asked about my political leanings, for instance, she actually blushed, as she might have had she asked if I had a boyfriend, and if we'd slept together. I told her who I voted for in the mayoral election, and when she asked me why, I said it was partly because he was so good looking and partly because I got a kick out of how a certain individual mimicked the way he talked.

A asked if I considered myself a supporter of his party.

I said I don't really see how his party differs from the others, since, as you know, everything they say sounds great but is dead-on boring.

Then A asked if I knew anything about my candidate's background, such as how he'd suffered for his participation in the Taiwanese democracy movement, even spending time in prison.

Prison? Isn't that a sort of investment gamble? Isn't it the risk you assume when you join an opposition movement against a third world totalitarian government? It's like when we invest in a friend's business, or when we buy stock: sometimes we make money, sometimes we lose it. Compared to members of the older generation, these people—still in the prime of life—have promptly reaped visible gains, so in my view, the returns on their investments seem reasonable.

That's how I answered A.

Wanting not to believe me, she kept the questions coming. Is that how all you new humans feel? Can you find even a little gratitude in your hearts for his sacrifices and his contributions to "the people," and just support him for that?

How naïve A seemed. Give me a break. It's not only marriages of love that have legal standing. Do marriages between families of wealth and status, undertaken for mutual benefit, have no legal standing? If this were a society in which every member of "the people" who voted for him were intelligent and selfless and did so for lofty and sacred reasons, there'd be no need for him to step in as savior or enlightened leader. Give me a break. My reasons for voting are as valid as anyone's, and she should have expected that at the beginning.

But do "the people" really have such a short memory? A asked.

Outside of a history course, they (at this point I too was beginning to describe unreal people) have neither the need nor the time to look back at the past. If that's a short memory, then the way they've overlooked the KMT's contributions to Taiwan's economic development also constitutes a short memory, but the fact that the KMT occasionally seeks public acknowledgment of their contributions disgusts you, doesn't it? Same logic.

But how can that be called "the past"? They're all still living, still around, not part of history. . . . A said patiently.

In my case, unless you force me to sit in a history class that outstrips my experience, I'm still at the kindergarten stage (I lowered my age five or six years), and that old dictator you folks still rail against is no longer around. When I was in middle school, there were times when protests out on the street made me so late for school I had to stand in class as punishment. A political party was formed the year I took the high school entrance exam, and during my junior year, rare was the teacher who wasn't listening to stock market developments during class time, and if I don't marry someone who owns a house before I'm fifty, there's no chance I'll ever have a place I can call my own. . . .

Meanwhile you people, you activists or entrepreneurs, sometimes both, incorporate idealism and a sense of mission when you do business, like my boss, and I simply can't imagine what you have to be worried about. Compared to people like me, who don't live with their parents, a "nomadic people" forced to wander the city in search of the next illegal attic to keep a roof over our heads, you already possess status and houses and cars that would take us a decade of scraping by to manage. That goes double for a certain legislator in the opposition party, a woman who doesn't do a damned thing but get up on stage from time to time to engage in antiauthority posturing, vowing to love this land and forcing everyone else to vow to love it as much as she does. Then one day, thanks to a sunshine provision in the law, we find out that this woman, who relies on lower-middle class contributors of fifty or a hundred NT to get elected, owns a dozen pieces of land and real estate, so no wonder she loves this land, and loves it so much. . . .

It's hard to say who's working for whom. I voted for him because I saw him on a TV variety show, where he was made to do the cha-cha, and he came across as both pitiful and lovable, and, give me a break, that was reason enough for me.

Not only that, I also managed to answer some questions I'd initially rejected as being silly, such as how to identify myself. Taiwanese? Chinese? Taiwanese and Chinese? Chinese, but in Taiwan . . . ?

In all honesty, if I could choose right now, I'd rather be Japanese, or spend the year in London with nothing to do, or go to Vancouver or Seattle for the summer. Or why not go to California, for no reason, like Faye Wang in the movie *Chungking Express*?

I also told A, who was ten years my senior, that I'd always thought that TV sets grew out of the walls in people's living rooms; always thought that the NT exchange rate was twenty-eight to the dollar and that it was the strongest currency on the China mainland and in Southeast Asia; always thought that the Zhongxing Department Store, which was the only thing that gave any meaning to "window shopping" and "fads," had always been there; always thought that there never was a President Chiang; always thought that the DPP had always existed; always thought that Chen Shui-bien had always been Mayor of Taipei—all you have to do is turn on the TV evening news and look at all the schoolchildren fighting to shake his hand or line up behind him to make "look at me" gestures for the camera to see I'm not exaggerating.

In my view, A's "short memory" was an integral and important element in the construction and consolidation of new memories.

Cuban Capitol, at 23.04 carats, which I consider to be the loveliest round-cut yellow diamond in the world, came from an African mine; it isn't set in jewelry, but has been inlaid in a pedestrian path in Havana, the capital of Cuba, and marks a military route.

Diamonds and revolution.

Diamonds and Castro.

It goes without saying that there's also diamonds and Russia—but here I'm definitely not referring to Paul I, the 13.35-carat purple diamond set in the Royal Crown of India, once the property of the Russian tsar and, named to commemorate the reign of Paul I, stored in a Russian diamond vault.

Russia is planning to begin manufacturing industrial diamonds next year in a 200-meter wind tunnel, built to test the reaction of rockets and ballistic missiles when they reenter the earth's atmosphere. The Director of Ballistic Technology in the Machine Manufacturing Unit of the Central Institute of Science told a Reuters reporter: "Our goal is to make this facility more economically viable."

More economically viable? He and his research fellows fed pieces of stainless steel into the wind tunnel collider and drove them into a piece of pig iron at ten times the speed of light; the collision created graphite chips that turned into diamond dust.

As a result, 250 grams of diamond dust were created on a 30-kilogram piece of pig iron. The director said they were updating the facility to create larger diamonds, estimating the largest to weigh in at 2,000 carats, or roughly four times the size of Star of Africa, currently the largest known diamond in the world. The institute plans to repeat the procedure 40 times a year, producing 15,000 carats each time, or an annual total of 600,000 carats of diamonds.

Russia and 600,000 carats of diamonds.

What was my hurry?

There was no turning back.

Just then, a curtain dropped in front of the modern museum at my bus stop, and a high-end boutique, work on which had been under way for a long time, opened. The riddle was solved: it was Tiffany's.

I was stunned. Never in my wildest dreams had I imagined that after all this time, this would be the confessional object I'd silently faced during my mental exile. It made me feel like a pagan worshipping the golden calf.

But that absurd feeling was quickly replaced by the magnetic attraction of the place. On an evening of freezing rain, when nearly all the traffic lights were out, my time facing it grew longer with each minute I spent waiting for the bus.

It turned out that the place offered more than just jewelry (which I discovered by gazing at the display window day in and day out). There were silver pen and pencil sets, tableware, exquisitely hand-painted pottery and porcelain, wristwatches, silk scarves, all false needs created by commodity aesthetics; before the curtain rose, I'd truly felt I had everything I needed, but now, thanks to my desires, I felt I had nothing.

I was like the little girl selling matches on the street, standing barefoot on a bitter cold, snowy Christmas Eve, looking in the window at a happy family in a warm house.

I decided to buy a Tiffany diamond ring for Valentine's Day, even if my desk at the office was noticeably bare of roses or chocolates.

Why Valentine's Day?

Long ago I'd decided not to participate in my co-workers' games, like when they asked, "Where will you go for your lovers' dinner?" The assumption—you must have a lover, so you're definitely going to have a lovers' dinner—disguised the questioner's real intent, which was to let me know that she was going to enjoy a lovers' meal—"lover" being the key word.

Naturally, I did not decide on Valentine's Day just so I could wear it on my finger the day after as a silent but unmistakable means of showing off in front of my co-workers.

> Labor produces beauty, but deformity for the
> worker;
> It replaces labor by machines, but it casts
> some of the workers back into barbarous
> forms of labor and turns others into ma-
> chines.
> It produces intelligence, but it produces idiocy
> and cretinism for the worker.
> It produces palaces, but hovels for the worker.

I return to what the *Manuscripts* said, that the slum created by my labor is located on the windswept rooftop of an apartment building, and it is as cold and dark as a dank cellar, and so the quixotic horse and sword, the coffeemaker, and the CD player at the head of my bed, which I move around with me, are all rusted beyond salvation; my precious Wedgwood handkerchief and red teacups from the same company are all streaked with wild berry patterns, but the ambience of springtime in all its fullness can neither cover nor conceal the books packed in two large cartons that I don't open because I'm afraid of moving. This is the table where I sit to drink and to write letters and journal entries. Dirty clothes under the cheap wooden bed that the landlord would not let me throw out, and which is covered by a navy-blue Elle towel, emit a strange odor that reminds me of when Xiao Ma and I lived together.

> The savage in his cave—a natural element which freely offers itself for his use and protection—feels himself no more a stranger, or rather feels as much at home as a fish in water. But the cellar dwelling of the poor man is a hostile element, "a dwelling which remains an alien power and only gives itself up to him insofar as he gives up to it his own blood and sweat"—a dwelling which he cannot regard as his own hearth—where he might at last exclaim: "Here I am at home"—but where instead he finds himself in someone else's house, in the house of a stranger who always watches him and throws him out if he does not pay his rent.

That is how *Manuscripts* portrayed my cellar room 151 years ago.

I flooded the room with every light I could turn on and lay on the moldy cotton Indian blanket to read magazines I hadn't yet opened, since the end of the month was rapidly approaching. I subscribed to four general-interest magazines of various types, including some from abroad, an indulgence of sorts. Even though I could read copies at the office or at one of the neighborhood teahouses, or could stand in a bookstore and read them off the shelf, for some reason, having my own copies gave me a greater sense of security than buying a pretty Chanel lipstick or doing aerobics regularly or swimming in a heated pool.

But it was predictable that sooner or later among them I'd come across A's fervid, assured observations of new humans, her descriptions so vivid and lively you felt as if you were hearing her voice or seeing her in person:

how the new humans carry no historical baggage, how traditions, good and bad, have been completely done away with, which has led to an absence of any concept of beliefs or values worth mentioning; new humans are nihilists, they have no interest in differentiating between politicians and political hacks, they view involvement in a democratic movement as commercial activity, in which profit and loss are one's personal responsibility; there is only success or failure, winning or losing, and that eliminates the need for either praise or scorn.

New humans worship the media, a god that determines all meaning and value. Any entity that has no place in the media simply does not exist. What that means, of course, is that any knowledge or wisdom can be discarded immediately after use (fifteen minutes of fame).

New humans have even lost touch with their emotions—they can neither give nor receive. Because they have never actually experienced poverty, war, or separation, their emotions are as pristine as the day they emerged from their mothers' wombs, no more and no less, which is why they must use high decibels and the exaggerated motions of deaf-mutes to express emotions and views that are either ill-defined or virtually nonexistent.

Among new humans, the men are like women, the women are like men—gender neutral (for my interview with A that day I'd had my hair cut short like the actor Lim Giong, and I was wearing a gold ring in one ear, straight-legged khakis, and ankle-high boots).

Among new humans, women are much more willing to take the initiative sexually and are not hung up on traditional gender differences (what if I'd said to A that day that sometimes my current boyfriend and I satisfy each other's needs by trying out new ways of making love in one of those MTV private rooms?), or, to the contrary, view emotions and desire as burdens, and, as a hedge against suffering, prefer to go without sex (like I told her that day).

I told A—as soon as I became conscious of the answer she might have been waiting for (such as what I occasionally or frequently did with a boyfriend in one of those MTV private rooms)—I gave her a different response. I told her that not having sex could signify an obsession over cleanliness, since you can't be sure that a man who looks neat and clean doesn't actually have bad breath, which, as you know, is certainly possible. Anyone with a job these days has an ulcer, pyorrhea, hepatitis, or insomnia, problems like that. Most important, how can you accept on faith that your partner may be a strong, handsome man, the kind you read about in romance novels, always ready to perform and always wearing clean, sexy underwear? And what if he can't get it up or is so-so in bed, leaving me unfulfilled, all hot and bothered, or wet and dirty? Give me a break, I'm not his wife, I have no moral or emotional obligation toward him or willingness to provide him with patience, sympathy, forgiveness, or consolation.

New humans also prefer images over the written word, by far (what if I'd told A that day that I'd watched the Japanese animes *Urban Hunter* and *Crayon Shinchan* many times and had gotten a lot of creative pointers from them?).

Having grown up in the wake of Taiwan's economic boom, the new humans have no concept of savings or of frugality, and are devoted materialists. They have an astonishing ability to spend, and on extended credit, and I urged her to read reports by Roper, the American polling company: new humans spend $1.25 trillion every year (if, what if, during our interview I'd worn a Tiffany diamond ring just like hers?).

I began making plans to buy a diamond ring.

Diamonds range from a subtle yellow and an off brown to the rare pink, sea blue, green, and other bright colors, but the finest ones are colorless, since, like prisms, they can break rays of light into their component rainbow of colors. Giving her a colorless diamond is the same as giving her a pure heart, is how De Beers puts it.

Purity—most diamonds have tiny flaws; the fewer the flaws and the smaller, the less they affect the reflective quality, and the lovelier they are. A diamond is more brilliant and transparent than any other gemstone. Flawless diamonds are extraordinarily rare, and therefore, very pricey. When selecting a woman—I mean, a diamond—the fewer the blemishes, the prettier and the more valuable, is how De Beers puts it.

Carat, that is, the weight, is, as everyone knows, one of the four Cs that determine the quality and value of a diamond, and it is the easiest to measure. High-quality diamonds are available in a variety of sizes and shapes, and we believe she will never object to the additional weight a high-quality diamond bestows upon her, is how De Beers puts it. (Master wordsmiths!)

In the refining process, diamonds are cut in a variety of shapes, depending upon the quality of the stone: round, olive-shaped, pear-shaped, oval, rectangular, and heart-shaped. Besides being the hardest object known to us, diamonds have unique light-dispersing properties; they can reflect light from their interior and separate rays into their component colors (dispersion), thereby creating a brilliant, dazzling luster and fiery hues. The responsibility for this, obviously, rests with the master diamond cutter, is the claim De Beers makes.

It was once thought that something as hard as a diamond must be indestructible. Until, that is, an Indian diamond cutter discovered that the surface of one diamond can be scratched by another, producing a special luminosity.

Then, in the fifteenth century, Belgian diamond cutter Van Berquem discovered that you could shave the facets of a diamond with a steel disk lined with diamond dust.

At the close of the seventeenth century, the Venetian Peruzzi discovered a way to cut fifty-eight facets into a diamond, and to this day that remains the benchmark for all forms of cutting.

On October 21, 1879, Thomas Edison invented a lantern that used a carbon filament (Give me a break—what does this have to do with diamonds?). Royalty and rich merchants who owned diamonds discovered that the wearing of diamond jewelry was no longer restricted to daylight hours, that displaying it in a lighted room during a social gathering enhanced its attraction. The popularity of diamonds grew.

In the early twentieth century, Marcel Tolkowsky used a mathematical formula to calculate the most appropriate angles and ratios when cutting a round brilliant diamond . . . that was what A wore on her finger and what I planned to own.

I'd saved up enough money—in order not to be like the country bumpkin in the joke who carried baskets of cash into town and asked, "How many pounds of this for a lady's wristwatch?" I went out and got a credit card. Before Valentine's Day rolled around, on the daily return to my poor girl's basement, I lingered in front of the rich girl's palace window, and it didn't take long to shift from appreciating the display and feeling breathless over the NT 100,000+ price tags for average-looking wristwatches to falling helplessly into all sorts of scenarios. . . .

The door, is it bulletproof? It looks heavy. No matter how natural and unaffected the man or how affected or coy the woman, they all must push. It doesn't move, so they wonder if it's an automatic door. They stand and wait for it to swing open. But it doesn't move, so they push real hard—hair flying, face red—not a very dignified start.

So I study the situation, trying to figure out how to open that really heavy glass door without making my face turn red or gasping for breath, appearing as casual as if I were walking into a convenience store.

This isn't the only door, but the other one is kept locked for some reason, and the last thing I want to do in my nervous state is try to enter through the wrong door. I've seen several sophisticated customers try and fail to enter through that door; they feel around for a way to go through the transparent door, even bang on it, but to no avail, and wind up putting on a Marcel Marceau pantomime.

Beyond this, the display case for the solitaire diamond ring I'm interested in is located in the far left corner of an area with two U-shaped counters; the distance between it and the heavy door is roughly six or seven steps by a man, eleven or so by a woman in heels, for me probably nine or ten. The floor is covered by a tightly woven Oriental rug with a faint dark pattern, removing any possibility of slipping as I walk, so, little sister, hold your head high and get over there, go on, don't look back. . . .

Sales clerks? That didn't seem like the right thing to call them. The men were courteous and reserved, like English butlers; and the women? They were like bank managers or flight attendants, each with a controlled facial expression, assuredly not people who would burst out laughing if asked, "Hey, Miss, how much for a pound of diamonds?" or "Color? I want 'A' grade."

No one, but no one, pays cash.

Only individual diamonds rate certificates, not diamond chips.

    . . .

Outside the palace, I considered everything that might occur during the purchase. It was more like planning a robbery than studying the multifarious phony and complex but necessary (why?) palace protocols.

No, you say? I even took pains to baby my hands by wearing thick, lanolin-lined gloves in bed at night, something I'd never done before, not to smooth out the loops and whorls of my fingers, but to avoid having someone think these were the hands of a slave when I tried the rings on.

I planned my wardrobe for the day, seeking a fashionably casual look; thanks to my survey of the lay of the land (the carpet I mentioned earlier), I knew I could confidently wear patent leather Mary Janes with heels, and not have to worry about slipping or falling (during the escape?). I bought a bottle of the newest Armani perfume at a tax-free import shop. (Was I covering my tracks the way a herbivorous animal rubs up against a rotting carcass to throw a carnivorous predator off the scent?)

All was in readiness, all but the D & G suede backpack purse, now selling at a 30 percent discount, soon to go to 50 percent, with its mossy color and feel, the one the fashion magazines were pushing as the essential accessory of the season, even though, from a distance, it looked like an army canvas bag. With one of those on my back, I was sure to look like a gung-ho young warrior. But what to put in it—a canteen? a hand grenade? a marching map? Hey, what difference could it make?

Everything had to be just right.

"The result is that man [the worker] feels that he is acting freely only in his animal functions—eating, drinking, and procreating, or at most in his dwelling and adornment—while in his human functions, he is nothing more than animal."

Xiao Ma. . . .

It's not too late to bail out.

The day before the robbery, every desk in the office was a sea of flowers; even I was the recipient of a bunch of champagne roses, sent by Xiao Jin from the print shop, who treats everyone the same, giving us all bouquets, sort of like the Mid-Autumn Festival, when everyone receives moon cakes.

While waiting for my bus, I stood quietly in front of the palace window, as usual, feeling nothing special about what I'd do the next day.

But what appeared to be a married couple inside caught my attention.

They were at my display case, sniffling from time to

time because they had to bend down to see the diamond rings. They were casually dressed, as if they'd decided to come on the spur of the moment. The man was holding an umbrella, minus its plastic cover, water dripping down to form a wet spot on the carpet. Yet they were focused on what they were looking at, probably memorizing the cost of each ring, spending much more time than most consumers did, on average, by my observation.

Eventually, they straightened up and signaled to the butler or flight attendant. While they were waiting, the woman looked at the man, who was sniffling loudly, and brushed something off his shoulder, probably dandruff, just as the flight attendant walked up and began taking out rings for the woman to try on, one after the other, each time both of them exhaustively questioning the flight attendant about something, and it was almost as if they were buying a house they planned to live in for the next thirty or forty years.

They'd probably just had a big fight—intuition.

Admittedly, it was also possible that this was a modern version of the story about the poor couple at Christmas: in order to buy her husband a chain for his pocket watch for Christmas, the wife cuts off and sells her long hair, and the husband, in order to buy his beloved wife a hair ornament, sells his pocket watch. . . .

I'd never let myself fall to that level, like a serf, not even for love.

Let me put it this way: one third of the money for which I rent my labor goes to my landlord; in the *Manuscripts* it says that landlords get rich on the bodies of the poor, but most of the landlords I've rented from have had to use the rent they collect to supplement their mortgage payments, and most likely their property has been financed by financial conglomerates.

"The worker's crude need is a far greater source of gain than the refined need of the rich. The cellar dwellings in

London bring more to those who let them than do the palaces."

To a property owner, a basement constitutes considerable wealth.

But enough about that. The remaining two thirds of my wages should be mine to spend as I wish.

But make no mistake about it, a third of the money I spend on food winds up eventually in the hands of property owners. Putting aside income taxes paid to the government, think about how much a cup of coffee costs, or a hamburger and a soft drink, or think about the standard French fare at one of our five-star hotels, and compare those to the costs in other countries (and please, don't give me Japan as your sole example).

Most of my clothing allowance goes to pay the rent of department store women's departments and clothing manufacturers.

A significant portion of the money I spend on taxis goes to pay the cabbies' rent, while property owners who pay no real estate taxes zip along in their Mercedes Benzes and BMWs ride down highways paved by income taxes I'm forced to pay, every cent of them.

At least 20 percent of what I shell out for subscriptions goes to pay the rent for magazine offices and warehouses, not to mention the factory rents for printing and typesetting, plus those paid by magazine employees and various workers—like me.

Beyond that, say we choose not to spend our money, but put it into a savings account in some financial institution, just so the real estate speculators can get megaloans and, reaping vast earnings, continue to speculate in properties we could never afford, no matter how long we lived, thereby forcing us and our descendants into lifelong backbreaking labor just so we can pay the rents we owe them.

We've already become a hereditary serf class without knowing it.

And still we consider ourselves to be freemen, in spite of the fact that we are fated to be no better off than the Russian serfs, who were inextricably tied to the land for life.

That is because the Russian serfs could direct their anger and disgust (or adoration or envy) at the landlord, while we neither see nor know the identity of the individuals for whom we work ourselves to death, even though we are surrounded by their castles and fiefdoms.

"Landlords, like all other men, love to reap where they never sowed, and demand a rent even for its natural produce."

"Landlords derive their power from force."

"They draw interest from the base habits of the impoverished proletariat, such as prostitution, drunkenness, money lending" (and buying diamonds?).

Most likely we manage to get through life only because we think we are free.

I don't know why Xiao Ma, who planned to spend his life in the opposition camp, stopped talking about the class issue.

I don't know how to avoid that sort of predicament, the predicament of the serfs, and regain my freedom.

The evening arrived. I opened the door and walked into Tiffany's. The door was exactly as I had calculated from long observations—neither too light nor too heavy—and I took exactly nine steps—no more, no less—up to the display case. In a word, everything progressed precisely as I had confidently predicted. Seventeen minutes, from start to finish, was a bit longer than I'd estimated, but that was because there were probably four times as many customers as usual on that Valentine's Day night.

The ease and speed with which I carried out my robbery amazed a woman beside me, someone who looked a lot like A in age and attire. She was bent over the counter, closely examining the diamond rings in the display case. She was not sniffling, but she did glance my way in a feigned nonchalant manner, and the look in her eyes said it all: "A new human, no wonder!"

Without making a fool of myself and without setting off an alarm, I walked out of Tiffany's, a modern-day tranquil palace, with my Star of the South, shouldered my way onto a bus, and returned to my basement.

I turned on every light in the room, untied the white ribbon, removed the robin's-egg blue paper outer box, and opened the Prussian blue silk box. There it was.

Its ID card described it: brilliant, round cut, weight— 39 points, overall quality good, clarity VVS1, a tiny flaw, H on the color scale, which is nearly colorless. Below that was a pompous description of its cutting ratio, like giving a woman's height, weight, and measurements . . . in a word, it went to great lengths to inform you how this diamond differed from all other diamonds in the world, the false individualism of consumer capitalist aesthetics.

Horkheimer. Adorno.

Smith's twenty lottery tickets.

Say's net income and gross income.

Such obscure puzzles and codes. . . .

Nonetheless, my Star of the South did bring indescribable brightness into my basement room. I picked it up with my right hand and slid it onto the ring finger of my left, slowly, the way a lover would do it, and my heart filled with a tranquil joy, like, like that of the little boy who was playing on the bank of the South African Orange River when he picked up Eureka.

Eureka originally weighed in at 21.25 carats, and was sparrow yellow; its discovery attracted a flood tide of greedy visitors to South Africa, vying with one another to mine for diamonds.

July 1995

HUNGARIAN WATER

This is something a middle-aged man who was about my age, looked a lot like me, and had pretty much the same job told me after he'd had a couple of drinks.

Obviously, in keeping with common practice, I need to set it in the proper time and place.

We met at a party thrown by a mutual friend—my college classmate and his high school classmate from the same town. The party was held in a little beer bar on a big illegal building site, and invited guests kept coming and going, with about a dozen people present at any given time. The guest of honor that night was the friend of our mutual friend, someone, I'd heard, who hadn't been back to Taiwan for more than a decade; this return visit was probably not part of the current love Taiwan fad, since we'd heard that he was either moving his company or being moved by his company to the Chinese mainland.

At a particular moment—when guests who drank were enjoying their liquor buzz and those who didn't, obviously bored, were sneaking looks at their watches—this guy I didn't know—I'll call him A—staggered toward me clutching an empty glass like a real boozer and, with a grin, first apologized for being a boor, then, in true boorish fashion, asked me, "How come you smell like that?"

By the time I realized that he meant exactly what he said, with a pretended show of politeness, I sniffed the sleeve of my comfortably cool wool suit, then spread my arms as a gesture that I couldn't smell anything.

A set down his glass and cordially helped me lift my elbow up to my nose for me to try again. He looked on expectantly.

So I sniffed again and, what do you know, I detected the rank garlicky odor of clams in wine sauce I'd spilled on my sleeve, and the cheap fragrance—cheaper than a certain toilet water, hardly worthy of the name "fragrance"—on the damp cloth I'd used to wipe it off. That and . . .

He spotted my "that and," and happily supplied the answer: "Citronella! I haven't smelled that in thirty years. Hungarian Water" A sniffed deeply.

It came rushing back to me: the late-spring rainy season had just begun, and my wife had discovered to her irritation what seemed to be evidence of termites, and had abandoned the camphor oil with alcohol she'd used for years and had gotten her hands on a bottle of yellow Vitali Tonic, on which the words "citronella oil" had been written; she'd used it to clean the closet, inside and out, and the smell was enough to suffocate everything within range, including termites and humans. Naturally, my clothes, especially my absorbent wool suit, were affected. But that was during the rainy season, and the suit had gone out to the cleaners no fewer than three times since then.

Ignoring my confirmation and implied praise of his sense of smell, A kept talking.

"At the time, up and down the entire street—in truth, it was the only street in the town—you couldn't avoid the smell of citronella oil, day or night, and it wasn't until I'd grown up that I learned it was extracted and exported to Japan. My aunt took me to do something, I forget what, and we went to the biggest general store in town—thinking back now, it couldn't have been more than sixty square feet—to buy me some clothes. The whole time we were shopping, she talked to the owner in Japanese. I put up with it because she promised to buy me a toy I'd been pestering her about, probably a plastic gun or a long-handled knife. . . . I haven't thought about my aunt for at least thirty years, just about forgot she'd ever existed, because not long after that they got a divorce, but for a time I lived with her, I shared her bed and she bathed me, even tweaking my little pee-pee while she was washing, just like a real mother. Where had my parents gone . . . ? I think she stuck so close to me during those days and nights because she didn't want to face my uncle. He worked out of town and came home only on weekends. While he was away, she and I slept like babies, at least I did. Some really scary noises woke me up once. My uncle was stomping on my aunt, and he looked like a giant on top of the tatami mat; she was crying, I think, and the only resistance she put up was to keep him from stomping on me or waking me up. . . . Now I wonder if that was an ordinary domestic fight or some kind of savage sexual behavior. They had no children and treated me like one of their own, that goes without saying, and she often called me her 'little treasure' in Japanese. When she had something to say to me, she'd bend down real low or squat on her haunches and straighten my clothes while she talked, just like housewives treated their husbands in Japanese movies we'd seen. . . . Honestly, I haven't thought about her in thirty years, even though I believe she was living in her family home not far from town, but you know, back then divorced couples were bitter enemies, and my grandmother forbade us to even talk about anything that involved the woman. My aunt always smelled so good; it wasn't citronella

oil, but now the smell of citronella oil on you has reminded me of her. She had a lovely figure, but maybe that was
because of the bindings. I saw her in her underwear once,
and it was a lot like our modern-day adjustable corsets,
squeezing her really tight to flatten her tummy and uplift
her breasts. I guess appearance was important to her. She
often took Japanese books and magazines to a shop where
she bought fabrics and asked the dressmaker to copy the
patterns, but somehow they always came out looking more
or less alike, a lot like the clothes my wife started buying last year, the sort of things worn by Jacqueline, who
had just died, Kennedy Onassis, that Jacqueline. Fashions
those days were strange, and now it all comes back to me,
when they went out they carried little rattan baskets painted in high-gloss soft colors. My aunt, for instance, owned
a butter-colored one, I think with a broken hasp—that was
my doing, so she gave it to me. I pretended it was a little
prison by keeping marbles or captured insects in it to tor-
ture them, but I also turned it into a nursery for fledgling
sparrows a few times . . ."

I listened patiently, praying, Do me a favor, please make
him forget I even exist when he sobers up, because the
last thing I want is to start up a friendship, even a bullshit-
ting one, with this sort of beginning.

After my shower that night I saw my wife frown at the
smell as she hung up my suit. She usually sniffed clothes
to see whether or not they needed to be cleaned, and that
always embarrassed the hell out of me, and more than
once I stopped her from sniffing underwear, or socks I'd
just taken off, saying that anybody with half a brain (nose)
could tell they should be washed without having to sniff
them, so why did she insist on doing it?

More than once she replied, "To prove to myself they need
cleaning." But that was when she was in a good mood.

I kept her from complaining about the garlicky smell by
asking her where the citronella oil had come from, and she

said a friend had brought it back from her native home in the countryside, saying it protected you against mosquitoes, and she wanted to keep the children safe from dengue fever and Japanese encephalitis, so she assumed that, logically, the stuff ought to protect against termites as well, and so she asked for a bottle, and asked me what I thought. I asked her if she didn't think it had a funny smell, and she glared at me: "Why didn't you say so before?"

I ran into A again not long after that, at a place, what should I call it, one of those places you see all the time in Taipei, designed to have a bar and several small tables, specializing in coffee, but over time, thanks to people like me who drop in after work to avoid rush-hour traffic, they start serving set-menu boxes, light snacks, even invent sandwiches with strange names and tastes that I'd never try, and later go ahead and start serving cocktails.

A and I were sitting a few tables apart reading our evening papers and, as we were both turning a page and yawning, our eyes met, but there was only indifference, and I secretly rejoiced that he hadn't remembered me after sobering up. Are you that way too? Now that I'm over forty, I no longer have the will or the energy to listen to other people's problems, and "other people" includes my wife and myself.

I often try to convince myself that this world is only one of a great many hells.

My pager beeped; it was my wife, she was at her parents' home; she often paged me to come get her after she'd been shopping or watching a soap opera with her parents during rush hour, then drive back to our suburban home, a trip that, at the peak of the rush hour, took two hours.

I tipped my head back, like I would if it was a real drink, and drained my cup of cold coffee, then stood up and went over to the bar, where the girl tending bar was making juice, and asked her to punch my coffee card.

"Citronella!"

Instinctively, I turned at the sound. What the hell, was that supposed to be my name or something?

It was A, of course, wearing a big grin, a complete reversal of the indifference of a few minutes before.

He wanted me to sit with him and would not take no for an answer. I had to give in, maybe unconsciously assuming the role of the aunt who'd bathed and shared a bed with him.

A ordered Long Island iced tea for both of us; I told him I didn't want one, but he let the order stand, and picked up where he'd left off in the conversation the other night, unhindered by the elapsed time.

"Later on I phoned her, my aunt, who'd retired the year before, but what hadn't changed, not a bit, was the primary school where she taught; I insisted on going with her once and sat in a classroom that probably dated back to the Japanese occupation, with straw poking through spots in the beat-up mud walls, but, strangely enough, so hardened I had to gouge with my fingernail to scrape off even a little piece. That was in the summer, and the ground in front of the classroom was cluttered with Burmese gardenias, I'm sure you've seen them, thick branches, far apart, the ones people call hen's-egg flowers, with white petals, a yellow core, and a subtle fragrance, but if you give me one, all I need is one whiff and I can recite the names of at least ten kids in that class, and if you supply me with the odor of a running sore on one of the students' legs or a whiff of gentian violet, I can conjure up a picture of every boy in the class."

The Long Island iced tea arrived. He picked up a glass, but instead of drinking, he breathed in the smell and muttered, "4711, X X." It sounded to me like a series of numbers, followed by someone's name in code.

A was lost in thought for a moment, until I was sure a current of air passed between us (maybe it was the smell of citronella oil on me) and brought a more familiar expression back to his face, and he continued.

"In the end, a member of her family, the person I'd addressed as kin when I'd gone to her parents' home with her, told me she died soon afterward, a scant few days after the death of my grandmother, and I assumed that their mutual enmity had led to a power struggle to see who would die first, like the Empress Dowager and the Guangxu Emperor, or Chiang Kai-shek and Mao Zedong, until, like those others, at some point they merged into a symbiotic unit, and when one left the scene, the other lost the will to go on living. I think my aunt must have blamed my grandmother for breaking up her marriage. You know that she, my aunt, was a reserved woman, to the point of being incapable of protecting herself or her marriage, whether my grandmother intended to torment her or not. I can recall how prone she was to sulking; she often stayed upstairs at mealtime, with the light off, either crying or sulking or sleeping, I didn't know which, but refusing to come downstairs to eat, so my grandmother would send me up with food on a tray, often pan-fried croaker, and once when I was on the stairs I did something disgraceful, I popped out one of the fish eyes and ate it, it was *so* nauseatingly fishy."

If you think he talked only about two old ladies who were dead and gone and the nauseating eye of a croaker, you're wrong, but at the time, I reacted pretty much like you would: I looked down at my watch as a sign that it was time to go (my god! I'd rather have been at my in-laws' house watching *Tokyo Love Story*).

Before letting me go, he begged, pathetically, I thought, asking me to bring along a bottle of citronella oil the next time we met (he said he worked in a nearby office). Without waiting for him to finish, I promised to get my hands on a large bottle of the stuff as soon as possible and rush it over to his office or his home (anything to avoid having to see him again).

A mustered up the courage, in spite of his embarrassment over my comment, to ask me to get him something—

anything I no longer wanted—from my dresser drawer, like a used handkerchief or a floppy sock I was going to throw away—Please, don't ask for a pair of underpants I've outgrown!—hurrying to explain that it wasn't just the citronella oil, but a mixture of other fragrances that duplicated the smell of his aunt ("I want to preserve that").

Except for my wife, I hadn't heard the sound of an adult about to cry for years.

I told him I'd do it.

In my drawer I found an environmental protection T-shirt a factory owner had passed out to celebrate Earth Day, but I was concerned that the smell might have been contaminated since the plastic bag was still sealed, so I asked him to assess it. He took it from me and sniffed it. "Thanks," he said, "a perfect mix."

A perfect mix, like I was a parfumeur, or, more correctly, my wife was. She regularly put nearly empty perfume bottles into our drawers, in a thoughtful, if seemingly random, manner, and I never found it strange, since I didn't realize they'd leave their smell on me, and even if they did, I'd have assumed that the various perfumes the women in the office wore would have overwhelmed them. My god, the air pollution they cause is worse than cigarette smoke.

He then told me a story that was much more interesting than the tale of the two old women and the nauseating fish eye, apparently to show his thanks.

"Strictly speaking, the disaster probably dates back to 1990—"

Nineteen-ninety? The seventy-ninth year of the Republic? I needed a minute to think back to what happened that year. At the beginning of the year, the president stunned everyone by choosing someone without a voice as his vice-president . . . a "horror story" about the National Assembly . . . stupid, ugly political power struggles . . . in mid-year, when everyone in the country said he couldn't do it, the president willfully picked a man in uniform as his premier. . . .

I didn't know if A's disaster had its origins in any of those. But given his provincial background, there's no way he was related to the cashiered Treasurer Zhang, Premier Li, or Military Commander Wang.

"—Nineteen-ninety, customs duty and commodities taxes dropped and the value of the New Taiwan dollar rose dramatically. Thanks to substantial imports, perfume was no longer considered a luxury item."

Ah, then it occurred to me that A's wife, like mine, probably could not control what we considered an irrational expenditure on perfume . . . but could this be considered a disaster?

"Have you ever heard the statement 'once in a decade'?"

I hadn't, so I shook my head, waiting to be enlightened.

"I forget if it's a Japanese saying, but it refers to how, owing to chance and karma, extraordinary, unforgettable sexual experiences come around only once a decade. No matter how many times we do it in a lifetime, starting in our teens—the pros manage to do it daily, while the amateurs or those who don't have a partner are good for at least several hundred times—when all is said and done, when you come to the end, there won't be more than a few times in your life that were truly unforgettable."

. . . That's right, only a few times in your life.

Actually, everything is repeated over and over, and if you forced yourself to record each experience, you'd likely run out of things to say after 300 or so words, or you could simply repeat what you wrote the time before, and the time before that . . . and just when was that? In the morning? Before bed at night? Lights on? Early morning, when the sky was blue-gray? . . . What CD was playing? Which pajamas was she wearing? How did it start? Was there anything out of the ordinary about it? . . .

Who can remember, even if it was the time before last?

Maybe, of course, this is inevitable in the lives of a faithful married couple.

I'm waiting for this guy I've only met three times to tell me about his once-in-a-decade experience.

"The difficulty in achieving or finding that once in a decade isn't the key issue. . . ."

He seemed not to know where to begin, and I couldn't help wondering if it might be the citronella oil and powder smell on me that was getting in the way.

"Um, my wife . . ."

That, as you can imagine, surprised me. His once-in-a-decade partner was his wife.

"Um, that wife of mine . . ."

It was clear that that wife of his was going to be a lot harder to describe than "that aunt of his."

"That wife of mine is a wild woman. We've got two kids still in grade school, and she doesn't care if we wake them up. And that's not all. You know, whenever a new perfume is imported into Taiwan she's the first to buy it, and she really *wears* it, laying it on thick and encasing herself in such a spray I can barely see her. Then that night, my god, she throws herself into it with all the energy of final exam week, like a fox spirit or sex demon, doing everything in her power to suck me dry, body and soul, before the light of dawn . . . and so, I guess you could say that this perfume history is my once in a decade. For instance, if you don't mind my saying so, you've got" (he laughed at this point) "the smell of Kenzo on your underwear; the fruit odors are gone, but the smells of wood and pungent Oriental spices still linger—"

A held up his hand to stop me from saying anything—even I wasn't sure what—in my defense, and continued the flow of words. "—That time in the bathroom I got her hair wet and washed off her light makeup, like the time we ran into a thunderstorm in the suburbs when we were dating. She wasn't yet forty and water beaded on her newly washed skin, and she knew that the bathroom was nothing but hard surfaces. Well, we did it twice, and we were so sore we couldn't get out of bed the next morning."

That reminded me of a similar incident . . . I smiled, my face must have turned red, and I had to explain why: How can you call that a disaster?

"Remember the perfume called Red Door? Reputedly, tens of millions of NT were spent on advertising when it first came to Taiwan. I'm sure my wife saw the print ads. She was on pins and needles until it went on sale—she bought it the first day and, as always, laid it on thick, even though she's allergic to ethanol-based perfumes, which cause a rash wherever they touch her skin, turning it red and itchy."

Needless to say, he went on to describe a sexual encounter that surpassed the previous one, its subtleties and shuddering effects, until I'd heard all I could endure. I interrupted him again, since I still didn't understand how any of this could be considered a disaster.

"Are you familiar with the ads for Red Door and their target audience?"

Of course I wasn't.

"They targeted bold, confident, ultramodern working women with strong personalities, age twenty-five to thir-ty-five—"

So . . .

"So, my wife was worried that the ads would work on the girls in my office, who'd all run out and buy a bottle of Red Door, and that spelled trouble!"

Why's that?

"You really don't get it, do you? She used it first, so if every bold, confident, modern moron in my office started using it, the aroma would remind me of my wife, and that longing would lead inevitably to another once in a decade. You can imagine, can't you, the sort of embarrassment that could lead to? You know, not every person, place, or situation is appropriate. Once, for instance, I was talking business with a factory owner over lunch, and his special assistant had on the perfume my wife wore several times during our honeymoon, which, I seem to recall, was no longer on the market. It was a gift her second brother, who was studying abroad, sent her when she graduated from college. I hadn't smelled it in more than a decade, and it really threw me; I nearly fell in love with that special assistant, and spent the whole afternoon like a dog on the make, trying to find my wife to take her to bed. Don't tell me you've never had an experience like that."

By racking my brain I recalled a girl who'd worked in my office for six months before leaving to study abroad—I can't even remember her name and had no particularly strong feelings for her. I believe she was a regular user of a subtle, slightly sweet perfume at a time when not a lot of women wore perfume, since it was still pretty expensive, and I assumed she wore it to mask a body odor.

Several years later, my wife and I attended a relative's wedding banquet, and the same fragrance suddenly reminded me of the girl, the lush, shoulder-length hair that covered her face when she was bent over her desk at work, only the tip of her nose and her chin poking through, and, once or twice, revealing a bit of cleavage. . . . She didn't appreciate the way her male colleagues teased her by telling stupid jokes. She'd just smile and complain, "That's stupid!"

"You see, that's what really scares my wife: a fragrance she wears reminding me of other women. Which is why she's tried every perfume on the market—that way, no matter what fragrance I smell on other women, I'll immediately think of her, something beyond my control, and if I ever have thoughts of cheating, the only way my wife will not be on my mind is if the other woman wears no perfume or makeup (unlikely) or wears one my wife hasn't tried (even less likely). Take, for instance, the girls at Flower X Flower Cocktail Lounge. Don't they all wear

Chanel No. 5, which the madam imports directly from Paris? Well, when the supplier learned that, they sent instructions that no more large orders from Taiwan were to be filled, to keep the desirability of their perfume from tumbling. So you see, with a lovely and desirable young woman sitting across from me, my mind was filled with the image of my wife in a purple satin negligée (see what a good memory I have), and you can imagine what that did to my libido. It killed it. That ended that. . . ."

A picked up the second glass of Long Island iced tea, sniffed it, and brought his remarks to a conclusion. "Of course, I had no burning need to stray, but when I considered the long road stretching out ahead of me, the thought that this possibility would no longer exist someday was too depressing for words."

So the idea of an extramarital affair depended upon finding a woman who wore a perfume your wife had never tried, right?

A muttered something before finally taking a drink from the glass he'd lifted to his lips several times, leaving a sniffable amount at the bottom.

"Now, would you call that a disaster or not?"

I couldn't be sure. Just then the dense mist of a strange odor enveloped us, and I discovered it came from the waitress who was removing our empty glasses and giving us a clean ashtray, and whose armpits were at the level of our faces.

A and I exchanged glances, like ants with their antennas, but said nothing until the waitress had cleared our table and walked off.

"What were you thinking just now?" A asked.

Curry rice. We were let out of grammar school at noon after the monthly exams, so I always went home for lunch. Mother would make fried rice with tomatoes or curry rice, filling a bowl and then turning it upside down onto a plate, so it lay there nice and round, like a cupcake, and I'd eat it with a spoon. My younger sister and I would try to talk like Americans while we ate. My god, the days were so hot then we had to be careful to keep our shoes from getting stuck in the soft, sticky asphalt . . . if that smell had lingered a few more seconds I'd have had more memories. . . . How about you?

"A dressmaker's shop. Ume-san's Dressmaker's Shop. Back then it was called a foreign tailor shop. My aunt often took me there, and once in a while my grandmother went there. Most of the time Ume-san came to our house to take my grandmother's measurements, but if she'd received a gift from a Japanese or some imported fabric or things made for younger women, Grandma would visit the shop herself, since Ume-san kept copies of the latest fashion magazines. The strange thing was, all Ume-san's fabrics were brand new, yet the overpowering smell of hundreds of armpits hung in the air of her shop. I wonder why? You know, she had a basket in which she tossed the remnants, and, as a boy of five or six, I was allowed to play in it. Sometimes I'd fall asleep, and all the new fabric combined to produce that smell. My grandmother and aunt would often gather intelligence on each other; my grandmother would casually ask Ume-san how many outfits my aunt had had made for the summer, and my aunt would step up to one of the racks to feel fabrics to be made into dresses for my grandmother, most of which had been given to her by Japanese, things that weren't available at any price. My aunt would be deeply envious, but my grandmother never treated her to any of those gift fabrics. . . ."

How did she die? What killed her?

A stared blankly, obviously still off in the tailor shop.

Your aunt, how did she die?

"Never asked. She was emaciated, and always on edge. If it wasn't cancer, it must have been a bad heart. . . . I've never understood death, like this minute, right now, I can describe everything about her at a certain time in her thirties in perfect detail, but what does that mean in terms of her death, of her no longer being there? I recall something a foreign writer once said: 'Death is the subtraction of me from the world to which I have been added.' For a time, I found that comment totally convincing, because I was constantly brooding over death. A Jew, maybe a prophet or something like that, once said: 'Death is simply pushing open a door and walking from this world into another,' but what if I get stuck somewhere in between? I was frightened and curious about every detail of death, such as what does it mean for me to remember my aunt so vividly? Does that also work for organ donating? Say her corneas or kidneys are still living in someone else's body. If so, then it's no longer a case of her subtracted from the world to which she has been added, is it?"

What could I say? The last time I'd heard anyone talk about things like this was probably in college with a studious girlfriend . . . now that I'm over forty, there are a lot of things I can't recall, and couldn't no matter how much time you gave me. I admit I can't recall the girl's name, and even though things didn't work out between us, I should at least be able to come up with her name. I'm superstitious enough to believe that if you provided me with an odor, I could recall her, at least her name and what she looked like.

"So what's the meaning of death? If there's anything more vivid than donated organs you can leave behind in this world, that is."

But seeking a smell tied to her would be far less easily accomplished than trying to come up with her name or appearance, since after all, finding a copy of a class yearbook wouldn't be that hard.

"Take, for example, that vivid memory I referred to a moment ago, sensory to the nth degree, olfactory, and how it's totally different from the abstract words or works left behind by artists and writers—"

What sort of smell would it take for me to recall her? Something vivid and sensory, totally different from the words and images of a class yearbook, as A just said.

"How about you? How do you see death?"

It can't be perfume, for back then, perfume was rare in Taiwan. Then how about the cafeteria outside the school gate? For a time, we regularly agreed to meet for lunch; or we went to the grassy area outside the library, and sometimes the caretaker was mowing the lawn, so maybe the fresh, green smell of newly mowed grass could spark memories of her; or a downpour on a summer afternoon, since we'd huddled together under one umbrella and, drenched, walked past her house many, many times.

What was her name? . . .

When I said good-bye to A that day, surrounded by the heavy aroma of organic coffee, that simple question droned in my head. I picked a leaf from the decorative plant on the table, rubbed it between my fingers to squeeze out a few drops, and held it up to my nose. Nothing about it gave rise to any memories. On weekends, when we ate at home, I'd sometimes search among the various vegetables for any thread that might help me solve this puzzle. Unfortunately, my wife was almost obsessively fond of Italian pasta and soup at the time, and I'd accumulated bottles of unfamiliar ingredients, with labels like "parsley," "sage," "thyme," and "oregano," but only their names were familiar, and I was reminded of a song that had been popular the summer after we took the college entrance exams, and I'd looked up each of these strange and unfamiliar names in a dictionary, at a time when my memory was excellent, which is why I never forgot them.

Overcome with boredom, I went out onto the balcony to visit my wife's potted plants. They were all leafy plants—no flowers and no fruit—twenty or thirty of them all together, and all different. But to me they were all the same. What *was* her name?

The next time we met, with some embarrassment, I revealed my simple problem to A: compared to his major question about death, my inability to recall the name of an old girlfriend showed I wasn't trying hard enough.

He invited me to go somewhere with him.

The visibility at seven o'clock on that summer night was perfect.

Like a cinematic sage and his disciple, or Holmes and Watson, we walked down a lane made barely passable by lines of parked cars or, where there were no cars, large potted plants used to reserve parking places. A reached out and picked a stem with leaves and a thick white flower from one of the roadside plants; holding it out as far as he could, so I couldn't smell the fragrance, he asked, What does that remind you of? The leaves were shiny green, almost black; I think one of those was among my wife's twenty or thirty plants. . . . I described it hesitantly.

A held it up under my nose and shook it to release its fragrance.

Ah, I said before he even asked, Zhu Meijun, who shared a desk with me in the first grade, brought one of those to school in her pencil box every day (A interrupted me to say it was a gardenia). Zhu Meijun was a cute girl, and smart, and every kid in the class eagerly followed her example by picking a gardenia from somebody's garden on the way to school and putting it in their pencil boxes. Zhu Meijun also kept the shavings from her Moonlight brand perfumed pencil in her pencil box, and so did the other kids who owned those pencils. In a word, we kept our little treasures in our pencil boxes, and we all had personal treasure troves on our desks, which we sometimes guarded like deep, dark secrets but on other times opened up for public display. In addition to the gardenias and perfumed pencil shavings, for a time the third most popular keepsakes were teeth, baby teeth that had just fallen out and were scrubbed clean, despite the fact that the cavities lent them a terrible smell, but which, when mixed with the flower and pencil perfumes, produced a captivating aroma. . . . Zhu Meijun, a name I hadn't thought of for thirty years, except once, when I spotted it on the college entrance exam announcement. I think she was admitted to Soochow University.

The fragrance of those flowers had stuck with me all this time, and as I regained my composure, my embarrassment was palpable, like someone seeing a hypnotist or psychologist.

"So I'm not afraid of coming down with Alzheimer's or winding up as a vegetable for one reason or another, because I believe that all I'll need to relive my past is exposure to my nurses' perfume, and it will be a truthful revisitation, like watching a movie, unaffected by the crafty revisions we impose upon our past as we grow older. I suggest that if your wife isn't in the habit of wearing perfume, you should make a point of using a fragrance yourself for a time. Some people call this a wet memory, and, of course, you needn't actually put it on your body, if that doesn't appeal to you, and you can find some other place for it in your life that feels natural. Storing your clothes in a closet or dresser with citronella isn't a bad idea . . . over time, a fragrance can help preserve a memory or preserve the woman in your memory, if holding on to memories of the past is something that interests you, that is, or is important."

A fondness for one's past, for one's memories, is no different than a fondness for one's present, one's future, one's life, isn't it? Could a compelling fondness for life be why A is so afraid of death, so mindful of it?

Even though he was no help in my attempt to recall the name of my former girlfriend, he had served as a catalyst for me in recalling Zhu Meijun, impossible though that seems, the girl I was secretly fond of in the first grade. For that I felt obliged to try to answer the question he'd posed the last time.

Here's what I think, and this is a hard thing to consider: everything dies, not just people. Look around you, everything dies: the flower you're holding, termites, turtles, sperm whales, moss, red cypresses up on Mount Ali, germs . . . actually, I don't know what scientists think, but if the goals of the medical and biology communities are to ease the difficulties of old age and make death less painful, I'm okay with that; if, on the other hand, they think that once they prevent the onset of disease altogether, they can keep death at bay permanently, then their naïveté is a little scary. I recall what a scientist who had studied medicine once said: insects are incapable of developing defenses against the ailments that will kill them. They are what they are, and when they reach a certain age, they die.

I couldn't go on, first, because my concern over death was so shallow, and second, because it felt funny to cite insects in a discussion of the death of humans.

"I'm delighted to hear you say that everything dies. That may be common sense, but it sounds fresh when you say it. Insects, what a great example! At any moment on this earth there are a billion times more insects than humans, and virtually all of them live much shorter lives than we do. In simplest terms, the frequency of death among insects is so concentrated that not a second goes by without their deaths, and yet they've developed no philosophy that we can detect. What I mean to say is, they don't struggle to keep living, however ignobly. You know those seventeen-year cicadas, well, when I was young, I got a kick out of finding their hiding places in trees. I just looked, I never caught them. Then a few days later, I'd see them lying belly-up on the ground, and if not for the occasional swarm of ants that tore off their limbs to make it easier to move them, they'd be so whole I wondered how they'd so easily accommodated death. It used to bother me, but now I envy them their willingness to just up and die—"

But it's not a matter of a willingness to just up and die, it could actually be a mechanism of dying. Someone once said, I recall, that animals have a built-in self-protection mechanism that, when death approaches, switches on to lead them to a painless death. People of faith might concretize this as the embrace and guidance of their gods or God's messengers. Don't heart attack victims who have been revived after several hours say that they passed through a tunnel into a gentle, warm, and merciful light?

I had to find a way to console A, in the belief that I'd rarely met anyone more afraid of dying.

"What I'm saying is, with or without a major war or calamitous natural disaster, the more than 5 billion people living on earth today will all die off within the next hundred years, and even though they cannot be compared to insects, which seem to do nothing but die, on average 50 million people die every year, yet we are witness to death only a few times in our lifetime, like you" (here I interrupted to agree that my only time was in the army, where one of our company's reserve officers committed suicide, but no one in my family has died yet), "but we separate these few deaths from the 50 million people who die off every year, and we attend their funerals, bearing our grief as best we can, recalling them tearfully, as if their deaths were unnatural, an exception, as if to say, if not for this accident or this illness or this age, they needn't have died. This petrifies me, increasing the horrifying aspect of death, a hateful, avoidable, strange and unfamiliar event. . . .

"So instead of saying I'm concerned about dying, or afraid of dying, you could say I'm concerned about and afraid of the way people avoid talking about it, how it's become the ultimate taboo."

I thought he was worrying too much, finding the time to ponder how other people deal with death, but here I discovered that there are two types of people in the world: one type isn't afraid of dying, or should I say has never given any thought to matters associated with death, yet they normally buy all the life insurance they need; the second type is like A, though they, surprisingly, shun life insurance.

The sky had turned dark, and we'd reached a small neighborhood park at the end of the lane; several mentally disturbed individuals (or so I assumed) were sitting in a daze in the park, in spite of a notice posted at the entrance that stated, with remarkable inhumanity, that the park was closed to the mentally disturbed, along with bicycles, peddlers, and pets.

We sat on a low wall bordering a flower bed, and I probably crushed some of the plants. I smelled crab mums; back in the third grade I'd ruined a bed of crab mums in the back yard by burying a dog that had died of measles, and then laying a bunch of the yellow flowers on the grave mound. . . .

I wondered if there were odors in A's memory that he was unable to find, the way I was unable to recall the name of my former girlfriend.

In the darkness, instead of answering my question, A began singing the opening lines of a song, which he repeated over and over, but the only word he seemed to recall was "Ramona." I didn't know the words to the song either, but it sounded like one I'd heard as a child, which had then been turned into a pop song, but now A had taken it back to what might have been a foreign folk song.

"My aunt, that aunt of mine, played this for me on her phonograph, called it a bad luck song. I asked her why, but she wouldn't say. When I threatened to go ask my uncle if she didn't tell me, she said simply that my uncle had a close friend in middle school who also lived in town, and he'd show up anytime my uncle had a new book or a new record; when my uncle was in vocational school, this 'Ramona' was his friend's favorite song. Later on, the friend was executed, and my uncle spent six years in prison for a different crime. I didn't learn that my uncle had served time until I'd grown up, and all my aunt would say was that his classmate had been 'popped' and every time he heard that song he called it a bad luck song."

I sniffed the night breeze to see if I could discover what had triggered this memory.

"It was fallen leaves from a camphor tree, swept into a pile on the muddy ground with a bamboo broom."

A explained:

"My grandfather loved to prune trees, all sorts of them. Every year he cruelly, ruthlessly trimmed them until there was hardly anything left. The sawed-off branches and limbs wound up in piles in the back yard between a star fruit and a mango tree, where they dried in the sun until they were ready to burn. I played in that wood pile just about every day. The first few days, when the leaves were still green and cool, and still fragrant, I lay on top, like a dead animal when the body heat has left it. There were all kinds of trees, but the camphor, eucalyptus, and Chinese magnolia smelled the best; the magnolia branches were actually more fragrant than their flowers. Sometimes we didn't burn them all. In the years before my grandfather had a gas line into the house, he used coal and kindling, plus these branches, and I helped him and the woman who cooked for him stack the dead wood. He was responsible for chopping up the branches; she bundled up the twigs and leaves to start fires in the stove. The branches, long dead, were still fragrant, no matter how they were split, stripped, or snapped in two. . . . My grandfather wasn't much older then than I am now."

Camphor, eucalyptus, Chinese magnolia, mango, star fruit, what do they get me thinking about?

Parsley, sage, rosemary, thyme.

Violet, Chinese lantern, orange, day lily, it was almost as if I could smell them more clearly from how they sounded, and they sparked memories, often appearing on the specials menu at the coffee shop where I passed the time at dusk during rush hour, the ingredients of a flavored tea called Star of the Desert, which the girls mixed, treating tea like a perfume by giving it a name.

"I'd love to be able to recall the girlfriend I left when I went into the army. One look told you her parents were from the mainland, like you. We met just before graduation and were madly in love, but I had to fulfill my military obligation. I can't say which was the cause and which was the effect, and what I'm trying to say is, I don't know if it was the short time before I had to go into the army that sped up the process—she wrote to me every day, which gave me a lot of 'face' in my unit—or if our passion, which lacked a foundation, died off because we were separated, but a few months before I was to be discharged, she went abroad to study, taking all the books I'd left at her place, all my letters, and the few pictures of us with her, or maybe she burned them. . . ."

Is that why you can't recall her?

But there ought to be some sort of formula, say, camphor leaves with eucalyptus, a bamboo broom, and mud, all swept together, which called to mind "Ramona." . . .

"There is. She came to visit a few times in Longquan, a little village on the outskirts of Pingdong and Neipu, and took a room in the best hotel in the area, across from where I was stationed. I found a way to sneak out of camp at night to be with her and keep her from being afraid, since for Taipei girls like her, there was plenty to be afraid of. You know, what they called the bathroom had no door, and was separated from the sleeping area by a curtain, a lot like the kindling shed, which also served as an outhouse, in my grandfather's mountainside quadrangle compound, where the tenant farmers lived. Whenever I was there at festival time, I refused to use it. There was no screen over the barred window, which looked out onto a vegetable garden and a pigsty, and all night long I heard the pigs moving around and smelled liquid manure. Because the fluorescent light was so ugly, she refused to turn on anything but a little lamp, one of those things farmers used thirty years ago, with a five-watt yellow bulb, to save electricity. And the comforter, well, it was the ugliest thing even I'd ever seen, and it had soaked up the sweat and other bodily fluids of who knows how many other people. How could anyone expect her to use that?

"She didn't want to go out during the day, so I rented dozens of Japanese robot *manga* so she wouldn't be bored. I went to see her one evening, earlier than usual, and maybe it was too hot, because she was lying on the bed in her underwear, her hair in braids, reading a manga. The sight was a real turn-on, like the femme fatale in a French movie, or the legendary Quemoy 813th—don't people say those girls used to read martial arts novels while they were servicing the soldiers to keep from being bored?—stuff like that . . . that was the first time we did it, and I was inexperienced at the time, and I don't know if it was her first time, but it didn't seem to bother her, for some strange reason. Afterward, after that, the room was steaming hot, so I took her out to walk around town, the town I'd lived in for a couple of years, and told her all about this place and that place, like the Western pharmacy where the daughter attended a business college in Kaohsiung, and came home on the weekends to help out, not bad looking, and people spent the week trying to come up with an ailment they could bring over to the pharmacy and ask the girl what they should take for it; I also pointed out a little eatery where I'd written the price list for the owner with a calligraphy brush.

"After a rain squall, all the trees and plants were green, lush green, saturated with rainwater, and I was in a terrific mood, though I neglected to think about how she was doing. We walked to the end of the town's main street, where the veterans' hospital was located, fronted by a grove of mango trees. Insistent upon eating some pickled mango, she told me to sneak over and steal some for her. I picked so many my hands were stained by the sap and wouldn't wash clean for days. We bought some granulated sugar and a little pencil-sharpening knife at a nearby convenience store, then went back to her room and made pickled mangoes: after washing, peeling, and slicing the fruit, we squeezed out the sour juice and added sugar, which kept us busy all evening. She ate every last one of them. I remember that after she returned to Taipei she wrote to tell me that she discovered blood from her stomach or intestines when she went to the toilet, probably caused by the pickled mangoes, but at the time I was so paranoid I assumed she was hinting that it was because she'd done it for the first time. . . ."

The smell of pig manure, pickled mangoes, an afternoon rain squall in May, soggy rented manga, a little knife . . . to which his sweat-soaked army uniform had to be added . . . we reminded each other of missing items and supplemented the lists, created a list of essential items, like devising a formula for a mysterious perfume.

Vertivert, oak moss, white pine, hyacinth, fingered utron, oregano . . .

Supposedly we humans can distinguish over a thousand smells. Is that more than you expected? Or fewer?

Sheepdogs have 220 million olfactory cells, 44 times more than we, and I can't help wondering if we've lost something because of that. Or maybe we've lost it by design. Say, like before I met A. What I mean is, maybe, over the millennia, our ancestors have passed down to us only those organs and functions they found useful, the precisely appropriate degree of memory, and that all we need are those things that are essential to our existence. And so the number of olfactory cells we have today can be likened to me before I met A, in that I was never interested in recalling long-hidden memories or those that had already vanished.

Not only that, a sense of fear lurks in the background, even though in these memories we've done nothing wicked or outrageous.

I vaguely recall something a foreign writer once said: "The purpose of literature," he said, "is not to educate." I am not saying that literature is unrelated to morality, but that it represents one person's morality, and that any one person's morality is seldom shared by the larger body of people to which that person belongs.

By substituting the word "memory" for "morality," we discover how frightened we are by the conscious or unconscious calling up of those authentic memories. My god! They are in conflict with collectively altered memories that can be made known to people, in such resolute conflict that one nearly feels oneself to be a traitor.

The best strategy for staying clear of danger is to hold on to utilitarian memory alone.

Suddenly, for the first time, I no longer felt that the game I was playing with A was either enjoyable or interesting.

I switched to a smaller coffee shop to avoid rush-hour traffic and wait for my wife to page me.

In a bookstore I found a popular science book on the sense of smell, in which I hoped to find relative rationality that would allow me to dissolve the mysterious atmosphere that characterized my relationship with A.

—Viewed as a whole, smell is a tiny Spartan-like chemical compound.

—In a rose garden, what makes a rose a rose is a chemical compound composed of ten carbons—related to vanilla spirits—and it is formed geometrically by atoms whose bonding angles determine its fragrance. The unique vibrations of these atoms or atom clusters within the odor molecules, or the chorus of vibrations in all the molecules, have all become the basis for a variety of theories, and this basis postulates that the "osmium frequency" is the origin of smell.

—If the external arrangement of any collection of atoms is identical, then no matter what chemical designation it is given, the fragrance may be identical.

—We don't know how odors excite olfactory cells; one way of looking at the issue is that odors poke tiny holes in receptor membranes and create depolarization, but other researchers believe that this element may have been confined by cells with special receptors and immobilized there, sending out its signal from a distance with a particular method, like the antibodies in an immune cell.

— . . .

Grape, Chinese lantern, rose, pulp . . . for Martinique, the coffee shop manager's recommended flavored tea.

I laughed.

Pig manure, pickled mangoes, an afternoon rain squall in May, soggy rented manga, a little knife . . . smells that cannot be formulated decreed that A would not be able to recall what his little French girlfriend looked like.

I couldn't help being curious during those days about which scent—something I could neither control nor select, whether vivid or functional—would aid me in recalling A, if one day, as he said, he was subtracted from the world to which he'd been added.

As I strolled alone in the lane we'd walked down many times, I picked a white gardenia that had nearly opened all the way, eager to know what memories it would spark. Ah, still Zhu Meijun, my first-grade "filial" classroom in Zhongshan Primary School, the parings of Moonlight brand perfumed pencils, baby teeth with cavities . . . plus our teacher, Wu Zhengying.

My god, our teacher, Wu Zhengying . . . I hadn't thought of her in nearly forty years, our pretty teacher, Wu Zhengying, Wu Zhengying, who was passionately in love with her boyfriend, and every time he came to see her at the teachers' dormitory, she had me go with her; he would sit at her desk by the window, so she and I had to sit together on the bed. She'd let me eat the treats he'd brought her, and I'd glare at him, trying hard to keep my animus in check, and he was never conscious of it, since all he could do was stare at our teacher and smile. She, on the other hand, kept her eyes on me, watching me eat and praising me: "Such a big head, a true sign of intelligence." I sort of felt that, in their eyes, for the moment at least, I was the son who would one day fill out their ideal little family, so I played along as best I could, at the same time lamenting every precious second of class break I was giving up.

Our young teacher, Wu Zhengying, with her shoulder-length hair, swept up in a sweet, happy atmosphere, did this boyfriend, or should I say future husband, treat her well?

Suddenly my eyes filled with warm tears, and I was in the grip of sentimentality.

The best strategy for staying clear of danger is to hold on to utilitarian memory alone.

But how can the brain differentiate and remember all those smells?

One theory of smell, J. E. Amoore's "stereochemical" theory, published in 1949, maps the connections between the geometric shapes of molecules and the odor sensations they produce. When a molecule of the right shape happens along, it fits into its neuron niche and then triggers a nerve impulse to the brain.

Musky odors have disc-shaped molecules that fit into an elliptical, bowl-like slot on the neuron.

Pepperminty odors have a wedge-shaped molecule that fits into a V-shaped site.

Camphoraceous odors have a spherical molecule that fits an elliptical site, but is smaller than that of musk.

Ethereal odors have a rod-shaped molecule that fits a trough-shaped site.

Floral odors have a disc-shaped molecule with a tail, which fits a bowl-and-trough-shaped site.

Putrid odors have a negative charge that is attracted to a positively charged site.

And pungent odors have a positive charge that fits a negatively charged site.

Some odors fit a couple of sites at once, and give a bouquet or blend effect.

. . .

Like a prophecy and like a poem, and, of course, resembling the words in a strange rap song.

I picked a green unripe grape from the bunch my wife bought for me and was unsure to which category its molecules belonged, but definitely not elliptical, or spherical, or rod-shaped, or disc-shaped with a tail, and since immature fruit that will die before it has a chance to grow to full ripeness cannot carry the negative charge of something putrid, then into which sites in the folds of my brain does it fit?

I pondered this question for a long time, until I was certain that the controllable part of my consciousness really did not contain the requisite material to deal with this; I pinched it, squeezed it, and rubbed it, then waited, like Aladdin anticipating the appearance of the genie from his magic lamp.

The fog rolled in, as expected, in Women's Association Village 1. . . . I sniffed the air, sniffed it again, and uttered the names of some playmates from several hundred years ago—now I understood why A, when he sipped his Long Island iced tea, had instinctively uttered what to him might have been a secret code. After the exodus out of the village following the flood, we spent our days in an outburst of anarchic hedonism. We'd wake up each morning to the news of which families had moved away, how the plants in a certain large garden could not be moved. A certain person's yard, where we'd risked our lives to steal grapes and longans, was now ours to leisurely ravage if we felt like it. Yet we weren't willing to let the fruit ripen, preferring, as before, to pick it when it was still green and no bigger than peas, so sour that more of our saliva fell out of our mouths than went into our stomachs.

Baoxin's older brother was a small, nimble boy who picked the most fruit by climbing quickly to the top of the bamboo fence. But when he jumped to the ground, a bamboo splinter stuck in his calf; he clenched his teeth and pulled it out, then rubbed dirt on the wound to stanch the bleeding. Just watching him made our skin crawl, but no one was worried he might die.

While we were exploring houses, we happened across an older, ghostlike boy and girl who were getting laid (that's what we called it then, but when I think back now, they were only hugging and kissing); the summer seemed endless, and our number kept shrinking. The new villages were not the same for everyone; as they left, some would shout a farewell: "We're going to Nanshijiao." Someone else would boast, "We're going to Shanzangli, where there's a hillside cemetery." We couldn't have said where these new places were, but there was no sorrow of parting, no promises to write, as if no matter where everyone went, we'd all meet again someday. Liao Ba, for example, sat in the cab of an army truck that was moving his family, waved with a show of bravado, and shouted, "I'll meet you in Nanjing after we've retaken the mainland!"

I never saw any of them again, nor gave them another thought . . . the sole exception was X X Liu, whose name I saw in the community section of a newspaper after he'd been sentenced to death for kidnapping a Japanese resident's child, whose body was never found.

Like me, X X Liu was a member of one of the last families to leave the village; he and I once caught a pet dog someone had left behind, killed it, cooked and ate it. The roly-poly little thing wagged its tail whenever it saw someone. God, Mao Wu and I had actually planned to raise it ourselves, without our parents' knowledge. It was Liu's job to do the killing. He didn't know the first thing about butchering, and blood wound up all over the place, really scary, and putrid smelling. Mao Wu and I hated the idea of being laughed at and called chicken if we didn't eat any, so, like initiates into a secret society, we ate under Liu's watchful eye, our mouths covered with dog blood. My one hope was that Liu and I would not wind up in the same village.

X X Liu didn't kill dogs only; he also dispatched rats, snakes, cats. . . . With all the insects dead and summer coming to an end, when night fell, no more than a dozen lights were on anywhere in a village that had once claimed several hundred households. Very rarely, someone's head-lights passed down the highway beyond the village, too far for us to hear the car; that was our only proof that the out-side world still existed. What was Papa was waiting for? Why couldn't he make up his mind to move to Nanshijiao or Shanzangli, or to the new villages of Dating or Neihu? What if there wouldn't be time for me to change schools? I'd have no school to go to, even though, as heaven is my witness, my fondest desire was for summer vacation to last twelve months a year, so I'd never have to go to school. But at this rate, X X Liu would kill a man sooner or later, then roast him and force Mao Wu and me to eat the guy's dick.

The best strategy for staying clear of danger is to hold on to utilitarian memory alone.

I threw away the green grape I'd squeezed into pulp and wondered why I'd absorbed its odor, with its positive charge, or why it wouldn't leave me . . . Did we kill a man or didn't we?

Some people were lost during an exodus that seemed like a panicky flight. Not until the night the Suns, a fam-ily with seven children, moved into their new house did they discover that their second youngest child was miss-ing. They went back to their old house and searched all night, unsuccessfully; undaunted, they returned to their new house and continued searching. Several days later, the stench from a dead rat in a public toilet on the village out-skirts rose to the heavens; the child of the Sun family had been taken off by a demon several days earlier, but there were plenty of ghost stories set in public toilets, so it didn't seem particularly unexpected; there was also Panpan's older brother, who failed to get in the army truck and turned up the next day, floating in the Dahan river, his ears and penis eaten off by fish, or so I heard from X X Liu, who ran over to see for himself; then there was Old Uncle, the bachelor former noncom who was in charge of emptying trash bins, and it wasn't until years later that adults who'd kept in touch determined, after years of assuming he'd moved to somebody else's village, that he'd actually been lost; obviously, no one knew what happened to the homeless guy who haunted the fringes of the public square or the weedy ground near the public toilet. . . . I saw how X X Liu tricked the homeless guy when his mother told him to take food out to him. Was he someone we killed? The homeless guy? Old Uncle, the former noncom? The Sun child? . . .

I quickly picked another green grape that wasn't ever going to ripen, confident that it would solve the great mystery of my universe. I stroked it, once again the fog spread all around . . . but it would only give me a single thread, which any breeze could snap in two: I had to return to that dusk, to the weeds that covered the ground on three sides of the public toilet and grew taller than us third-graders. We were assaulted by the strong odor of what might have been long grass belonging to the fleabane family, since it resisted our stomping and snapping; we often had contests in that grass to see who could catch the most ladybugs, and when we had several of the frightened little bugs in our dirty, sweaty palms, they released foul-smelling droppings. Sometimes we went crazy looking for lost treasure, because some older kid swore that a couple of days before, so-and-so had found a gold ring while taking a dump in the wild, and we believed every word of it, because all the grownups, including our parents, told us to stay away from the wilds, since that was where thieves went to divvy up their loot, and if you stumbled upon them, they'd have to kill you to shut you up.

Kill you to shut you up. . . .

Disc-shaped molecules with tails that have positive charges are unwilling to tell me anything more, except, except to return to a night wind in a weed-covered place like that—a night wind contains your and my dream; in the dream, time is borrowed and tightly embraced, the dream embraced is like a gust of wind, like a gust of wind—

In the dream, time is borrowed, I'm positive I've been hypnotized. I can't wake up, I want to see A again, I honestly do, I'm sure he'll be a hypnotist who can awaken me with a snap of his fingers.

After work, I headed back to the little coffee shop we used to frequent, and as soon as the automatic door slid open, all the familiar odors rushed up to me, as if I'd never left the place.

But A wasn't there. . . .

I didn't even know his name. . . .

While I waited for him, like a disciple reading the scriptures without a purpose, I opened a popular science book and read with quiet assurance.

—Odors, an undesired exchange of signals between people—

—They say that schizophrenia is a result of misreading signals, one's own and others', which is why a person cannot distinguish people from reality—

—Legends say that schizophrenics have an odor not found in other people, and science has recently confirmed that their sweat contains N_3—methylhexilic acid.

—Olfactory receptors, which serve as links among all living creatures, are extraordinarily important in building symbiotic relationships, such as that between crabs and sea anemones.

Such as between A and me.

A once said that most perfume ads use music as a metaphor for the compounding process; some ingredients, or some groups of ingredients, for instance, are equated with musical notes, or harmonies, or musical instruments; the initial scent is like a melodic high note, and after the alcohol has dissipated, you can discern the mid-range notes of perfume, usually floral; the low notes come last, and sometimes they remain on the skin for as long as two or three days.

Then A said, Actually, perfume is like sex: foreplay, action, climax, consolation, and finally staying on the skin for as long as two or three days, and almost all of it comes from animals—and not from one's sex partner—usually it's ambergris, beaver, civet cat, musk . . . messengers of ancient smells, accompanying us as we pass through woods and across plains, as someone once described the occasion poetically.

Someone even said that giving a person perfume is like giving them liquid memory.

The Latin *perfumum* informs us of its origins: *per* (through or by) and *fumum* (fumes). The burned body of an animal, sacrificed to the gods, is like the second son of Adam and Eve, Abel, in the fourth chapter of the Book of Genesis. Abel was a shepherd, Abel wanted to offer up the lard from firstborn lambs; Jehovah looked favorably upon Abel and his offering. . . . Beyond that, he used it in an exorcism, to cure illnesses, and after sex.

Records of the use of incense in old Egypt, Mesopotamia, India, and China have come down to us in ancient texts or on relics; at first it was only the gods, but at some point high priests began using it, and after that came sacred leaders, then mortal leaders . . . the earliest perfumes were mixtures of fragrances and ointments, and then in the 1370s, alcohol was added to the incense and the mixture called "Hungarian water." When the Crusaders went east, they brought back spices and knowledge of Arabian skills in alchemy and distillation. Perfume was very popular during the reign of Louis XIV.

Louis XIV kept a stable of servants to perfume his rooms with rose water and marjoram, to wash his shirts and other apparel in a stew of cloves, nutmeg, aloe, jasmine, orange water, and musk; he insisted that a new perfume be invented for him every day. At "The Perfumed Court" of Louis XV servants used to drench doves in different scents and release them at dinner parties.

In the waning years of the empire, Napoleon III successfully pursued the Spanish beauty Eugenie, thanks to a creation by parfumeur Pierre Guerlain. An edict was promulgated, conferring on the Guerlain family the hereditary title of Imperial Parfumeur and Cosmetician.

Even though we do not need to use smell the way animals do—marking territory, establishing hierarchies, distinguishing among individuals, or determining when females are in heat—if you look at the vast amounts of perfume we use and the psychological effects it produces, it is clear that smell is an old warhorse in our evolution, one that we groom and feed, and won't let go of—

I groomed and fed my old warhorse and wouldn't let it go, as I waited for A to show up.

I ordered Long Island iced tea, A's drink of choice, in order to think about him, or to recall the name he might have mentioned when we first met and introduced ourselves. I groomed it again and again, but my thoughts were on the cold, clean-scented soap my wife used after returning from a year-long solo trip abroad. I forget what had caused the two- or three-month cold war between us, but all I was allowed each and every day was to know what she smelled like after her bath, not to be near her.

I paid close attention to the girl with the underarm odor, breathing in deeply when she came over with a clean ashtray, but my thoughts were on the curry rice I'd had for lunch at home after the monthly exams one day during primary school.

What in the world did I want A to help me recall or to conceal?

I thought deeply about the homeless guy X X Liu and I might have killed, as I hummed a song over and over in the strange, shifting sunset clouds that moved like a violent aesthetic: Tonight's wind, and tomorrow's dream, what traces have they left in your heart? Tonight can I borrow some time, borrow the night wind to deliver my love straight to your heart? After so long, for the very first time I recalled the theme song from the movie *Shanghai Nights* without relying upon smells. In the movie the impoverished songwriter plays his new song on a violin on the rooftop, and the sound travels on the night wind throughout the city, down to vagrants, one-time wounded soldiers now in rags and reduced to begging, who are drawn out from under a bridge by the music to look off into the distance. A year or two after that, many of them probably emigrated to Taiwan with the Nationalist government, and, for one reason or another, landed in Nanshijiao, Shanzangli, or Neihu, and may even have ended up being slaughtered.

Tonight's wind, and tomorrow's dream, what traces have they left in your heart? God, for the first time in so many years I really missed those mothers, all those mothers from various provinces who hummed and sang songs like this one, made famous by Bai Guang and Zhou Xuan. Do you believe they actually wore *cheongsams* all the time, even when they were in the kitchen cooking or performing household chores (think about our wives, who dress in expensive casual chic)? For a while, my kid sister, who was collecting gold, silver, and other treasures, insisted that I take her to a playmate's house. Back then all the mothers were doing needlework, like embroidering beads or patterns; someone came periodically to distribute materials and the money the mothers earned to help out with family expenses. Even I could tell that some of them didn't know how to do embroidery, and, like young ladies from wealthy families, tried hard to copy from memory the adroit ways of needlework by maids and elderly servants in their hometowns. Beads and sequins were often scattered all over the floor, and my kid sister would quietly retrieve them, with supreme patience, convinced that our family would be "rich" once she collected enough of them.

Sometimes, when they wore their hair in a bird's-nest style, those mothers would be prettier than the Shaw or Cathay Film Company's starlets whose pictures appeared in *South Country Cinema*. All decked out, they'd hail a pedicab and go into town to attend military aid parties at their husbands' offices. We'd stop playing and watch them like idiots when they passed by.

The third stanza of the song goes like this: The love in my heart, is it the dream in your heart? Can we borrow a bridge to connect us? On this borrowed bridge, the I of tomorrow, the you of tomorrow, will we embrace again like today?

Some mothers worked hard to learn the song, hoping to win first prize at the party, a Tatung electric fan or a U.S. Army blanket. I recalled how they embroidered with their eyes lowered, singing at the same time. The heavy smell of saliva and the rancid odor of children's urine seemed mixed in the remnants and discarded thread that littered the floor. I found it hard to imagine that those women had ever been younger than they were at that moment, even harder to imagine that after that they would keep growing older. They no longer existed in the memories of hometown relatives, nor were they understood or sympathized with by children who had set down roots here. Borrowed time, borrowed evening breeze. Most are probably no longer around by now.

A once said that a Greek writer from 2,500 years ago had the following recommendation: "mint for the arms, thyme for the knees, cinnamon, rose, or palm oil for the jaws and chest, almond oil for the hands and feet, and marjoram on the hair and eyebrows." Going through all that trouble to widen their presence and extend their territory. But A never did any of these, so I couldn't recall him via any scents (such as the smell of citronella oil on me, which I couldn't detect)—it turned out to be so easy! In the warm, thick mist of coffee that could immediately improve your mood, a tiny thread of—A called out to me from behind, "Hello, Citronella Oil."

Now that I knew he also had a smell, I couldn't wait to ask him if he'd been using that Oriental-scented perfume all along. I thought hard and presumed: "It's got pepper, honey, benzoin, tonga bean, cinnamon, fir, and no animal fragrance."

"It's camphor. My wife likes to store clothes in a camphor chest."

Before either of us could ask, we began telling each other all about our recent disappearance.

"I made a trip to Longquan in Pingdong."

A mighty sword on the wall, and the dragon roars.

Maybe I needed to make a trip to Fuzhouli (I'm still not sure if that's how to write the name of that place, since over the past thirty years I've never read any memoir or report that mentions it), if I really wanted to get to the bottom of whether we'd butchered and eaten X X Liu, no, I mean the homeless guy.

"I picked an appropriate season and chose not to drive; instead, just as back then, I boarded a bus by the Pingdong Train Station and rode to Longquan through Neipu, the same trip I'd made twice weekly in the army. I didn't recognize most of the sights, because the place was congested with new houses so ugly they were beyond salvation. But as soon as I closed my eyes and opened the window, the smells—all the plants mingled with insects on summer nights, you know, like the smell of the air on the day after a typhoon, with the fragrance from broken branches and the clean smell of water—so dense they seemed to be solidifying, cascading toward you, blocking your eyes, ears, nose, and mouth to the point of suffocation.

"How could I not know about that sort of late summer night wind, the kind you get when the kissing and touching arouses you and makes you all sweaty, with an erection that comes and goes several times, then you have to get her back, before the curfew, to the dorm or her home on the last bus with all the windows open to dry the stickiness in your crotch, blowing away the desire and awakening your feelings, until you can't help but whisper in her ear heartfelt vows, except that the vows are blown away by the same wind? It wasn't our fault."

But at least you should finally be able to recall that little French girlfriend, right? I asked A.

"I even forced myself to stay in the same hotel. The owner, obviously worried about me, kept having his wife come over for one reason or another—bringing me toilet paper or lighting the mosquito incense—maybe thinking that I planned to take poison. The hotel hadn't changed much, except for the addition of a TV set with lots of cable stations, which probably meant that no one would rent manga to read any more. Citronella Oil, I just can't recall her—"

It was because there were no fucking moist, dirty mangas! I pestered him with an accusing tone, even more afraid than he was of failing to recall the little French girl.

"Of course there were! I found a pile of them. I even picked some mangoes. God, the veterans' hospital was doing better than before, with a throng of senile old folks sitting under trees. I also bought some granulated sugar and a little paring knife; I had everything. You remember I told you about the pharmacy beauty—"

But was there still a vegetable garden outside the room for raising pigs? In this day and age, I find it hard to believe that anyone would do something that stupid.

"You're right, there wasn't. There was a three- or four-story building where men and women of all ages sang karaoke all night along. But a farm smell lingered in the air, the liquid manure of vegetable gardens. I guess the soldiers were still raising pigs and growing vegetables. That's what we did back then, to introduce some variety into our meals, and besides, we were truly bored. You know, don't you, that back then the most common phone conversation we had with our brothers in the MP company guarding the arsenal by our barracks was: Hello, hello, hello, recon company, your pigs have jumped the fence again—"

So what went wrong? My attention was diverted to thoughts of the evening wind of my youth, filled with sexual urges, which I dearly missed. It had been ten or twenty years since I'd last felt that way. For one thing, I had few opportunities to take the bus; for another, now that buses were air-conditioned, the windows could no longer be opened. Besides, in today's Taipei, where can a bus go forty or fifty miles an hour? Lend me the same kind of evening wind, and maybe I'd remember another two or three girls I've been nuts about.

"Citronella Oil, I read a terrifying report a while ago that said that Alzheimer's patients often lose their sense of smell along with their memory."

God, doesn't that mean . . .

"Yes, that means death will come earlier than you expect."

And not just our own deaths. Anything that's hidden, asleep, or undiscovered will fly away like swarms of buzzing bees, for when they're no longer remembered, they'll truly fall into a slumber and disappear forever.

I was disconcerted by their second, unavoidable, true deaths, which, sooner or later, would occur. I really didn't know if they were leaving without us or if we'd abandoned them.

"I've been thinking about this for some time, about how old folks aren't actually unafraid of dying. Didn't you once say that the death switch has been activated? Well, I think they're not afraid of death, not of a year later or five years later, not even the sudden, unanticipated death that can arrive at night. They don't fear death, because over there, in the world of the dead, there are more friends and relatives, even more than they have now. Don't you think that the unknown world of the dead with all its friends is actually quite appealing? I wouldn't be surprised if they secretly welcome the opportunity—"

What, after all, is death, except for no life? That's what death is all about.

"Citronella, what would you most like to do if there were still a little time before dying, a little remaining sense of smell, and of course a little remaining memory?"

What I'd most like to do is. . . .

"I mean the first thing you can think of, not the rational actions of taking care of your will or personal effects."

I want most to, I want most to gather together my playmates from that last summer. We'd forget all our past grudges and wouldn't be curious or reminiscent or criticize how we looked now that we're older, but would return to our secret weedy ground. You couldn't know this but, in addition to searching for wild tomatoes and hunting for treasure, we also dug a tunnel, convinced that, if the direction was right, we could successfully dig all the way to America, so long as no one feigned sickness or got lazy. I really miss them, I mean it, I'd really like to see Liao Ba, Mao Wu, and X X Liu again.

To my surprise, I actually started sobbing like an old drunk.

I have no idea why everyone was so intent on going to America, I mean back then.

"After returning from Longquan, I went to see my maternal grandpa, because I'd spent part of my summer breaks with him. He was a real pack rat who kept everything, including letters from his grandchildren, our diplomas, award certificates, useful or useless tuition receipts, even a return receipt for a postal package from more than two decades ago. I found letters I wrote home when I was in the army, plus a notebook that was part diary, but included my friends' addresses, the amount of money people owed me or I owed them, with occasional scribbles of some ideas. Know what I discovered?"

No doubt about it! You found your little French girlfriend's photo or her letters!

"In the notebook I wrote: A smells so good (I have a habit of assigning each girlfriend a code to avoid complications). I wrote: A smells so good. I asked which shampoo or soap she used, and she said she used a perfume called j'aiosé; A must have come from a wealthy family—"

Say no more. All he had to do now was quickly find some j'aiosé. Since A's frenzied, overly possessive wife hadn't yet appeared, whatever was attached to that j'aiosé would be purely, without adulteration, the memory of the little French girl. That is, as soon as you opened or applied a bit of j'aiosé perfume, it would be like, well, just like rubbing Aladdin's magic lamp, and the French girl would have no choice but to obey and appear, like the genie.

"The problem was, I searched all of Taipei's perfumeries, department stores, direct import shops for authentic goods, boutiques, consignment shops. Some said they'd never heard of it, while others said they'd stopped selling it. Citronella, I'm afraid the fragrance is no longer available."

On this day, September 4, many days later, A and I met again as usual at the coffee shop with the girl whose armpits emitted a strong curry smell. Together we pored over the classified ads in two major newspapers: "Wanted: a bottle of j'aiosé perfume, open or unopened, huge reward for any kind person willing to part with one; Please call (02) 2932–1832."

Confirming that not a single word needed to be corrected or changed, we planned to run the ad indefinitely, until, needless to say, j'aiosé turned up.

We didn't squander the days of waiting either. Every day we each prepared at least three different items, and then, by way of example, A waved the first item of the day in front me with my eyes closed, and I said, "My teacher, Ren Wenwei." I opened my eyes and saw a square of ink that primary school students use to practice brush writing. My fifth-grade calligraphy teacher, a tall, pretty, single woman from Shenyang, was Ren Wenwei. Looking back now, I think she was no more than forty, but back then we thought she was very old.

A closed his eyes, while I placed before him a magnolia my wife had put into a crystal bowl with fresh water the night before. After a long while, A opened his eyes, which shone moistly: "Grandma. In the evenings, when Auntie was making a cook fire, my grandma liked to pick one of two varieties of magnolia to wear in the buttonhole of her blouse."

My turn: grave mounts, fishing, catfish, poor earthworms. The pungent and strange leaves of the alpina flower of the ginger family.

"Rose, jasmine, Joy perfume, X X Hotel, Victoria Harbor—" A was slightly embarrassed, but the precision with which he identified these smells told me it must have been one of those once-in-a-decade experiences his wife had carefully designed.

"My office," I sighed, exhausted, and opened my eyes to see a sheet of fax paper.

Of course there were smells without memories to accompany them.

I cut open a hard, green berry, but even after a long time, A could only say, "Some kind of plant."

It was a chinaberry. In the summer, chinaberry trees flanking the main road in our village were chock full of lilac-hued flowers, so many they gave off a toxic smell. We stood under a tree, stewing from envy as we watched the homeless guy eat a small dish of Heavenly Tyrant ice cream. At the time, we were about to embark on an exploration of Women's Association Village 2, alongside the north-south highway, each of us armed with a homemade slingshot on our belt and some chinaberry ammo.

We also prepared two draft copies of a classified ad we'd carefully put away so it could be quickly published if something happened to me. The ad read, "To all the boys from the Zhongshan Primary School who lived in Women's Association Village 1 during Typhoon Gregory, please gather at the bus stop at Fuzhouli at X time on X day of X month. No one leaves until we see each other, Zaizai."

Naturally I wished I could have added to this draft my own lyrics from the song, "Evening Breeze":

The love in my heart, is it the dream in your heart?
Can we borrow a bridge to connect us?
On this borrowed bridge,
The I of tomorrow, the you of tomorrow,
Will we embrace again like today—

With such meticulous preparation, A and I could wait with our hearts at peace until the end, with each other as company, outlasting heaven and earth, until yellow rain pours down, until no one leaves unless the other shows.

September 1995

THE OLD CAPITAL

*I was at St. Mark's Square, watching the acrobatic flights of angels and the dancing of the Moors, but, without you, my dear, the loneliness was unbearable.

—*I. V. Foscarini*

Is it possible that none of your memories count?

Back then, the sky was much bluer, so blue it made you feel as if the ocean were close by, drawing you to it, and making the cumulus clouds seem even whiter, like castles sculpted out of snow. The sun shone intensely through clean air that threw up no barriers, but strangely, you didn't feel its heat. You just stood there foolishly in an unshaded spot, not knowing where to spend the afternoon, yet showing no signs of heatstroke.

Back then, bodily fluids and tears were as fresh and clear as the dew on flowers; people were more willing to let them fall if that was what felt natural.

Back then, people were so simple, so naïve, they were often willing to sacrifice themselves over a belief or a loved one, whatever their party affiliation.

Back then, before commercial real estate had led to an unrestrained opening of new roads, a building boom, and land speculation, trees could survive and grow tall and green, like those in tropical rain forests.

Back then, there were few public places, virtually no cafés, fast-food restaurants, iced tea shops, or KTV, and pubs were virtually unheard of, so young people had only the streets to roam, yet they did not surge through town like white mice.

Back then, on summer nights you could see the Milky Way and shooting stars, and watching them for a long, long time spawned an awareness of the vicissitudes of life and death, of dynasties rising and falling. Especially foolish spectators vowed to do something spectacular so as not to end up wasting their lives.

Back then, your background music, if you had a brother or sister in college, would likely be the Beatles. If it was the beginning of the 1970s, you'd be playing "Candida" nonstop, then in the next year it would be "Knock Three Times" by the same group. If it was late 1969, then you'd have listened to "Aquarius." Every third song played on the TV show *Happy Palace* would be by the black group The 5th Dimension. If it was a bit earlier than that, you'd have heard "Can't Take My Eyes off of You" by The Graduates. People who missed it then could have heard it in the bar scene in *The Deer Hunter* ten years later.

Since you were fond of Don McLean's "Vincent" and "American Pie," we need to move the time forward two years—let me check my data: "Vincent" made it to the pop charts on May 13, 1972, so this makes it the summer of 1972. You turned a deaf ear to "Joy to the World" by Three Dog Night, the hottest song at dance parties, and, of course, you ignored "Black & White," an even bigger hit by the same group, which came out after that summer, because you were engrossed in the *Donghua English Dictionary* you'd just bought to look up the meanings of words in the lyrics.

Starry starry night. . . . On the same kind of starry night, you and A were lying on a wooden bed. You still recall how the moon shone through the window and cast its light, along with shadows of wisteria and the window screen, on your bodies. You forget what led up to it, but you recall saying, "I'm not getting married, no matter what." A laughed in the dark. "That'd be terrible for so-and-so." So-and-so, a student in the same grade as you at the boys' school, was bombarding you with letters. A gentle face with a large nose and big eyes floated in front of you. A long silence before A added, "Wonder if it'd be fun to be gay." You didn't reply. Maybe you'd had too much fun during the day, and so you fell asleep without exchanging another word, the young bodies of two seventeen-year-olds, like purring cats.

*The first lunar month in the seventh year of the Xianfeng reign, a major snowfall in Tamsui.

Neither of you ever had a chance to learn if it'd be fun to be gay. You were too busy; in the space of a year or two, the emotions stirred up inside and all those tears that weren't necessarily shed in sadness constituted a great deal more than the sum total of what you would experience over the next twenty years.

You two left town whenever you felt like it. If you rode the train line that had been completed the first year of the century, instead of taking empty seats, you sat on the stairs by the door and sang songs you'd just memorized into the wind. If it was the summer of the following year, you'd surely be singing "Tie a Yellow Ribbon Round the Old Oak Tree." Sometimes you took the bus. Back then, North Gate had yet to be tyrannized by an overpass, so you could walk past it casually, feeling like one of your ancestors heading out of town a century before. You'd walk past the railway office and board the bus at Izumi-machi, I-chome and within a quarter of an hour you'd arrive at Dadu Road, which, fifteen years later, would be famous for motorbike racing.

Traveling sixty miles an hour, the bus would roar through Guandu Temple Pass, where the wide river appeared before you, and each time you would be deeply moved, or you would breathe in the damp river and ocean air before saying to your companion, who was seeing it for the first time, "Doesn't that look like the Yangtze River?"

When the bus passed Zhuwei in the afternoon, the setting sun would send its rays across the rippling surface from the Guanyin Mountains on the opposite bank. Sandbars overgrown with yellow hibiscuses and mangroves, as well as the small egrets, buffalo herons, and night herons perched on them, would call to mind the lines "Clear streams meander through the Hanyang Woods/Fragrant grasses spread across Parrot Islet."

You did not go to see A's male friends every time. They were hard to find, in spite of their large numbers. Some lived, commune-style, in traditional farmhouses, all but tilling the land to grow their own food. One of them lived in Youchekou on the outskirts of town, which gave him a perfect excuse to miss classes, and that made him even more difficult to find. They said he spent most of his time at the Mountain Work Club. When he wasn't busy, he'd be out sketching terraced rice paddies by Xinghuadian or pencil-drawing old houses along rebuilt streets. Another one lived in town above a pool hall. Sleeping during the day and going out at night, he was incomprehensibly careless about his appearance. Photographs he'd taken filled the walls in his room, mostly faces of weatherworn, unisex-looking old folks. But you saw a photo of A, who bared her shoulders, with only a scarf draped across her chest. You wondered about when she'd had that picture taken, as well as . . .

It didn't matter whether you found her friends or not, and eventually you'd end up on Qingshui Street, after passing through the traditional open market that scared you witless. You did not go to Longshan Temple, even though one of A's boyfriends, an architecture major, took great pleasure in inviting you to eat salty peanuts, boiled in their shells, under the pillars in front of the temple, where he'd tell you all about the temple's history and architecture. With mixed feelings of curiosity and sympathy, you'd walk past small hotels manned by old pimps and arrive at Qingshuiyan Temple. You never drew inscribed lots, nor were you interested in the faithful, men or women. Instead, you'd walk past the gilt-paper incinerator, which was shrouded in white smoke the year round, and onto the narrow path halfway up the hill. On the right were either stone walls covered with weeds and moss or residential brick walls; on the other side was the spot where the wide river met the ocean. You ignored the single-ridge southern Min–style houses, with their slanted roofs, agreeing that it was a San Francisco sort of view, even though neither of you had ever been there.

When you reached the end of the path, you'd have to pass through someone's kitchen to return to Chongjian Street, the oldest street in town, the one you couldn't wait to get away from. Resigned to a return to reality, you'd walk past fresh fish stalls, pork sellers, giant cauldrons that fried fish the year round, and Fuyou Temple, built during the reign of the Yongzhen Emperor, before coming to narrow Zhongzheng Road, where you'd take care not to be hit by a bus. Before long, you would be following familiar steps up the narrow alley facing the ferry landing, where lush green seasonal weeds forever peeked out through the cracks. It was as if you were going home, except for the part about calling out to the folks at #2 and #4, "*Tadaima*"—I'm back.

The wrought-iron gate on the wall around Red Mansion was locked sometimes, but you could always get in. You two would sit on the low wall facing the river, and neither the chinaberry nor the flame tree, not even the grove of unruly bamboo, could block out the sun or the ocean winds. Sometimes, when a sea of fiery red flowers covered the flame tree, you felt as if you were in Spain or some small Mediterranean town.

Red Tower, beige in the colonial style, had been a shipping tycoon's mansion at the end of the previous century, and his descendants did not know what to do with the place. It was currently the lair, à la the People's Commune, of a bunch of boys, all students from the nearby university and vocational college. Some of them skipped class and stayed in bed until the afternoon, then stood bare-chested on the balcony, staring down at you like idiots. Others, who had just awakened from erotic dreams, whistled or shouted menacingly, "Hey, didn't you see the NO TRESPASSING sign on the gate?"

You'd look up at them nonchalantly. Their underwear would be drying on the balcony, flapping in the wind like banners.

From where you sat, on the short wall, as if on a ship about to set sail, you could almost see the captain enter in his log: "6:30 AM, N34°26′ E17°28′, a 20-knot western wind, heading 330. . . ."

A, who shared your feelings, gestured a lot when she talked. You wished you had her body, all 5'6" of it, with the square shoulders of a swimmer and long, lanky limbs. She had breasts too, but they were more like an athlete's muscled chest. You hated your body, with its narrow waist, full breasts it was impossible to hide, and girlish hands and feet. Paradoxically, you sometimes wished you were more like Song, A's best friend in junior high, whom she talked about all the time. Which book, which teacher, which movie Song liked the best, what kind of food she hated, and what kinds of boys disgusted her. Song was an only child. She and A agreed that they just had to get into the same senior high, but Song was sick during the month before the entrance exams and only made it into a girls' high school on the city's south side. . . . You hadn't met Song, but no one ever existed in this world as clearly and unambiguously as she.

One time you and A skipped class to see a double feature at Qingkang for 20 NT, because one of them starred George Chakiris, A's current obsession. When the movie ended, you heard someone call A's name. It was a tiny yet clear voice, and you knew instinctively it must be Song. You were right. Dressed in a lime yellow school uniform, Song was so tiny that A reached out and, in dramatic fashion, picked her up and spun her twice in the air. When A made the introductions, you were attentive to Song's eyes on you—very big, very dark, and very empty.

Without the least hesitation, A walked with Song to the bus stop and saw her home.

Refusing to walk alone across the quiet, gray baseball field, now that there was no game, fearful of being reminded that those ballplayers, who were about your age, were also getting old, you crossed to the other side of the street, which, to your surprise, was overgrown with weeds. Five years later a giant billboard would be erected on that spot, outlandishly claiming it as the future site of the largest hotel and shopping mall in all of Southeast Asia. Another five years would pass and the hotel complex would be completed, and then even later you would actually be married in one of the banquet rooms of the "outlandish" five-star hotel.

Walking alone on the weedy path and looking at the fiery red sunset, in a tiny voice you sang to yourself "When the Sunset Rages in the Sky," a song your school choir had been practicing. When you got to "My love, my love, let me wish you the best . . . ," snow flurries filled the air.

*In the disgusting green and slippery damp city, the aging Governor had ancient eyes.—D. H. Lawrence

But this is how the Hundred Flowers Calendar described the lunar seventh month: in the seventh month, the hollyhocks turn crimson, corfu lilies caress the head, crepe myrtles are submerged in the moon, hibiscuses face the sun, knotweeds bloom red, and waternut flowers grow full.

In any case, in order to create a contrast with the Wedgwood blue September sky, all the flowers in the red category bloom: South American purple jasmine, Oriental coral tree, large-blossomed crepe myrtle, red ixora, lady's slipper, Chinese hibiscus, canna. . . . In particular, the Chinese hibiscus, known for reaching over walls from under eaves, left a deep impression on the group of young and middle-aged men who arrived in 1949, and the Portuguese and Spaniards who came to save souls and obtain pepper 300 years earlier. The later group, away from their homelands for so long, were driven to the brink of madness as they recalled similar blue skies, white walls, green trees, red flowers, black hair, dark brows and lashes, and love songs like "Let me look at you, girl from Lima, let me tell you about the glory of dreams, dreams that awaken memories of ancient bridges, rivers, and forests. . . ." The name of the song might well have been "Cinnamon Flowers."

Actually, nonred flowers also bloomed, including Burmese gardenias, which we called egg flowers, with their white petals and yellow pistils (you could, for instance, spot them in the courtyard of the Presbyterian church on Shijō-tō or at No. 2, Lane 3, Tai'an Street). Their subtle sweetness, with a slight medicinal odor, often stirred up a bit of melancholy in mothers who were rushing to work and sending kids to school; about how they could, as in so many Septembers in the past, go to school with new uniforms, new classmates, new classrooms, new teachers. Everything was new and unknown, thus filled with endless possibilities. Even though people set up rules telling you what to do and what not to do, you could be completely free, truly free outside of the rules. Not the sort of freedom you think you have now in choosing between a job at 42,000 or 45,000 a month, and definitely not the sort of freedom to choose between a Montessori or Flubber kindergarten or the American-style Orff school for your kids.

You would take full advantage of that freedom. Twenty years later, politically correct writers, when dealing with this period, would surely have you participating in such activities as demonstrations against the Japanese occupation of Diaoyu Island or the million-hour-contribution movement initiated after Taiwan's withdrawal from the UN or the Aboriginal Service Club. If not, the writers would arrange for you a father or grandfather who was a victim of the incident of many years before, or have you secretly distribute flyers for Guo Yuxin and Kang Ningxiang. Or you would be a conscientious reader of *Free China* or *Grand Learning Magazine*, which would lead to enlightenment. If not that, at least you'd be itching for a fight over the termination of diplomatic relations with Japan, scheduled for the end of that year. Like most people around you, you were ignorant about everything mentioned above. Around 400 A.D., people stopped believing in Zeus; by around 1650 A.D., no one believed in shamans anymore; in 1700, doubts about God's revelations began to spread. Isn't everything like that? The glory and suffering of an age always belong only to a few sages, shamans, and sorcerers.

You couldn't have cared less about school starting. Like fun-loving people of every generation, you could always find ways to skip school, no matter which one you were attending. Your school was located in Bumbu-machi and the first thing you saw when you left the school grounds was the Governor-General's Office. The building was less than four decades older than you, but it gave the impression of being old and decrepit. Without giving it a second thought, you assumed it had a history going back at least a century or two, but at other times you assumed it had been built by the Nationalist government, which came over with your parents' generation.

You reached Hon-machi, Book Street, after passing the square in front of the government building, which sometimes was packed with commuter buses and at other times was deserted. You seldom had time for the bookstores, especially the dark, gloomy, coldly ancient bookstores that felt like Chinese herbal shops, for they reminded you too much of the literature or history class you'd just gotten out of.

You usually took the train, where you sat on the steps by the door, oblivious that you were blocking the passage. How could so many housewives be getting on and off, all going grocery shopping? The train traveled through the ugliest part of the city, so the petulant families, as if by prior agreement, lined the tracks with their back doors, illegal constructions, public toilets, vegetable gardens, and garbage dumps, steeping the area in a village flavor, even though the train passed through Kensei-chō, Owari-machi, and Hōrai-machi, the most prosperous districts of a bygone era.

Sometimes you left the train at Miyanoshita, but if you were too absorbed in your conversation, you got off at Shilin. The small station at Miyanoshita was like other small stations along the line. Most of those still standing ten years later would appear in coffee commercials or short-subject government documentaries to advertise economic accomplishments. The vacant ground in front of the platform and station office would often be carpeted in Korean grass, with its exotic fragrance, and several pretty flowers with a Southeast Asian flair, like multicolored purslanes, lantanas, poisonous leopard lilies, and monthly roses. The occasional attempt to plant Chinese peonies and tree peonies was doomed to failure. Equally difficult to grow were temperate-zone araucaria and arhat pines, which, seen against the whitewashed wall and station house built of stained fir, brought solace to many homesick soldiers.

For the same reason, a 10,000-cherry-tree movement was initiated during the war, hoping the islanders would, like the soldiers, fall in love with the unique, tragic, and resolute beauty of cherry blossoms. They planted an enormous number of *hikan* cherries, *omisha* cherries, double cherries on Grass Mountain, Wushe, and Nanfang'ao, which is how this particular station came to have a row of hikan cherry trees. Except for a week of hasty blooming around the Lunar New Year, their pale, bare figures were hidden under mastlike betel palms, as if inflicted with an autistic lack of confidence. Yes, there were definitely betel palms, as in a photograph of soldiers from the end of the previous century, in which an oxcart moves slowly under the shadow of trees that sway in the wind, as if cut out of paper. The corner of the photo is inscribed "Impression of the South," making you feel like taking a bath in the afternoon and cooling off in *yukata* and *geta*.

There had to be betel palms, for they could be seen around public schools, post offices, government buildings, and churches built in the Taisho or early Showa periods. At least there had to be fan palms, coconut palms, and date palms, which are similar in shape and style. There were more than a dozen fan palms in front of the rickety classroom building at your primary school, which was built in the fifth year of the century, isn't that so? You could more or less sense the age of the school, or else why did you run over to dig beneath a banyan tree after school, convinced you'd find an antique treasure to enrich your parents, who had fled the war and come to this side of the strait, bringing with them nothing of value? Your persistence sustained you through the third grade, but the results were far from satisfactory, for you were rewarded with a scant few shards of dark green pottery from an unknown period, which you entrusted to your mother for safekeeping. The yellow earth, smoothed by bare feet over decades, was cool and solid to the touch; the banyan fruit, no matter how pretty it looked, was wormy. When you opened it, you had to carefully lick the wormless part with the tip of your tongue for the sweetness; those palms, whose leaves were used to make fans, swished in the wind and made you sleepy; the shiny green nuts were so hard, so solid you cut them with a broken tile, smashed them with a brick, even gnawed them with your teeth, eager to know what treasure was hidden inside. There also had to be ocean dates, Taiwanese ocean dates, or else how could those men 300 years ago gaze upon a coastline teeming with Taiwanese ocean dates and shout, "Ilha Formosa!"? It didn't matter that this was said to be the twelfth "beautiful island" they'd so named on their eastbound voyage.

A shimmering ocean; a beautiful island.

You really missed the time when, in that dark, red brick auditorium that was scheduled to be demolished, several hundred primary school children shouted your school song at the top of their lungs, "Bailu Mountain and Neihu Hill Are Our Best Shields." The song was rhythmless because you were shouting. Back then you had no idea that, except for Bailu Mountain, the public school located by Neihu Hill in Seven Star County was completely unknown to the seventh principal, Kobori Yoshihei, who had taken over in the seventh year of the Taishō era, after the end of the war in Europe. Nor did you know that Akanabe Misao, an earlier principal, had later described Neihu as a "purple mountain with clear water." Your only concern was that neither of your two best friends in class took the same route as you, making it impossible to goof off on the way home once you were out of the student monitor's jurisdiction. On sunny winter afternoons, you took turns jumping from the path onto farmers' haystacks. One of your best friends belonged to the Gangqian Route, the other, the Shisifen Route. The Shisifen Route had once had about ten students, but she was the only one left, since those in the higher grades had to stay after school to study and those in the lower grades went home at noon. She told you she had to walk two hours on a mountain path to get to school, and in the winter, she had to get up before dawn. Two hours! Wouldn't that take you all the way to Taipei city?

Later on you learned to read grownups' newspapers. When she was late for school, you had trouble listening in class, because you were afraid she'd run into bad people and be raped on Bailu Mountain. Hey! Where was Shisifen, you wondered. And Hey! again, what about Donghu, which you heard was also two hours away on foot? And the ones from Donghu were always the last to pay their tuition, usually when the semester was half over and after being beaten daily by the teacher. But Donghu students were indispensable during school celebration sports meets. There were usually Donghu boys in your classes; they were dark and quiet, like oxen, and none of them cried or screamed under the teacher's savage beatings. Sooner or later, the teacher would curse them: "Are you taking mute medicine?" You felt sorry for them, but were never romantically involved with any of them.

If they hadn't sold off their land over the next twenty years, they'd have been billionaires by now.

*Beyond the yuccas and Chinese hibiscuses was the ocean.

One night twenty years later, when you were blind drunk for reasons you can no longer recall, you lay prone in your dark, silent bedroom, where, with eyes unfocused but absolute mental clarity, you watched as your seventeen-year-old bodies, clad in school uniforms, book bags on your backs, took a danger-laden path under a gourd trellis in a yard teeming with chickens and ducks (neither of you knew how to speak Taiwanese, and you were afraid you wouldn't be able to explain to the farmer who owned the house that you were using the trellis as a shortcut and had no intention of stealing his gourds). The ground beneath your feet had turned to soft, yellow, fine sand, making for tough going on the gentle slope. Dirty Chinese hibiscuses were abloom with giant yellow flowers, blocking the cold rain that had been falling for some time. The seasonal change of uniform had yet to take place, but you didn't feel the cold in your short-sleeved shirts. Wasn't it always like that back then? You didn't feel the cold, you didn't feel the heat, you were never hungry, and you were never fatigued, so long as you had enough to occupy your mind and heart.

So with enough to occupy your mind and heart, you walked past the Chinese hibiscuses, cut between the yuccas and sisal, which occasionally nicked you with their serrated leaves but didn't hurt. Giant, two- or three-meter-long stamens covered in big, white, fleshy flowers rose out of the centers of the sisal. Against the ocean, which was not far off and easily visible, the stamens looked like ships' masts, a scene nearly identical to that which the Canadian doctor Mackay had seen a century earlier upon his arrival from the province of Ontario.

Beyond the yuccas and Chinese hibiscuses was the ocean. You told yourselves not to forget the password repeated to you over and over by one of A's boyfriends the first time he took you through the secret passage. Summer was over and the coastline was again under the tight control of the coastal defense garrison, so that was the only way to keep from being seen by naval personnel on the base. You could not know that, at the same time on the same day, 88 years earlier, the French navy launched an attack on that spot, their ships' big guns covering the 800 marines who came ashore at Shalun. The defenders fired from makeshift battlements to lure the enemy inland. The French fell for the trick and entered a dense forest of yucca and Chinese hibiscus, where their machine guns and cannons were ineffective, leaving them no choice but to engage in hand-to-hand combat with knives. You had memorized Qing history for the exams, so you knew every big and small battle and the subsequent treaties from the beginning of the Daoguang reign, but you could not recall this life-and-death skirmish or its outcome in the dense forest of yucca and Chinese hibiscus.

Unlike the ghosts of the French soldiers who were lost here eighty-eight years earlier, you passed through the yucca and Chinese hibiscus with ease under their envious gaze.

Most of the time it was only the two of you. Purple ipomoea flowers blanketed the ground, at the end of which was the ocean, the bright gray ocean. Moist air turned the place where the ocean met the sky misty. Already drenched, you walked side by side on the beach, each singing your favorite song to yourself, engrossed in similar scenes in your favorite movies, so there was nothing to talk about. It was no one's fault that you'd always believed that this ocean was the largest in the world, and that filled you with boundless fantasies of pirates and adventurers from centuries ago.

The low, cloudy sky that seemed to press down on your brows and lashes usually reminded you of *Ryan's Daughter*, but if it had been ten years later, it would have been *The French Lieutenant's Woman*. Like repressed, dark, gloomy England, with its raging undercurrent, it was the opposite of a summer beach.

Salt-filled breezes over a summer beach, especially after sunset, seemed to possess you and wouldn't let you leave. The sand, retaining the dying heat of the sun, caressed you as music flew in all directions. Sometimes the music was real, coming from the portable cassette players of lingering visitors. Dispersed by the wind, the music seemed to come and go lazily. How wonderful if it happened to be playing Frankie Avalon's "Why." Whoever missed the song would hear it repeated twenty years later in Edward Yang's movie *A Brighter Summer Day*. In any case, under circumstances created by these combined factors, plus a fire burning with driftwood collected by an industrious individual, you'd wish you had a boy next to you, so the two of you could lie on the beach oblivious to how people might see you. You'd feel so warm and secure in his arms that you'd happily be turned into a woman, no matter who he was.

You looked at A, next to you, and wondered why she'd never been the object of your fantasies.

When the sky merged with the ocean, you lost your sense of direction and, without realizing it, wound up at the headwater of the Gongsitian Stream, where you were stopped, and Guanyin Mountain leaped into view as you turned around. When the weather improved, you could see clouds on the top of the mountain. And when a strong wind arose, the clouds raced across the sky, as if Guanyin Mountain were performing Daoist breathing exercises. Few people lived on the mountain back then, and only one house about midway up turned on a light when it got dark, which made it appear as a lonely glistening tear coursing down a cheek, like that night when you were all liquored up for reasons you can no longer remember, and you shed tears too.

With calm composure, you listened as A chattered away about her boyfriends. You didn't care; the only taboo topic was Song. You would feel the damp coldness from your clothes travel down your spine the moment she mentioned Song; then your heart would shrivel, like a tiny fist, smaller and smaller and smaller and smaller, until it hung forlornly, beyond all help.

The beach was deserted in the fall. You were oblivious to the spirits of the dead wandering around you, including the one who went swimming one winter a few years before and was swallowed up by a shark, and the Samaritan who drowned while trying to save someone at Xinghuadian a few years later, including your own.

*When the Qing government took over Taiwan, there was talk in the court about laying waste to it.

When there was a hint of fall in the air, you'd get off the train at Miyanoshita Station, or Jiantan if you were taking the bus—Jiantan was less than half a mile from Dalang bengshe at the northern end of the Tamsui River, where the natives rowed their boats in and the channel was wide. A tree called the nightshade was so tall it blocked out the sun, so big it required several linked arms to encircle its trunk. It grew by the lakeshore. A Dutchman was rumored to have stuck his sword into the tree, which grew around it; that's how the place got its name, Jiantan—Sword Lake.

Of course that didn't square with what you knew about Jiantan. When you were five, your parents dressed you up and took you for your first visit to the zoo and the children's amusement park. After getting off the bus, you didn't want to go anywhere else, for there in front of you was a carnival square, so big, so bustling there was much more joy in the air than at Disneyland, to which you would take your daughter thirty years later. The air seemed filled with colorful balloons, bubbles, and music; there were smells and shouts from all sorts of food stalls; and giant billboards blocked out the top of Maruyama, or Yuanshan—Rounded Hill. The billboards were unremarkable: no pictures, just words, ads for the few national enterprises, such as Tatung electric fans, White Flower Oil, Ta-hsin Raincoats, or inspirational slogans by the government. Tiny structures that looked like ticket booths were crammed full of toys that, looking back, must have been truly cheap and ugly, so no wonder your parents had refused to buy you any.

Within the next two or three years, the remaining Japanese Shinto shrines would be cleared away from Maruyama and replaced by the Chinese palace-style Grand Hotel for foreign VIPs. The illegal buildings at the foot of the hill would be razed, like a circus that, as soon as the performance is over, packs up its tents and moves out overnight. Not until twenty years later, on a visit to Cairo, did it dawn on you that the peddlers had actually migrated to Egypt. You were on a tourist bus, the air conditioning going full blast, when you discovered that the traffic-clogged streets were packed with booths where ugly snacks, plastic toys, and other unknown objects were sold. You had no idea who would want to buy that junk, but then you saw a young couple with dark skin and big eyes who were holding the hands of their child and studiously asking the price of this and that. You pressed your face against the bus window, unable to peel yourself away from the sight.

There was a hint of autumn in the air. Back then, neither of you had ever left this island, where it never snows, even in the winter, so how could you have known what autumn was like?

In the ninth month of the lunar calendar, the chrysanthemums bloom, the hibiscuses wither, the campions grow fuzz, leaves of the calthrops and lilies dry out on the river, the oranges appear, and the yams turn milky. . . . No, no, it's definitely not because there were chrysanthemums and osmanthus (if your father had come from another province), or hibiscuses and tree orchids (if your father was local Taiwanese), or wisterias and arhat pines (if your ancestors had spoken Japanese), or eucalyptuses and breadfruit trees (if your ancestors had fought in the South Pacific, even Australia, as imperial soldiers). You'd know autumn was here when you stood on the Meiji Bridge, designed by Togaro Katarō, and could feel the wind coming from somewhere far, far away; how very sad. If it was a clear day, the sky would be incredibly vast. When you were feeling low, one of you would recall a line of poetry or an adage from a wise man you'd read a few days before. Then you'd turn vague and illusive, which was enough to prove that autumn had indeed come to the island.

Additional proof was in the fragrance of sweet gum trees that lined the narrow path, even though they remained a scorched yellow and never turned bright red. But that was enough for you. You walked down Chokushi Avenue, completed at the turn of the century, imagining you were in one of the thirteen New England states. It was all the fault of the MAAG dormitory, with its whitewashed walls, large windows, chimneys, and lush green lawn, a typical scene from a 1950s Hollywood movie. It was all the fault of off-duty GIs, who were seen on the street from time to time, and who chatted you up, gentlemanly. It was all the fault of those of you who were engrossed in the TV show *Peyton Place*, with its small-town affairs. If you didn't loaf around after school, you'd get home in time to see the show. It really didn't matter if you missed some episodes, since it had been running for more than two years and the plot hadn't progressed much, even though you'd watched it from the age of fourteen or fifteen all the way up to seventeen. You weren't that crazy about Ryan O'Neal, who would become famous later; you felt somehow that you were more like Mia Farrow's character, Allison, who was intent upon leaving the small town for Boston or New York to be a writer. You felt something acutely similar between you and her, since for no identifiable reason you wanted to leave the place where you were born and raised.

Even though the sweet gum trees did not turn red, you felt that autumn had arrived, and so you walked to Hotel Loma, where you crossed the street diagonally. Usually there were lots of GIs standing outside waiting for taxis. You were too shy to look closely at the sculpture on the hotel façade, and wondered why two babies were suckling on a dog. Roughly twenty years later, when you were reading Greek and Roman myths to your daughter, it occurred to you that the sculpture was a Roman creation myth and that "Loma" actually was "Roma." Across the street from Loma was Caves Bookstore, but you did not go in. Among the bookstores you did not visit, besides Caves, were Gold Mountain and Linkou Book Company, since they sold only English books. For you they were like a foreign concession, where Chinese and dogs were forbidden entry. In the concession near St. Christopher's Church was an Oriental arts and crafts shop that targeted foreigners. There were also Qingguang Market; Fuli Bakery; Rose Marie Restaurant; Meiqi Hotel; Dream Café; CAT, the airline owned by Chen Xiangmei, widow of Flying Tiger Claire Chennault; The Roundtable; and the fountain in front of the Jiaxin Building.

One day, A wanted to buy a pair of genuine Levi's® jeans allegedly brought out from the PX, so you entered the maze of Qingguang Market. Feeling that every woman in sight was a bar girl, you had no time to dispense sympathy; instead you studied them wide-eyed, amazed to discover how ordinary they looked, and how they were fond of rice-noodle soup and pork-liver sausage. You must have also gone into Fuli Bakery, where there were pastries and candy you found only in translated novels, and which gave you the feeling of being in a foreign country. For example, Christmas puddings that were available only at year's end, bread made with strange spices, abundant meaty products, butter, a variety of jams and jellies, black tea. . . . Enough for you to fantasize about a life ten times better than the KMT could supply, though in reality your allowance would have been used up by buying a single chocolate-covered nut. No wonder one of you vowed to splurge on chocolate with your first paycheck.

Strange how all this had nothing to do with nationalism.

At the end of that year, Japan was about to sever diplomatic ties with the island. The government, in order to calm the people, produced one slogan after another, which moved you so much you started up a donation campaign during one of the class meetings. You donated your chocolate money. You also launched campaigns to give blood and sign petitions in blood, and would have performed such public service as sweeping the street in front of the school gate and assisting with traffic control if your class monitor hadn't dissuaded you from doing so.

The donation of a single piece of chocolate candy did not provide adequate outlet for your energy or patriotic sentiments, so you went with A to look up her boyfriends at the university, where you casually cut your finger, supplying enough blood to draw a stroke on one of the characters written on a giant sheet of white cloth. With emotions still raging, you followed them as they thronged to the campus store, an old, dark, frosty warehouse structure likely left behind from the colonial era, which made you wish you could grow up fast. Or maybe it was the vines you thought were holly that covered the window, or the surrounding tall paperbark trees found in temperate-zone countries, for even the air was cool and dry. You noticed that one of the boys, who looked a little like Ryan O'Neal, had been stealing glances at you, and you smiled, pitying him for no apparent reason.

Strangely, though, none of this was in conflict with real life. You continued to stroll in the Concession and watched as a man with fair skin and a high nose took one of your female compatriots by the arm like an old imperialist after the Opium War. As they walked along, he tickled her and made her cackle. You didn't sense anything out of the ordinary about the scene, seemingly having forgotten the accusations and protest written on the cloth that included a bit of your blood.

A great deal more than that was not in conflict.

On the same evening 20 years later, you and your husband would go to a gathering purported to have been attended by 100,000 people. You racked your brain but could not fathom where that soccer stadium had come from and what the place had been used for before the stadium materialized. And that wasn't the only thing that puzzled you. Your original intention had been to donate some money, a meager contribution to help unseat the ruling party, like giving blood for a single stroke on a written character years before, and then leave. In the end, of course, you couldn't make your way out through the crowd. More importantly, your husband of nearly 20 years wasn't about to leave. When you looked at him, his blurred face displaying the same expression as the tens of thousands of faces around him, he could have been a total stranger who was shouting and clapping in response to the spotlighted speakers. Finally, when a campaign aide said something about how people with a provincial background like yours ought to get out and go back to China, your husband cast you a frenzied glance, as if afraid you'd be identified and driven off by the people around you.

That night, with the residual excitement still raging inside him, your husband attacked you with movements and rhythms the likes of which he'd never used before. You lay in the dark refusing to shed a tear, while he did what he wanted. It had been many years since you'd last cried, because tears were too salty. Sweat was salty too. You couldn't say when it started, but a strange and repellant odor slowly began to appear on you. At first you thought it was the result of childbirth. You'd spent a week in the hospital and come home with a pleasant mixture of smells: the hospital's fresh, clean disinfectant; baby oil; medicine; and breast milk. But it didn't take long for the fragrance to disappear. The first time you discovered that the strange odor clung to you, you returned assiduously to the shampoo, hand soap, and laundry powder you'd used before. But twenty-odd years of the same odor was gone; it had been with you for over two decades without your noticing it, and you realized you'd had it only after you'd lost it. What remained was a salty odor that easily crystallized; the dirty, salty smell must have had a completely different molecular structure than the salt in the ocean. There were things you could neither avoid nor change, like bodily fluids or sweat, but not tears, and that is why you refused to shed them.

You couldn't help but think of the five failings of a deity: ears turning deaf, eyes going blind, nose getting dull, facial complexion turning sallow, splendid clothes covered in dust.

Refusing to admit that your ears were turning deaf or your eyes going blind, you decided to go alone to the football stadium on the postelection holiday, in the daytime, for you were shocked and distressed to be unable to recall what had originally been at the site, even though you'd spent most of your life in the city's eastern district and hadn't been off the island for a single moment over the past twenty years.

You got off at the bus at Jiantan one ordinary winter afternoon, just as you'd done at the age of seventeen. Except for the absence of the friend who'd skipped class with you, you were immensely pleased by the smell of late autumn in the air. You nearly said "Long time no see" to the trees, which were much taller and much greener now, and you quickly contained your shock and disbelief at the sight of the MRT station, ugly and gigantic beyond belief, for it destroyed the skyline's beauty. When you were seventeen the sky wasn't all that different from the one seen by ancestors who had followed the Tamsui River to fish, hunt, and farm 4,000 years ago, and the same as that seen by the Spaniards who followed the river upstream one night and discovered the Ketagalan tribe 330 years ago. The station and newly completed MRT tracks destroyed every sliver of imagination. The track built at the turn of the twentieth century ran parallel to a long stretch of red brick sidewalk. As a pedestrian, you'd fought to control your urge to wave at a train as you watched it go by, envious of the passengers inside, as if they were embarking on a long journey. When there were no trains, the silent tracks seemed especially friendly, for you could cross them or lie down on them anytime you wished. The broad, even fields on the far side of the tracks were not much different from those the Tongan people saw 120 years ago, when they were defeated in skirmishes in the wild. The river was out of sight, but you knew that it was nearby and you could follow it to the ocean, which made you long for far-away places.

You had no idea when the incessant longing for far-away places, the desire to go on a long trip, to fly far and high, first came to you. In fact, you'd been off the island less than a month altogether, like an island savage or an ocean pirate. For many years you had actually found life bearable only by regularly imagining some part of the city, some section of a certain road, or some street scene as some other city, one you either had or had not visited. It was like so many men who, regardless of how they feel about their wives—good or bad—have to imagine them as another woman before they can perform in bed.

You never tried to deal with this feeling, nor did you dare mention it to anyone, especially since there were always people who wanted to know whether or not you loved this place, even wanted you to hurry up and leave if you didn't.

"If you want to leave, leave. Go back to where you came from"—as if you all had a place just waiting for you to return to, a ready-made place to live, but you kept hanging around, to your shame.

Was there such a place?

*No need to go ashore, no need to shave your head, no need to change your clothing style; sending tribute and being a royal subject will suffice.

Hideo turned his steps toward the bridge at Shijo where he had first met "Chieko's Naeko" or "Naeko's Chieko," but it was hot under the noonday sun. He felt like strolling across the bridge at Shijo, so that was what he did. Leaning against the rail at the end of the bridge, he closed his eyes. He listened, not for the echoes of the crowds or the trains, but for the almost imperceptible sound of the flow of the river.

Unlike Chieko, you stood on Shijō Bridge in the wind and cold, which, according to the digital display on a nearby building, was 4° Celsius. You were looking down on lovers along the Kamo River who were immune to the cold and seemed to never leave.

The only difficult decision was where to take your afternoon tea—Fauchon, in the basement level of Takashimaya, or Rakushō, by the entrance to Kōdaiji Temple. The afternoon tea at Fauchon—a scone and a cup of house blend coffee or black tea—cost 500 yen, a price that had remained the same for years, whether the value of the yen appreciated dramatically or dropped precipitously. You deeply missed the seats, so few that there was usually a long line. You'd often see neatly dressed old couples, in their seventies at least, taking their meals solemnly, as if conducting a ritual of sorts. They talked in whispers and did not look or act like the average Japanese. You were pretty sure they were probably Deng Xiaoping's classmates when he studied in France.

But you missed the waramochi at Rakushō even more, so you made your way to Gion. A traveling monk asking for alms stood motionless at one end of the bridge. You weren't sure if he was the same one you'd seen before. He wore the same summer attire. You never gave him anything, not ever.

Minamiza Theater was still showing a movie by Ban-dou Tamazaburō, so there was no point in going. The green light was blinking when you suddenly decided to cross the street to look at Shirakawa-minami-dōri, where flagstones were being laid the last time you were there. Shirakawa-minami-dōri parallels Shijo; you and your daughter walked down it that time you followed a geisha on her rounds. The Shiri-kawa flowed past the back doors of the houses, which, if it had been Taiwan, would have been the perfect place to dump trash and dirty water. Koi lived in this stream, which was not quite two meters wide and less than half a meter deep, with willow and weeping cherry trees flanking the banks, toward which shop own-ers oriented their view, raising or lowering their bamboo curtains based on the intensity of the sun. You told your daughter that southern China was just like that. When had you ever been in southern China?

The flagstone road was finished. If you hadn't seen the construction with your own eyes, you'd have thought that the street, like the Kiyomizu Sannen-zaka or Ninen-zaka in Higashiyama, was also 100 years old. You sent A a pic-ture you'd taken with your daughter on one of the small bridges at Shiri-kawa, as a belated response to the Christ-mas card she'd sent you a few years earlier.

Like so many people who vowed never to part and to remain single, you and A never saw each other again after college. The last time had been during the graduation cer-emony procession. You were both in the company of fam-ily members and boyfriend. A introduced her boyfriend to you, while casting a passing glance at the man next to you. You didn't know if she had been thinking the same thing—so, someone like *that* is what you left for.

When you checked your luggage, the hotel manager told you that the flowering season might be delayed a week because it had been unusually cold that year. No wonder the flagstone path was deserted and the charcoal gray branches of the weeping cherries and willows looked so lifeless. Even so, community shops had all contributed lanterns and vats of liquor; peach red and willow green bunting had been hung at an angle on utility poles, while electric lamps had been placed at just the right angle under older, bigger weeping cherry trees.

You had no idea what A was thinking. She hadn't been back to Taiwan for two decades, but she studied Taiwan. This time she had to make a trip to Japan for a paper she was working on, and when she heard that you were coming here, she had someone send you a fax with the simple request to reserve a hotel room; ideally, you'd share a room and sleep feet to feet, just like in high school. The rest would have to wait until you saw each other.

That is why you hadn't brought your daughter or invited your husband along.

Regret set in as soon as you stepped on Tatsumi Bridge on the way to Kyomoto-machi. The street lamps were turned on earlier than usual because of the dark, cold weather, and in that light, the smooth surface of the water was mirror clear, showing the fish suspended motionlessly. If your daughter, who loved fish, had been there, she'd have taken out the bread she'd saved from breakfast to feed them. You recalled the first time you'd brought her here. She'd just learned to talk and knew nothing about fish, but when she saw them fighting over food, she gestured anxiously and shouted, "Fish, *bai-bai* fight!" *Bai-bai*—"don't"—had been the only Taiwanese phrase her father had taught her that she still remembered. Told to wash her face? "Bai-bai." Asked to give something she liked to others? "Bai-bai." Time to go to bed? "Bai-bai." Now she was about to graduate from primary school. Over the years, she'd become friendly with the big koi in the Rakushō garden. This time she'd asked you to touch the one she called Japanese flag, a koi that was white all over, except for a big round red dot on its head. She'd noticed that it was always slow to get to the food, so she'd push the other fish away with one hand and feed this one with the other; it never swam away from her.

On several occasions, you sat inside drinking coffee and watched her through the window as she squatted by the pond, so preoccupied with feeding the fish that she tilted toward the water until all you could see was her little fanny in floral underpants sticking up into the air.

Unconsciously you quickened your steps and decided to take a shortcut, as if you'd be able to see your five-year-old daughter squatting by the pond feeding and touching the fish, so long as you reached Rakushō before dark.

You took the stairs up to the Yasaka Shrine; it was dark, gloomy, and deserted. The dense trees swayed like ocean waves. Reminding yourself that you weren't in Taiwan anymore, you walked unworried past the trees, not forgetting to pay a hurried tribute before the shrine, tossing a coin and clapping your hands. You put your palms together and closed your eyes, praying for the deities to wake up and listen to your wish that this trip not turn into a disaster.

The inclining sun of the peaceful spring shone on the dull, weatherworn lettering of the sign, making it look all the more forlorn. The thick cotton shop-door curtain was faded white, with heavy threads dangling from it.

"Even the red weeping cherries at Heian Shrine have times when they are lonely, subdued by this kind of feeling." Chieko hurried away.

Why had the word "disaster" occurred to you?

Except for her usual rashness, you simply couldn't fathom what A might be thinking. The last time you'd heard from her was when she'd sent a Western-style wedding announcement, informing you that she and so-and-so (you tried to come up with a plausible Chinese name from the romanized spelling) would be married in a certain church in such-and-such county in the state of New

Jersey on such-and-such date. It would be the first time A had lived with someone legally. You weren't even sure if she was still married now, but of course this had nothing to do with the looming sense of disaster.

If not, what was it then? You finished your coffee before it turned cold, but you couldn't stop yawning. With the trouble you'd had to go through early that morning, the three-hour flight, and the evening chill, plus your low blood pressure, you knew how you must look without checking the mirror. Tiny lines created by icy winds spread out like cracks on ice over a porcelain face that usually did so well with cosmetics. Your hair was fuzzy and coarse, there were dark circles under your eyes, and your lips were either ashen or turning purple. You no longer had the energy for frenzied activity; now you required a full nine hours of sleep and took three kinds of vitamins plus deep-sea fish oil and beta-carotene. Afraid that people would detect a salty odor that seemed to deepen by the day, you bathed and washed your hair religiously. You couldn't guess what A would look like now. She had the perfect body type for putting on weight, and quite a few pounds of flesh could hang on that 5'6" frame, with its broad shoulders, compounded by twenty years of American dietary habits.

You could no longer travel the way you had at seventeen, going off with her for a few days, sometimes not taking a thing, not even toilet articles, along. You would agree to meet at the east or west bus station, empty-handed except for a collection of poetry or a copy of Schopenhauer, which you didn't really understand. What little traveling money you had was tucked inside the back pocket of your jeans. Strange that you didn't seem to need to wash your face or brush your teeth, or, for that matter, bathe. When you woke up, you were hale and hearty, eyes bright, mouth fresh. And you never gained weight, no matter what or how much you ate.

That was why you hesitated over accommodating A's request to share a double room. Spending several nights with her in a Japanese business hotel room that was barely big enough to turn around in was virtually unimaginable. Nor could you face the salty odor and hair that would surely linger in the bathroom, or tolerate the body odor you were sure A would have acquired by now. You'd sleep with your back to her and even in your sleep you'd have to be careful—no talking in your sleep, no wild dreams. Your purrlike snores probably had not gotten any louder, but now they were probably more like a machine with a screw loose and in need of repair, a sort of metallic noise.

But A's snores would surely have gotten much louder.

You had given up on ever seeing A again one day. After going abroad, whether she was studying or working, she seemed confined to small towns like those visited by Allison in *Peyton Place*. During the early years, she'd sent you maple leaves, beautiful leaves the color of red peppers or of red roses, and so big she'd mailed them in large manila envelopes, so big, in fact, they actually disappointed you, because they were so different from those you'd created in your imagination. But you put them away carefully, then generously gave them to your daughter when her primary school class collected specimens. Ten years, and the brightness and color hadn't faded a bit, as if they were plastic or silk. Like you, your daughter was amazed that leaves could be so big, big enough to cover her face; they were nothing like the takao kaede maple leaves she'd collected here over several autumns, or the ones from those fragrant maples she found on the island.

Beneath the specimen, your daughter wrote in uneven characters that made it look as if the writer had some sort of handicap: "Fragrance maple, Chinese witch hazel . . ."

You were filled with regret. Why had you chosen to meet with A rather than spend the precious holiday with your daughter?

The road was rather long. They avoided the trains, taking the more distant route around to Nanzenji Temple Road, passing behind Chianji Temple. Then they passed through the rear of Maruyama Park, walking the old narrow path to Kiyomizu Temple. At that moment, the sky was covered in a spring sunset.

When you paid your bill, the owners, two sisters, reminded you to put on a coat, for it was quite cold out. They were so friendly you wondered if they remembered you. You didn't get a chance to touch "Japanese flag" for your daughter, since the door and windows were all closed and heavily draped. The Fuminosuke Teahouse across the way had already lit their big black lanterns. A few customers who didn't mind the cold were lined up outside. You'd never been there, maybe because every time you walked by the place you had thoughts of your five-year-old daughter squatting by Rakushō Pond to feed the fish, so engrossed that her little fanny stuck up in the air, even though she was always right beside you when your thoughts were of her.

You decided to take the opposite route from Shinichi and Chieko, turning left out of the lane by Saigyōan and Kikukei Pavilion and cutting across the front of Higashiō Temple to go into Maruyama Park. That's where most of the cats were.

Unlike your daughter, on your first visit you were surprised to find that they had brazenly, in your view, used the same name, Maruyama (Yuanshan), for the park. She, on the other hand, had gone on a kindergarten outing to the Yuanshan (Maruyama) River Park and come home to ask why we had given it a Japanese name. Stumped, you couldn't answer, while your husband teased her about forgetting her own traditions.

The buds were still hard on the hundred-year-old weeping cherry in the center of the park, so, reluctant to leave, you bought a hot drink to warm yourself, like all those hardy night visitors.

The weeping cherry was like a weeping willow before buds appeared. Floodlights had been set up, just waiting for the tree to awaken. One spring you and your daughter had enjoyed a picnic lunch under the cherry trees near sculptures of Sakamoto Ryōma and Nakao Shintarō. From where you sat at a distance, you could see the hundred-year-old weeping cherry. Under the floodlights, it seemed to float high in the sky, like a freeze-frame shot of fireworks or one of those beautiful yet lethal jellyfish. You didn't dare let your eyes linger too long for fear that the tree might have acquired supernatural powers that could suck out your soul.

As you ate and drank, you told your daughter the story of Sakamoto Ryōma and Nakao Shintarō. During the daylight hours, you had followed Ryōma's route through the capital city, visiting places like the teahouse at the alley entrance to Kiyomizu-zaka, near Sannen-zaka, where Ryōma and the late Tokugawa patriots had held their secret meetings. It sat atop one of the thirty-six peaks of the Higashi-yama Range, where they could see the Nijo gate of the shogun castle open, which meant that gendarmes were coming to arrest them, and that gave them time to jump through windows and flee. You walked by Sanjōgawara-machi, where a stele on the roadside indicated that was where Sakamoto Ryōma and Nakao Shintarō met their tragic ends. Ryōma's tomb was not far from the upper hill of Ryōzen Kannon in Ninen-zaka, where your daughter once found a giant cocoon like that of a *mosura*. It left such an indelible impression on her that later, whenever you walked by Sannen-zaka or Ninen-zaka, she'd rush you over to Ryōma's tomb to see if she could find another cocoon, since you had lingered, unwilling to leave, standing by the entrance of Ninen-zaka, the old residence of Takehisa Yumeiji, where you could gaze down at the city scene and market site below.

In fact, you could not have had any special feelings toward Sakamoto Ryōma. You recalled the day before you were scheduled to return to the island, which was then embroiled in ugly political struggles, and that prompted you to tell your daughter about Saigō Takamori, a political adversary of the Meiji Emperor, each of whom treated the other with respect. That was also how the Kangxi Emperor viewed Koxinga: an official of the Ming, neither a rebel nor a traitorous official of his own.

Your daughter, a second-grader at the time, was moved by the story.

. . .

The primitive aborigines knew nothing about farming, shooting down flying creatures and hunting those on the ground to provide for themselves and for their offspring. They worshiped totems.

In the beginning, here is how the Spaniards and Dutch described Taipei: weeds long, air foul, many residents are sick.

The Kangxi Taipei Lake.

Later, Yu Yonghe, who came for the sulfur, described Taipei in his *A Record of Travels in Baihai* as follows: no place for humans. But that was 1697, and you really couldn't blame the city. During the same period, one could ride an oxcart through the Jiayi-Tainan Plain and feel as if they were traveling underground (how wonderful!).

Toward the end of the Kangxi reign, Lan Dingyuan, who led an army to put down the Zhu Yigui rebellion, said that the Taiwanese are habitually rebellious; you quell them but they rise up again.

Even Shen Baozhen said: Taipei is a pestilential place.

Li Hongzhang: the birds don't sing, the flowers have no fragrance, the men are ruthless, the women are faithless.

. . .

Dissatisfaction with the place did not begin with you.

You really did not want to go back there.

"Chieko, let's sell off this shop and move to Xizhen, what do you say? Or else we could find a small, quiet house near

Nanzenji or Okazaki, and the two of us can think up designs for kimono cloth and obis, how does that sound?"

You recalled the unfinished trip you'd made the day after the big election. You reached Yuanshan, but saw passageways everywhere, in the air, on the ground, and you were lost among them, not knowing how to locate the route you'd taken hundreds of times at seventeen. Meiji Bridge—later you learned that's what it was called. The brass lamps from the Meiji Bridge had been purchased during a round of reconstruction by Li Meishu, who installed them in a Buddhist temple in Sanxia. The handsome, straight, and even bridge, now overshadowed by a new one, was waiting to be demolished. The new rulers, who had criticized the *ancien régime* as an occupying power, had been in office four years, and the way *they* behaved was exactly like an occupying power. They acted as if they were just staying for a while and could pick up and leave at any moment; otherwise, why had they taken down the two rows of fragrant maples that had been there before any of you living now had appeared on the scene? No wonder you nearly forgot the FORTUNE-TELLER sign that had been faintly visible in the dense verdant shade. It was the first long word you'd learned after mastering the twenty-six letters of the English alphabet in junior high school. You'd made a tiny vow to yourself that you'd have your fortune told one day when you grew up, stubbornly, unquestioningly believing that there would be a mysterious, alluring Gypsy beyond the wall who would unveil the secrets of the universe for you in her crystal ball.

Surprisingly, the children's amusement park was still there, but the gloomy late autumn air raised the question of whether or not it was in operation. Oh, how you wanted to go inside. If the dragon boat, with its rotten planks, replete with the smell of urine, were still there, you were certain you'd see the five-year-old you, who exposed her underpants as she bent over to touch the water. You wondered if your daughter, who had been to Disneyland countless times, would accompany you here, the paradise of your childhood when you were her age. You tried to tell her that it had been just as much fun as Disneyland. In fact, you did more than that; you took her along on your search for your childhood village. It was in a northern suburb, not far. Ultimately, as you stood amid rows of remodeled public housing, you had to use the distant mountains to position yourself before you could locate the likely site of your old home—now flower beds outside a convenience store. You took your daughter to the hills where you'd run wild and celebrated the joys of childhood, only to find, to your surprise, that the hills had been swallowed up by five or six ugly apartment buildings. What remained was a tiny hilltop you could easily walk across. Standing on the path, you pointed to a culvert under the highway and told your daughter that was where you'd buried your dog. You tried your best to reconstruct that autumn day: the fields submerged in arista weeds, lonely smoke rising up from fires the farmers lit to burn the weeds, and your inconsolable mood. Strange how dogs all seem to die in the autumn.

And that wasn't all that had disappeared.

You and your playmates had once baked sweet potatoes you'd stolen from the farmers after the harvest. Untiringly, you took turns running back to the village to steal matches from home so you could start a fire. But you were so bad at it that after using up five or six boxes of Freedom matches, you only managed to burn a small pile of chaff, while the bright red sweet potatoes lay unscathed at the bottom of the pit. Left with nothing to do on such a long and boring day, you decided to walk aimlessly away from the village. The more you walked, the larger the airplanes flying overhead became. Overcome with excitement, you speculated that an airport must lie at the far end of the field, so you agreed to walk over there. If you actually made it to the area's one and only airport, it would be like going abroad. Just what did it mean to go abroad? It seemed to you to mean that an airport was a better shortcut than the tunnel you were constantly planning to dig all the way down to America.

You walked and you walked, and pretty soon, none of you felt like talking anymore; you hadn't expected it to be so far. You passed a huge manure pit, then you walked by a farmhouse with a howling dog, even reached a gourd trellis, where you were forced, like tightrope walkers, to cross a bridge made of a single rotting log. If not for the encouragement lent by airplanes flying just above your heads, you'd have given up. When the youngest tagalong started to sob and complain, you wouldn't let him cry, afraid that would shatter your morale. But the few sobs attracted some kids a ways off. One of them turned out to be a classmate who sat in the second-to-last row, someone with whom you'd never exchanged a word. Hers was the godforsaken Beishihu Route—Oh, no, had you actually come all the way to Beishihu?

Your classmate's family operated brick kilns. Row after row of crab red or grayish green bricks, some fired, some not, stood in a broad open area, the perfect place for a fight. So you divided into two "nations," the Beishihu Nation and the Loyalty New Village Nation. The two sides fought long and hard, until it turned dark and the Beishihu Nation was called home for dinner by angry parents.

When you returned to your village, you all told your parents and the older kids the same story: you'd walked all the way to the airport. You described the giant monsters you saw there, claiming you'd have gone abroad if the Keelung River hadn't blocked your way. I mean it, we were that close, a matter of inches, you repeated emphatically, guessing that they probably didn't believe you.

You wouldn't see the name Beishihu again until thirty years later, when you were helping your daughter with her third-grade field report. Beishihu was associated with building materials for Taihoku (Taipei) at the end of the Qing dynasty. Some said the stones were mined at Beishihu Hill in Dazhi, that the bricks came from kilns in Beishihu and Fangliaozhuang, and that the lime was produced by lime kilns at Hegoutou in Dataocheng. But another version had it that the stone came from Anshan rocks in Qili'an, the bricks were bought in Amoy, and the mortar was Dutch clay. The latter was made of glutinous rice steamed with brown sugar and lime, and resembled the material used to build the Chikan Fortress and other Dutch sites on the island.

Japan tore down the city wall ten years after the Qing built it.

You never returned to Beishihu, dreamlike Beishihu.

The Japanese were no different from the Manchu Qing court; if it wasn't "perhaps we should level the place," it was "sell Taiwan for a billion dollars." They disassembled the bricks and tiles laboriously fired in Beishihu and built three-lane streets, along which were planted nightshade trees, which were popular all over the island, and betel palms and coconut trees to give them a southern flavor, 150 of them on Aiguo East Road and 100 on Xinyi Road.

Half a century later, the nightshades had become a green wall, the demarcation line where your all-girls high school made peace with one of the all-boys high schools. You and A often arranged to meet boys there. The wide safety island was paved with red bricks; white wrought-iron benches encircled the tree trunks, and the streetlights, no matter how bright, could not penetrate the dense shadows from the nightshade trees, making it a convenient place for the boys to smoke cigarettes, and for you to evade the nosy military education teacher who was always following you. Most of the time the boys brought books or the latest copy of their school publication, or vice versa. With much greater enthusiasm than you invested in your textbooks, you recited and memorized the difficult and obscure lines, savoring them as if relishing candy. When you bade one another good-bye, you never forgot to agree on an end-of-the-month outing between your class and theirs.

Back then there were few cars, so there was no need to worry that headlights would expose the boy who held you in a passionate embrace and explored your body at night. You cooperated without reciprocating, hoping he'd quickly finish what he was doing and return to normal, so you could go back to the evening study hall, where you'd finish memorizing a history lesson for the next day's exam. His sweat and body odor were as pungent as the nightshade trees, which sent your thoughts wandering to unknown places. The boy would straighten your clothes and pick up your book bag with a sparkle in his eyes. A would definitely hear about this, and you felt reassured.

Chieko suffered a tremendous blow. She was so fond of going to the village, so fond of looking up at the pine-covered mountains. Maybe it was a summons from her father's spirit. The girl from the mountain village told her she had a twin sister. Is it possible that her biological father was worrying so much about the abandoned twin daughter, Chieko, that a misstep had caused him to fall from the fir tree?

The Japanese who had originally thought of selling Taiwan for a billion dollars not only covered Kitayamasugi with trees but also tried to grow them all over the southern island. They didn't just plant annual flowers and plants; with an unworried certainty, they put down saplings that would take a century to show any resemblance to trees. Strange how they seemed not to have planned to simply eat and run.

Eat and run. That reminded you of the dissident who had been exiled for thirty years because of his resistance against the totalitarian government. That was then, this is now. Once he became the county head, reminiscent of others before him, he converted the island's last piece of

wetland into a polluting industrial site that consumed tremendous amounts of energy.

How was he any different from the foreign power he'd
criticized and hoped to overthrow? How else would he
have dared do what he did? When you walked by your
green wall one day you discovered—oh my god—the century-old nightshade trees had disappeared overnight, all
for the ostensibly justifiable reason of widening the street.
You were so grief-stricken, so distressed, you felt as if
you'd lost your best friend.

It became virtually impossible to recount to your daughter the traces of your lives in this city: the village you'd
lived in; the spot where you'd buried the dog; the studio
where you'd learned to dance; the memory-filled suburban
movie theaters, with their double features; the site where
you and her father had had your first date; you and your
best friend's favorite coffee shop; the bookstores you'd frequented as a student; the house you'd rented when you
and her father were first married. . . . Even the two kinder-
gartens (same location, different ownership) where she'd
been enrolled not so long ago had disappeared (it was now
a small restaurant called Home of the Geese).

Must all this have an either-or relation with progress?

It was getting really cold, so you went back to the hotel
to check in, deciding to take a single room for the time
being. When A arrived, you two could move to a double
room or she could get a single for herself.

This simple decision instantly eradicated your hesitation and anxiety over the past few days. As soon as you put
your luggage in the room, you felt the pangs of hunger.

So, following your old habits, you first went to pray,
palms together, at Nishiki tenman Temple in Shin-kyō-
goku-dōri. Lanterns the size of giant vats hung all around
the temple, and you had no idea what deity they wor-
shipped here. Most of the stores on Nishiki-koji, across
from the temple, were closed. Shopkeepers at the few fish

stores that still had lights on were busy washing the countertops and corridors, but yelled out when they saw you walk by, "*Irasshai*, irasshai, welcome."

Clutching your money tightly and quickening your pace, you made yourself out to be someone in a hurry, a professional woman hurrying home to make dinner after a day's work at the office. You walked all the way to a small shop in Takeda City, where you bought two pairs of thick, brand-name socks that were no longer fashionable. It was colder than usual, so a kerosene heater warmed the shop, which was shrouded in the aroma of fish soup. The owner's school-age granddaughter was crowded into the space by the cash register so she could watch TV while doing her homework. The sight, of course, reminded you of your daughter.

The rear section of the Nishiki Market was already quiet and deserted, so you were forced to cross the Yanagibaba-dōri to return to Shijō-dōri and, out of all the places to eat, you picked Doutor Café across the street, where you normally ate your breakfast.

You ordered a cup of the day's special coffee and a kō-gen hot dog sandwich. Since the window seats were taken, you sat at the large round table inside. The heat and cigarette smoke quickened your heartbeat, but that could also have been caused by the thought that you might see your daughter's back as she bent over her homework.

If she came when school was in session, she had to bring her schoolwork in order to keep up. And since there was so little space in the hotel room, she often came here to do her homework at the large round table. At first you helped with her arithmetic, but you were out of your element when she reached third grade. The two of you speaking a different language did not draw the attention of other people at the table, or maybe it just didn't register on their faces. They all wore an expression that said they'd seen enough strange things not to be bothered. Too many people, too little space; they fought crowds on commuter trains, in department stores, and in coffee shops. Constantly thrown into situations where interpersonal space was limited beyond the range of tolerance, they developed an indifferent, expressionless mask, which they donned with their clothes and hat when they left the house. Otherwise, how could they survive?

But that's how you liked it: everyone ignoring everyone else. Probably there were mental patients among them, but you felt perfectly safe. With skill and tact, you sized up an immaculately dressed middle-aged man, two Chanel-clad young women who were heavy smokers, and a handsome young professional who could have been Takeshi Kaneshiro's brother. Taking a sip of the hot coffee, you said to yourself, for some strange reason, "Tadaima, I'm back."

*There were King Arthur, who was as tall as a tree, a colorful Egyptian bas relief, giant sculptures of kings, and a portrait of the real Sphinx. It was like a dream world.—Freud

Your kind of weather has lush and pungent greenery, azure skies, and blinding sunlight, but now you were invariably in a room chilled by air conditioners, or in a car, or inside a coffee shop, or in a room by a window, and that cost you your sense of reality, causing you to mistakenly assume that the temperature outside was the same as inside—cold. That and the striking contrast between light and shadow produced the illusion that you were in a country you'd wanted to visit or one you'd visited before.

For instance, when you took the MRT, which you'd once vowed never to take, you sat in a three-story-high train that lopped off the sight of most of the disgustingly ugly, old, five-story apartment buildings, and seemed to have returned to an age when there were only single-story houses. A large chunk of the sky was exposed, creating a sense of vastness and reminding you, for the first time in years, that from the beginning, this was an oceanic country, and that the nearby ocean, there at the edge of the sky, fired your imagination. Sometimes the train cut across the midsection of small hills on the edge of the basin. If you succeeded in remaining unperturbed by the junkyards or potter's fields below and concentrated on the cassia forest swaying in the sunlight, then you were reminded of a small Mediterranean island in late autumn, carpeted with olive trees. Sometimes the train stopped at a station that rose above the mansion of an ousted official who refused to move. If you tried your best to ignore the dillenia grove, with its equatorial rain forest flavor, the arhat pines, standing in contrast with the sea-blue sky, would surely recall for you and many people memories of camping on the beach at Jinshan. But buildings that were a dozen or more stories tall obstructed your view of the sky. On dark, gloomy days, when the train slithered between colorless tall buildings and squat illegal structures, trumpet music would sound from the bottom of your heart (and, you believed, others' hearts as well). It was the background music from *Annie Hall*, "Sleepy Lagoon," where Woody Allen reminisces about his childhood days, living under a roller coaster. The mood of the melody contradicts its lyrics, which are about an equatorial moon, a sleepy coral reef, and you . . . you wondered why they'd picked a song about a tropical island.

Experiences like this were becoming increasingly rare. Except for the one route that was indispensable in your daily life, you had become reluctant to roam, afraid of discovering more things like the disappearance of a line of century-old nightshade trees, afraid to face the overnight disappearance of old 30-foot maple trees on which sparrows and emerald eyes perched the year round. The latter had been replaced by a gigantic billboard, selling upscale housing at 100,000 NT a square foot. Directly across from it, in Lane 243, Jinhua Street, a row of 50-year-old eucalyptus trees had been taken down by his Excellency the Mayor, who never stopped crowing about how much he loved this island and this city. Even more ironic was that the place was immediately turned into a small community park with tiny trees.

Since you were no longer willing to walk down unfamiliar streets and alleyways, the routes available to you were getting scarcer.

You walked past 145 Jinjiang Street, behind Taiwan First Bank on Roosevelt Road; a sign on the wooden gate proclaimed in couplet style: GOVERNMENT PROPERTY, NO TRESPASSING. For the very first time, you wished that this administration would maintain its low efficiency and have no time to deal with public property, so that the birds and lush, tall camphor and coconut trees could continue to occupy the space. There were other pretty ruins like that: Nos. 1 and 7 of Lane 22, Pucheng Street (their mutual neighbor, No. 3, was used as book storage for the National Assembly, but in essence it was no different from a ruin); across from the Huamao Hotel in Alley 30, Lane 83, Section 1 of Zhongshan North Road was a place where fragrant cedar, bougainvillea, grannylike mango trees . . . stood; on Changchun Road, sparrow banyan trees spilled over the fence of No. 249, where the door was guarded by mulberry and eucalyptus. No. 249's neighbors, 251 and 253, were occupied; yellow gourd flowers were blooming at No. 255. Then there was the place kitty-corner from No. 18, Lane 63 of Linqi Street, where a paper mulberry, a banyan, and a breadfruit tree formed a triangle, while an arhat pine cowered in the corner, and you could imagine the autumnal feelings of the person, a onetime resident of South Asia, no doubt, who had planted the trees.

Then there was a house, one corner of which was an illegal construction of long standing—No. 2, Lane 140, Section 3 of Roosevelt Road. Another one, overrun by feral cats, was No. 3, Lane 26 of Taishun Street, where the calicoes and tabbies would come out and let you feed them, while little black kittens sat in the dark like owls. Some houses had collapsed walls, and it was easy to spot the materials and construction style of Showa-era houses, like No. 244, Section 1 of Heping East Road and Nos. 143 and 145, Chaozhou Street. There was also an entire lane that hadn't changed in decades and served as a moat to curb the Nationalist government's propaganda apparatus, such as the Central Broadcasting Company or Central TV; that was Lane 212, Section 1 of Jianguo South Road, where a family of dogs lived in No. 59. The mommy dog was alert but timid, a typical mutt, but the amiable smiles of the five tan-and-white pups showed that their daddy had Akita blood (no hidden meaning in this passage). A host of ghosts lived at No. 49, a family at No. 53, a yard full of kids at No. 37. The house beyond that was taken by master squatters, who had no house number and no mailbox. Were they humans or fox spirits? The neatly trimmed gardenias, pomeloes, loquats, and tallow trees in the yard told you that the person who planted them must have been a fox spirit from a province other than Taiwan.

There were also houses that had deteriorated so badly they had largely turned to dust and been blown away by the wind, leaving a yard, a fence, and a door frame. On the doors were miniature forests of horsetail in colors somewhere between gray and green, a plant that had seen the existence of dinosaurs. One such house was located at No. 7, Lane 92 of Taiwan Normal University Road, directly across from Guzhuang Park.

To be sure, some places were well maintained by their occupants, who could have been officials or servants, or their descendants. One example was the former residence of Chiang Junior, located at No. 20, Section 1 of Chang'an East Road, facing the rear entrance of the Presbyterian church, established in 1937 A.D. Japanese indulging in all-night revelry had left the lingering pungent smell of urine at the base of the outside wall. Antitheft barbed wire atop the wall was intertwined with pink coral vines and hemlock at 75, Section 1 of Hangzhou South Road; the male head of a family, having neither been killed nor turned up missing, returned a year after the war ended and planted a giant breadfruit tree at No. 9, Lane 61 of Linqi Street; another planting by a head of household was of South Pacific firs at No. 1, Lane 44 of Linqi Street; yet another was by a South Pacific returnee who chose to plant Burmese gardenias at No. 2–1, Lane 3 of Tai'an Street; there was also a family whose status was impossible to guess; No. 3, Lane 2 on the same street spread out until it was the size of a row of apartment buildings; parallel to that sprawling house was No. 1, Lane 6 of Tongshan Street, with banana shrubs and mangoes stretching over the fence, reminiscent of your paternal grandfather's house. But more like his house ought to be the one at No. 11, Lane 24 of Pucheng Street. Many people's old photo albums would have a faded black-and-white photograph in which, with azaleas and longan trees on a small patch of cement as a background, a child sits on a tricycle with younger siblings behind. There were also Nos. 23, 7, and 1 in Lane 264 of Ruian Street, which should have been a better location for the imposing mansion on Roosevelt Road that was searched by the female protagonist in *Dodder Flower*, a Guolian Film Corporation movie you saw as a girl, one that was based on Qiong Yao's novel. If not, the only other possible places would be No. 10, Lane 11 of Qingtian Street or No. 4, Lane 9 or No. 1, across from it.

Some residents carefully maintained the original looks of the houses, opting not to cement up the ox-eye openings in the courtyard walls or the skylights, such as Nos. 7 and 9 in Lane 91, Section 2 of Ren'ai Road; No. 4 in Lane 62, Section 2 of Ji'nan Road; and No. 71, Alley 1, Lane 24, Section 3 of Ren'ai Road. The owners even set down strict rules about trees; they planted only cherries, arhat pines, and South Pacific firs, while preventing the growth of a variety of mulberries and sparrow banyans, whose seeds can sprout anywhere and thrive once they are dropped by birds. Such an immaculate house was located at No. 34, Lane 97, Section 1 of Xinsheng South Road, where fired tiles and a black fir wall served as backdrop for an arhat pine, which was close to a completed flower arrangement. It resembled the tradesman's house you were used to seeing on Higashiyama Gojo. If it had been a bit bigger, it could have served as a small community museum, like the salt museum in Shinano Ō-machi.

It didn't matter whether or not they cemented the openings in the wall, planted varieties of mulberries, or picked and ate the berries in the yard—all these families had one thing in common: on their wooden gates, painted or unpainted, written in chalk, were the names of newspapers: *Lian* (*United Daily News*), *Yang* (*Central Daily News*), *Lian-Yang, Lian-Guo* (*China Daily News*), or *Guo-Min* (*Minsheng Daily*). You would never see *Zi* (*Zili—Independent News* or *Ziyou—Liberty Times*), nor *Tai* (*Taiwan Times, Taiwan Daily*). No exceptions, up or down the alley, and it was reminiscent of the Ali Baba story, where the forty thieves marked people's doors to determine whether or not to kill the residents inside one of these days.

One of these days, the houses in these lanes and alleys would be returned, at a high efficiency rate, to the new administration, which also loved Taiwan, to build, with plenty of corners cut, a dormitory for the Postal Administration or for the Customs Office or for professors at such-and-such university, or residences for government officials. . . . By then, except for Lane 52 of Wenzhou Street, any other street you'd trod would have disappeared, and you'd have no place to walk, no memory to recall. And it didn't end there. You recalled something by a writer with the same background as yours: "It turns out that you cannot call a place your hometown if none of your relatives has died there." You weren't as picky as that; you just wanted to ask humbly and deferentially: wouldn't a city, no matter what it's called (usually something related to prosperity, progress, or, occasionally, hope and happiness), be in essence a city of strangers if it had no intention of retaining the traces of people who had lived there? Why would anyone want to cherish, treasure, maintain, and identify with an unfamiliar city?

The Daimonji on Niyoigatake Peak on Higashiyama is the best known, but there were actually five mountains where fires were lighted. The "Left Daimonji" on Okitayama near Kinkakuji, the "Myoho" on Mount Matsugasaki, the "Funagata" on Akimiyama in Nishigamo, and the "Toriigata" on a mountain in Kamisaga. In all, five "sending fires" were lighted, bonfires to direct the spirits of the dead back to the netherworld. For the forty minutes of the events, all the neon lighting and advertising in the city was turned off.

Chieko could sense the color of early autumn in the sending fires and the glow of the night sky.

When you woke up, the caws of crows flapping their wings in the mansion gave you the feeling that you were in an ancient temple deep in the mountains. You could gaze at far-off Higashi-yama through your window. You would not need to cool off at Kamo-gawa if you came in August. At night you could sip cold sake by the window and watch the bonfire on Daimon-ji to send off the spirits.

The water boiled, so you made a cup of green tea using the Uji tea bag provided by the hotel. You turned on the TV, from which emerged that language you did not understand, but which, mixed with the fragrance of the tea, comprised part of the smells in your deep memory. Sometimes there were also the mixed fragrances of all the brand-name perfumes in a department store; sometimes there was the cheerless aroma, devoid of the smell of food, from the tea and Kyoto incense lit at an old fruit shop; sometimes there were the smells, in closed spaces like a train or a coffee shop, of bath soap, body lotion, and eau de cologne on men and women obsessed with cleanliness, or simply air freshener in rooms with central air. . . . Smells lingered above the city, not dissipating, and maybe the indispensable odor of crows should be added, all of which would, before you died, fill you with nostalgia over these familiar smells.

You were standing at Tanba-ya at the entrance to Teramachi-dōri to the left of Otabisho, unsure of which kind of rich *mochi* to buy—those covered in *ogarumame* and rolled in yellow bean powder, or the green ones with ogarumame filling. In the past you would buy a box of six, split them with your daughter, and eat as you walked to wherever you were going: Fumishi-inari taisha, Shichijo keihan, the entrance to Gion's Nawate-dōri . . . since your daughter was not with you, you probably couldn't finish a box by yourself, so you decided to wait until A arrived, then split a box with her.

Spotting the entrance to Fuyamachi-dōri, you decided to cross the street to buy some coffee spoons and forks at Alba, counting up all the people who had praised your crescent-shaped utensils in the past. You'd also finally made up your mind to buy the Italian Taitu platter with its painted leaves from all kinds of deciduous trees in autumn. The style was the same as that on the little plates used for handmade rice cakes by the owner of Saloon Ko-hi-kan, located at the alley entrance to the old residence at Shiganaoya. You'd looked at it for years, but it had always been too pricey for you. But then, when you returned to the island, where autumns were rare, those autumnal leaves always appeared before your eyes in all their beauty.

The shop clerk, who could tell you were a foreigner when you spoke, packed the platter with extra care to make sure it wouldn't break during the flight home. You hadn't been this happy in a long time. With these ever-lasting leaves from green hard oaks, chestnuts, mountain elms, oak trees, poplars, alders . . . you could face many winters back home.

Here is how winters on the island have been described: in the last month the winter sweets bloom, the tea flowers spread, daffodils sprout, plum buds appear, camellias blossom, and snowflakes fall.

But the reality was: the day after the gubernatorial and mayoral election, you were pacing outside the bleak amusement park of your childhood, not sure whether to go in or not, when you spotted a stone stele covered in intertwining banyan roots, climbing figs, and sedge. On it was carved: OLD SITE OF TAIGUCAO. This was where Chen Weiying, the famous Taiwan Confucian scholar, had retired to undergo self-cultivation. The inscription revealed that Chen (1811–1869) was born during the Jiacheng reign of the Qing dynasty, at Gangziqian in Dalongtong. He was widely read in history and well versed in all schools of thought. In the ninth year of the Xianfeng reign he passed the provincial exam, the second highest rung, and later worked as head of the Min County Confucian School and Head of the Grand Secretariat. After returning to Taiwan, he took charge of the Yangshan and Xuehai academies, teaching more than a thousand students. At the age of fifty, he moved to Taigucao, where he lived the life of a recluse. According to legends passed down from the colonial period, Taigucao, surrounded by water and mountains, had taken its name from "mountains quiet as Taigu." But others said that it was the birthplace of Taiwan's aborigines. A more reliable explanation would be that during the Jiaqing and Daoguang reigns, the place was called Taige Hut, with a large concentration of lepers. *Taige* in Taiwanese sounds like *Taigu*. After the death of Chen Weiying, the place fell into disrepair and decline. In 1906, the Japanese cut into the north side of the mountain to build a bridge. Taigucao, being in the way, could not escape the fate of demolition.

Casting a glance at the ghost of Chen Weiying, who stood shoulder to shoulder with you, you read the inscription and were tongue-tied. It was an allegory belonging to all ancient cultures: you lack the knowledge, even the historical knowledge, but live with it happily and in harmony until you gain the knowledge to understand it and, feeling slight remorse (even though you had always liked it), you treat it better; but it will never be the same, never the same as before. Was this a case of middle-aged nostalgia, which all people and all cultures experience? Unwilling to admit that was so, you believed that Chen Weiying shared your view, and believed even more strongly that the Meiji Bridge, buried beneath you in the eternal darkness of the eighteenth level of hell, did too. Over half the sweet gum trees, which had been as old as Chokushi Street, were gone; the beautiful Miyanoshita Road had grown into such a state that it was like countless incurable tumors—ugly, ugly. Mournfully, you avoided the area, but what had died, of course, included part of you.

The same sort of annoying knowledge told you that the original site of the soccer field that had sprung up out of nowhere had been a stadium built in 1923 to welcome the Showa, then still the Crown Prince, on his southern inspection trip. In the early years of the Nationalist government, it was lent to the Seventh Fleet Military Assistance and Advisory Group. On one soccer game night, the mayor-elect described his blueprint for the city's future, in which the soccer field might be used as the site of a stadium. By then, you, along with many more sweet gum trees, would have to join ranks with Chen Weiying.

When had the Meiqi Hotel become the Shanghai Commercial Bank?

Cities are bases for banks and prostitution, strewn with

weedlike skyscrapers. That is what Frank Lloyd Wright, who designed the Imperial Hotel, once said.

Like someone who's been abroad for years, you sighed as you wondered why you could not recall what the site occupied by a row of wedding photo studios had been used for. Then you saw that St. Christopher's was still there, looking like its old self. Vulgar and virtually identical oil paintings for export hung on its wrought-iron fence; as before, winter sunlight streamed through the trees and cast shadows on the paintings, coloring them in such a way that they became an indispensable vista. That had been part of your youthful fantasies: roaming the world to sell your paintings and perform as a sidewalk musician.

The people selling paintings here were all deaf-mutes (it wasn't until much later that you realized they could simply be sellers of paintings). The good friends who had sworn to roam the world with you, earning a living as street performers, were all abroad now. Some had become virtuous wives and good mothers; others were ensconced in upper-management positions with computer companies. One followed her famous chef husband from state to state, working in Chinese restaurants and living like gypsies. One, like A, never returned, while another came back to Taiwan every summer with children who could not communicate with your daughter or become good friends, as had the older generation, and that disappointed all of you.

You went out for a meal or for afternoon tea, and you talked about your current lives. But you never brought up the past, for that was too much like the nightshade and sweet gum trees, which had been either transplanted or taken down.

So you preferred not to reminisce, not because there were so many new things—new shops, new idols, new scandals, new opportunities to make money, new lovers of so-and-so's husband, a new dynasty, and new officials.

You suspected that, precisely because they could not recall what had existed before, they easily established harmonious relationships with new things, good and bad. But not you. You weren't even willing to lament how "The Way We Were" had changed or how Eslite Bookstore had become Sesame Wedding. For you, compared to the real past, all these were simply too new, and you wanted nothing to do with them, not to buy a magazine or enjoy a cup of coffee, since that would surely lead to the beginning of something that would soon disappear; otherwise, why would you have offered up so many lamentations wondering how to enter Qingguang Market? A location you vaguely recalled was now overrun by McDonald's, Giordano, Sanshang qiaofu, Nicai Boutiques, or Wendy's, 7–11, Michelle Fashions, and Hang Ten. You felt like the Jin dynasty fisherman from Wuling. . . .

Chieko recalled that incident as she walked the lane toward Nonomiya. A notice along the way read, THIS PATH PASSES THROUGH A DEEP BAMBOO THICKET. *The sign was not very old, but what once may have been a dark footpath was now bright and open. There was even a vendor in front of the gate who called to Chieko.*

The small shrine, however, had not changed. It was described even in the Tale of Genji.

Had not changed was only the beginning. Even more worshippers had come after Ayanomiya, second son of Emperor Akihito, and his wife came to plant trees a few years back. The visitors were all praying for a great marriage, but not you. Across the tracks, there were far fewer people, maybe because it was so cold. You'd seen the NHK weather forecast that morning and learned that the high would only be 5° or 6° Celsius, so the cherry-blossom festival might require an unprecedented one-week postponement. You worried that A, given the shortness of her visit, would not be able to see the cherry blossoms—oh god, you might see her when you got back to the hotel that night.

You hoped she wouldn't lard her speech with English, like so many people who had been out of the country far too long, because that would only increase the tension in your exchanges. You also hoped she wouldn't be dressed sloppily and attract attention, like most Americans. Of course you couldn't imagine A in stuffy clothes like a suit or a jacket and silk scarf. No way to know if her hair was long or short. Women of your age normally wore their hair in one of two styles, no matter how much attention they paid to it—short *obasan* style or long obasan style. God, it truly had been years since you'd last seen each other. A stopped sending pictures after a while. The last one you sent was of you and your daughter on the Shirakawa-Tatsumi-bashi at Gion. You could not help but be afraid that you might sit in different corners of the hotel lobby, glancing at each other for the longest time before exclaiming silently, "My god, have I become as hard to recognize as she is?"

After Bamboo Grove, there were only ordinary residences. In the garden, facing east, stood some oshima cherries, their white peachlike flowers struggling to bloom. Since it was too cold for visitors, the small gift shop near Rakushisha that sold figurines was closed, but the long wooden bench, covered in a red blanket, hadn't been taken inside. You decided to follow the Kyorai Cemetery road; you recalled that the Seiryōji Festival would feature a *kyogen* performance on a given Saturday or Sunday in April.

The Kyorai Cemetery was located in a grove of eighty- or ninety-year-old fir trees, where your daughter had once picked mushrooms and wild berries, though you had no idea whether they were poisonous or not. The wild turtledoves were unafraid of humans, making it even harder for your daughter to leave.

The fields by the fir grove were sometimes blanketed by buttery yellow rape flowers, and at times like that, even the nearby peach trees bloomed. Sometimes the farmers would be burning leaves and grass, and the persimmon trees in Rakushisha would have shed their leaves, leaving only sunset red persimmons hanging here and there on the dark branches. The scene ought to have been exactly the same as the one the poet Bashō saw several centuries earlier. . . . Every time you went there, you vowed that if somewhere near your house there might be a fir grove that would remain unchanged for fifty years, and your daughter were to spend her life playing there, not learning how to read or to work, you would not object.

Would that be such a difficult wish to fulfill?

The bamboo tool shop in front of Nisonin was open; a toasty kerosene burner was lit in the sealed glass room. You remembered to buy a garden rake for your father, who disliked the Japanese but felt that the little rakes made wonderful gardening tools. The owner, maybe noticing that your lips had turned purple, said politely, "It's cold." You understood but could not respond, so you just smiled foolishly.

The lane from Nisonin to Seiryō-ji was your favorite route, and you wove your way along in a zigzag fashion so as not to miss a single alley along the way.

Except for the color tones of the different seasons, every house remained fixed in eternal memory. There had been some notable changes during the years of the bubble economy; some families bought a car and converted part of their yard into a parking space. Fortunately, that was about all that had changed. Lush ivy covered the tops of the stone walls on some houses, while ferns blanketed the areas near the ravines. You reached out and picked a fleshy stalk with a dull glint; the cold, meaty sensation reminded you of your daughter's fingers back when she was still willing to hold your hand. Some people with large yards were burning branches and leaves they'd trimmed from fir trees. You were nearly hypnotized by the enchanting aroma of the smoke, but managed to keep a steady pace, not wanting to be pegged as a tourist by two obasans, who, cheeks red from the cold, were chatting while cradling grandchildren in their arms. The Akita at the big house where clusters of dry reeds hung on the earthen wall the year round, the one by the bamboo grove, stared at you, just as before, but did not bark. Not one family's cherry trees had hard little buds. If there were flowers anywhere, they were white magnolias the size of large bowls, or blood-red Chinese toon flowers, which, at their fullest, fell with their stems to the green moss below, creating an air of tragic beauty.

There are more shrines and temples, large and small, in the ancient capital than anyone knows. People favor one over the others for reasons of their own. You liked coming to the Seiryō-ji, too small to merit mention in some guidebooks.

At first that fondness stemmed from sympathy, for the temple, like its name—cool and remote—was bleak and deserted the year round. Beyond that, there was a burial stele for Toyotomi Hideyori by the main hall. When a fire raged through Osaka, Hideyori committed suicide at Tenshu Pavilion, but the whereabouts of his body remained a mystery until a few decades ago, when a dormitory for a nearby girls' school was being built and a carefully wrapped human head was excavated. Based on the family crest on the wrapping cloth, it was determined to be Hideyori's head and was reinterred in Seiryō-ji. Except for fees to pray in the main hall and the Treasure Room, visitors were free to come and go, so they used the main gate and side gate as shortcuts. Of course, you had also seen a college boy on his way to class come rushing in with a small carton of milk to feed a large cat. You had also seen middle-aged salary men stop off on their way home to pray, palms together. But most of the visitors were students from the Sagano Primary School, who rode over on bicycles, wearing shorts and skirts even on cold days, their red cheeks puffed up like Fuji apples. They fought to outdo each other with their boasts and arguments, shouting at the top of their lungs, like the little imps who worked for Fujiko Fujio. In addition, you saw young women in lace-trimmed aprons walking their dogs, plus a large number of older folks.

As time went by, you grew more sympathetic. Often you'd sit on a simple, crude wooden bench and let your daughter run wild like a puppy. If you came right after the rainy season, you could pick ripe yellow plums in the untended grove by the old bell tower. As the plums ripened, the side facing the sun would glow a lovely bright red, but the plums would be unspeakably tart. Unable to turn down your daughter's invitation, you ate them till your teeth seemed to turn upside down.

This is how it was: if a little time and a little memory remained before you died and you could choose where to go, like so many people who are anxious to leave a hospital and return to a familiar place, usually their home, you'd likely choose this place, and that was because, because it was only in places where you had left traces of yourself, where everything connected to you existed, that maybe those things would continue to exist and the significance of your imminent disappearance would be diluted—isn't that so?

You once read someone's autobiography about life on death row. He said he saw the usual sunshine outside his window and heard familiar tunes from the guard's radio, and knew that if they reappeared the next day as usual, his death would be of little consequence.

But why not choose the city where you were born, grew up, gave birth, and raised children, and began to show signs of aging?

Why wasn't it the city you came from? . . . You sat on the bench, freezing cold, as if sitting in water.

On the wooden sign was written: THE SAGA BUDDHA KYOGEN WILL BE PERFORMED ONLY ON THE SECOND SATURDAY AND THIRD SUNDAY OF APRIL.

Maybe everything belonging to that with which you were familiar, everything you remembered, died before you.

Thinking about it now, with an ocean between you, you were convinced that it was some sort of strange river with no navigational landmarks. Living on it, you often entertained crazy thoughts about fishing for the moon or marking the side of the boat to locate a lost sword. For instance, the month before you arrived, a neighboring country undertook missile tests in the ocean north and south of your island. The island was thrown into turmoil, everywhere the buzzing of a disturbed beehive. You belonged to the group who believed that war might come, but were not afraid. Of course there were other groups . . . those who believed that war would come and were very afraid, those who did not think war would come and therefore were not afraid, and others who did not think that war would break out but were still afraid.

You were unafraid simply because you realized early on that, when faced with weighty matters, particularly those concerning life and death, there is little a person can do. For instance, a volcano erupts in some country, yet for some strange reason, the residents living in the danger zone do not flee. You never could figure out who was fighting whom in Central Africa or the Balkans, but the people strangely did not leave their countries. And in Kaohsiung, where cases of dengue fever occurred at a high rate, several million people continued to live without an apparent trace of fear. Or, how could the people of Dongshi County, which is flooded half the year, be so resigned to their fate?

Knowing there was nothing you could do, you followed your normal 24-hour-a-day routine. None of you had any real estate to sell and no private stash to convert into U.S. dollars at the bank, so you could only hope, like so many other people, for the first time, that the technological standards of that country's national defense apparatus were as good as Uncle Sam's during the Gulf war, accurate enough to send a missile unerringly to the house of the person they considered the prime culprit and ensure that no innocent people became collateral damage. Some people actually believed that to be the case; one of your husband's coworkers, a renter, moved out and rented a new place beyond the 500-meter parameters of The Residence.

During those days, filled with jokes and clever ideas, there were times when you would be waiting for the light to change at an intersection (one day you waited a very long time because the premier was on his way home for dinner) and, gazing at the street scene, you could not help but wonder if that would be the last sight you saw it. If so, commit it to memory . . . but then you'd realize how hard that would be. If you didn't take pains to remind yourself, you'd look off to the left and to the right, and, without exception, be distracted by five-, seven-, or thirteen-story mixed-use buildings covered with all kinds of strange, ugly signboards, and by the sidewalks and overhangs crowded with motorcycles, betel nut stalls, fire hydrants, and trash cans. My god! Are these signs of early onset dementia? Where is this place anyway? Sanchong? Zhonghe or Yonghe? Xinzhuang? New Developments in Taizhong or Tainan?

It was a river with no navigational landmarks. But you refused to believe that and many times thought of sticking your foot into that same river. Three thousand years, and still no change.

*When I die, you'll find white oaks imprinted on my heart.—Thoreau

White oaks can grow as high as thirty-five or forty feet, and with their serrate leaves, they are beautiful temperate-zone trees. When the season is right, the ground below is covered with lovely acorns. When your daughter was still at an age when she went gaga over the anime character

Totoro Dragon-Cat, each day she'd fill her pockets with acorns that she pretended were chestnuts. They spilled from the hotel room table onto the carpet, but the house-keeping staff never treated them as removable trash.

Honestly speaking, what would have been imprinted on your heart before you died was not white oaks.

So what would it have been?

As you walked past a run-of-the-mill barbecue shop, hot, smoky tears welled up in your eyes. Maybe, maybe this was that So-and-so Eatery. Sometimes "so-and-so" was the owner's name, Ah-shui, or Ah-wang; sometimes it was the name of the town, like Tongluo. From north to south the signs were a faded blue that could have been in-tended as the color of the ocean, with red fish and curled shrimp painted on them. They were virtually identical, like the franchise stores you see everywhere these days. The eateries were usually located in the busy center of town, often by the north-to-south line train station. When your grandfather went to see patients in some far-off place or went north for a reunion with his classmates from the Taihoku Imperial University Medical School, your grand-mother would shed her identity as a doctor's wife, plun-der some of her private stash, and take one of her favorite third-generation kids (for a long time it was you) to the eatery, where she'd order half a sliced cold chicken in but-ter and kidney cooked in sesame oil. Grandfather, who watched Grandmother's blood pressure closely, would not normally allow her to eat too much of either. They cer-tainly weren't your fare—you were fixated on jawbreak-ers and pickled guava, so the little sundries shop under the eaves at the train station was your hallowed ground. Shrugging out of Grandmother's hand, you ran to play under the eaves, greasy chicken skin you couldn't swal-low still in your mouth. You wrapped your arms around a smooth juniper pillar and rubbed your face against it affectionately. You sensed, at an early age, that the solemn air of the train station was out of step with your boring, underdeveloped town.

Similarly out of step was the post office. Sometimes you'd tag along, insisting upon going there with your grandfather's pharmacist. You didn't dare make a scene under the high-flying roof of the post office, with its dark, cold, severe airs, like an official's residence you read about in stories. Your instincts were right. A hundred years earlier, the third Chief of Civil Adminstration, Gotō Shinpei, cited two lines from a Tang poem—"Not seeing the magnificent Imperial Residence,/How would you know the stature of the Emperor"—and carried out what he'd read without hesitation. Over the next ten years, train stations and post offices you either loved or feared were built all over the island. Even though your grandfather did not live in the old capital, still the local train station had a Renaissance-style pediment gable, while inside were substantial but smooth and intricately carved columns, minus the grooves. If you ignored the Japanese-style wooden posts and windows and the pastel blue window lattice, it would constitute a standard architectural type.

Was the confusing style all that different from the structures in Sanchong, Yonghe, or Taoyuan, which were neither Western nor southern Min nor Taiwanese nor illegal constructions? Why had the demolition of the former and new construction brought such sorrow, created such trauma? Was it simply because they harbored memories? If so, then your daughter's generation would surely have its own warm recollections of things. So what were you worrying about? Maybe you were like people who, as they begin to age, unwittingly fall into the trap of nostalgia—was that it?

. . . But there must have been differences. Separated by an ocean, you were able to simplify the complexities and clearly see the sites of your daughter's activities: school (it was only six years old, but had undergone two reconstructions simply because it had had two principals; the entry-way and statue had been moved for no apparent reason, while the poor, totally innocent trees had been dug up and replanted elsewhere), home (unoccupied high-rises had been built on a nearby hill by a business conglomerate), friends' houses (to play on the computer), classmates' houses (to play on the computer), cousins' houses (to play on the computer), fast-food restaurants, department stores. . . . When you can order fast food, all with the same taste and at the same price in eateries decorated in exactly the same style, the same tones, the same tempera-ture in a country where even the birds don't lay eggs, what irreplaceable memories of this McDonald's moving one street over or that 31 Flavors ice cream shop going out of business could possibly be out there for your daughter?

Once this land no longer held anything irreplaceable that stuck to the people, they would stay because they had no choice, not because they wanted to. The new rulers surely sensed this, which is why they shouted slogans about community into the skies, hoping that would get the people to at least heed the "Buddha" (the land and the people) even if they ignored the "monks" (the state machine, the rulers). Who would dare challenge the po-litically correct status of the peasants? Had the opposition party, which criticized everything under the sun, ever ut-tered a word of displeasure about the land and its people, as far as you knew?

Your daughter would remember that which belonged to her generation, or she would feel sad and traumatized over its disappearance. And what would that be? What would be imprinted on her heart?

The pretty white oaks? The bright red, overripe plums? The tumblebug cocoons in front of Ryōma's Tomb? The Chion'in, where she wailed after the pedometer tied to her waist fell into the toilet? The wild clams in the viaduct at Biwa Lake along Tetsugaku no michi? The "Japanese flag" koi in the pond at Rakushō? The big weeping cherry appearing in Okumura Dogyū's painting by the gate at Daigo-ji? The Doraemon feature-length movies shown once a year on the fifth floor of Takarazuka at Sanjōgawara-machi? The rice cakes at Seigoin yattsubashi? The flocks of doves or picking up gingko leaves at Higashi-hongan-ji? The Doutor Café, where she did her homework? Or the Japanese paper shop across from Saga Station? She was so unconcerned; on the train ride there she'd plan what kind of paper to buy this time. A turn around the corner and there it was, always open, never disappointing her. A few doors down from the paper shop was a small coffee shop called Hirose. A family-style eatery with no more than fifteen seats, it was always shrouded in cigarette smoke and coffee steam, messier than any house, with newspapers and magazines strewn all over the place. Once there, she could hardly wait to open the newly purchased paper and start folding it. Looking out at the street scene through the gauzy curtain, you felt as if you'd never left, even though it had been a year or several seasons since you were last there, even though you had aged from twenty to forty-one.

Maybe that was the reason Seiryō-ji would be there forever. The seventeen temples of the World Heritage Site, such as Tenryū-ji, Seiryō-ji, and Enryaku-ji, would always be there; Higashi-hongan-ji, Nanzen-ji, Tōfuku-ji, with their cultural artifacts and designated cultural heritage, would always be there; the Nonomi-ya in Nijōjō would always be there, so long as it was located in a place with traces of human habitation. Is that so rare?

Hadn't many grade A, B, and C relics been designated on the island in recent years? There were, for instance, Longshan Temple, built in the eighth year of the Xianfeng reign, where you and A always lingered and were always reluctant to leave. Or the Qingshui Patriarch Temple, where the nose of the patriarch fell off to alert the people in Tamsui and aid them in defeating the French. Or the Western-style missionary's dormitory on Zhenli Street across from Tamsui High School. One summer, A was wearing an off-the-shoulder T-shirt and jeans, and you were dressed in a short white skirt and sandals. The two of you were sitting on the balcony railing of the white Western-style building, talking and laughing about something, unaware that A's current boyfriend, an architecture major, had snapped a photo of you.

For a long time every summer you took time out to enjoy a bowl of shaved ice made from agar-agar or green bean soup at the corner of English College Road and Qingshui Street, sort of like now, when you went to the Sannen-zaka, you'd be sure to go to the main branch of Segoin for some soba and the free rice cake and green tea. Sometimes you'd get off at the ferry landing and squeeze into the crowds of tourists buying fishnet, fishing gear, fish balls, and "iron eggs" that were cooked so long they shrank drastically. You were neither anxious nor concerned; you just climbed the stairs up to the white hut on the hill. Not a soul under the melia tree, where you sat the whole afternoon, the way you'd sat in Seiryō-ji, which was cold like water. Guanyin Mountain lay quietly before you and to your right was the spire of the Presbyterian church and Mackay Hospital, showing a bit of roof. The giant banyan trees and Burmese gardenias by the hospital, built in 1880, weren't all that different from what Lu Jizheng and Yang Sanlang had seen several decades before, when they made their sketches. Now you felt as if you'd never been away.

Until that year you took the person you were going to marry to visit your secret garden. Just as before, you followed familiar paths and walked beneath the big banyan tree by Mackay Hospital. Telling him to watch out for the wet, slippery moss underfoot, you took his hand and traversed the shaded slope, until suddenly an open space appeared before you—Zhenli Street, no, it was the obligatory four-lane Zhongshan Road in every town, city, country, and village. All of a sudden you couldn't recall what it had been before. Like an eyewitness who, after going to the police to report a dead body, returns to the scene only to see there was no body, no blood stains, everything normal, you told your future husband in a sobbing voice that the place was never like this or like this, that it should be like that and like that. In a panicky mood, you pointed here and there aimlessly; in a word, you were lost.

During the Taiyuan Reign of the Jin Dynasty a fisherman of Wuling once rowed upstream, unmindful of the distance he had gone. . . .

You never went back.

Maybe this was the reason: you would never be disappointed or shocked when you walked through the ancient gate of Seiryō-ji, not caring if it was a two-star or grade A relic or a designated cultural treasure. No matter how cold it was, there were always neighborhood residents lined up to buy tofu at the door of Mori Yoshi. One day, after you die, they will still line up here in the evening to buy tofu, and it is comforting to know that after one dies the world of the living continues in predictable fashion. You weren't the only person with such thoughts. A film director who wrote his autobiography two or three years before he died said that, as he faced death, which confronts old people every day, his only wish was to rise up in his coffin once every ten years to read the paper, that it was enough to know that the world would continue to function as usual.

It is simply not enough to have cold, spotless, well-preserved relics.

You were suddenly gripped by a desire to see A, a simple desire, mindlessly believing that she was your dearest friend, someone who had been closer to you than your parents or anyone else when you were fifteen.

It was getting dark, and it looked like snow. Not another soul on the Togetsu Bridge, which was normally packed with tourists. The bridge seemed to be very long and to reach very far. You tightened the scarf around your neck, your shivering body and hesitant steps reminding you of Yoshinaga Sayuri in a still from the movie *Akan*, several years earlier, in which she was walking across this same Togetsu Bridge. But the broad, vast mountains and rivers, the house lights along the banks, the lantern-style street lamps, and the chilly, unending wind so special to bridges seemed to take you back to a moment before you turned five. Your maternal grandparents were holding you by the hands as you all stood on a large and very similar bridge. You'd been asleep, but were awakened to get out of the car. Grandfather pointed to the Dajia River, central Taiwan's largest, and as you stood on the newly finished bridge, Grandmother said something in Japanese to Grandfather, heavy with emotion. Maybe she was saying "It's so big," or "It's so beautiful," or "It's so cold." Still wrapped in the powdery smell of Grandmother, who had been holding you, you weren't sure what you were afraid of, maybe the darkness or maybe Grandfather.

Snow began to fall, as expected, and as you walked slowly down the Togetsu Bridge, the same sad longing, from that moment before you turned five, forty years earlier, now filled your heart.

The hotel's English-speaking desk clerk told you there were no messages, phone calls, or faxes.

You went up to your room and turned on the TV; no news of an airplane crash. It's not that you were overreacting, just that Americans, like A, were supposed to be punctual, to keep their word.

For the first time you sensed something strange about how the arrangements had been made; it all felt like it belonged to an agricultural age, a time when you waited even when you knew the other party was not going to show. To begin with, you didn't know her flight number, not even which airline she had taken; all you had was that faxed message. And A hadn't asked how she was supposed to get from Kansai Airport to the hotel, relying solely on the address, which you had faxed to her. Maybe she thought this was a tiny ancient city. Compared to the metropolis where she lived, it was no bigger than the small towns the two of you had roamed as youngsters.

Then it occurred to you that it could have been a spur-of-the-moment invitation. A might have run into a problem at work or had a fight with her husband, the man she was living with . . . anything was possible. Hadn't you been gripped by a mindless desire to see her no more than an hour or two before, feeling closer to her than to your parents, even to your husband and your daughter?

You put on your warmest clothes and applied a thick layer of windscreen lotion, deciding to have some crab ramen at the corner of Tera-machi and Rokku-dōri, even though it was way past five o'clock. Before five, a set menu of a big bowl of crab ramen and a salmon *donburi* cost only 890 yen.

After eating the noodles, you were full and you had warmed up; the sad longing you'd felt all evening now seemed far away. It turned out that had something to do with low blood pressure. In the evening, low blood sugar and low blood pressure had created a physical warning, which in turn had prompted you to think of important things, like life and death.

You walked all the way to Honnō-ji before turning back. High school girls on spring break from all over the country came to brightly lit Sanjō-dōri to buy local specialties. Their uniform skirts were short, but they didn't seem to mind the cold as they crowded into the Ōnishikyō Fan Shop, possibly planning to pick out a pretty Kyoto fan for their mothers, just as you had done many years before.

You'd passed the shop many times without going in, but it was always there, and that gave you a comforting sense of certitude.

From Sanjō you went to Kiya-machi, but then you weren't sure if you should turn in or take the next street, Bonto-chō, which paralleled Kamo-gawa.

Green buds showed on the willow trees at Kiya-machi, which, under the streetlights, looked especially green and lush. There had been many streets like this in the city where you grew up, pretty streets you liked so much you found it hard to choose one over the others. Oftentimes, when you and A walked along Chongjian Avenue, the oldest street, you looked all around as you went down the stone steps. Every little alley you crossed made you feel as if you'd missed an opportunity and would live to regret it. Then there were streets on which A had lived: Yuanhe Street, Chaozhou Street, Xiamen Street, and Hangzhou South Road. Hailing from central Taiwan, she had been renting ever since starting high school. Her landlords were usually aides-de-camp or husband-and-wife servant teams left behind to collect rents for retired government officials now living abroad. Depending on their size, the houses were often divided up and rented to several students at once. You sometimes spent the night at A's place, where you listened to phonograph records that were at least ten years older than you, all left behind by the landlord's children, who had also gone abroad, to school. Records back then sounded as if they'd been recorded in a big, empty room (like when Nat King Cole sang "Too Young" or "When I Fall in Love"). If anyone missed the songs, they'd have a second chance to hear them forty years later in *Sleepless in Seattle*. It really did feel like an empty room, for even Paul Anka's "Dance on, Little Girl" sounded terribly sad and bleak. Seated on a cypress floor mopped by the old servant woman until it sparkled, the two of you sang along by following lyrics printed on the album cover. The trees out in the yard were too dense for the chirps of cicadas to be carried in on rays of summer sun. Parts of the frame house were rotting, emitting the subtly sweet odor of mushrooms and fungi, together with the smell of green moss beneath the window, and the curved, knifelike, allegedly poisonous flame tree pods. You and A had exchanged a short-lived vow about remaining single. Which of these things would A manage not to forget?

In college, A was assigned a dorm room, but she kept her place on Jinhua Street, the last place she rented, as storage for her overflow of clothes and books. But more importantly, it quickly became a trysting spot for those of you who were madly in love. Once you waited for A outside a classroom in the College of Liberal Arts and asked if she was returning to the place on Jinhua Street. If not, you'd like to borrow the key. She said another girl, so-and-so, had the key, and she complained about so-and-so, who never folded the quilt and left food around, which attracted swarms of ants. You replied that you and X X X would make sure everything was neat and tidy before leaving, X X X being your boyfriend at the time. A gave you a look. The first month of the seventh year of the Xianfeng reign, a heavy snowfall.

You and X X X were hoping you'd be lucky, and you weren't much good at birth control techniques, so he ejaculated onto the wood floor. You tried to wipe the stain clean, but it had already seeped into the wood. X X X flipped through A's books and lost interest; he then picked up the records belonging to the landlord's children, "Sukiyaki" by Sakamoto Kyū, also recorded in a big, empty room. Twenty-year-old Sakamoto whistled on the record, unaware that he would die in a domestic plane crash twenty-three years later, on August 12.

*The Taiwanese like to rebel, like moths flying into a fire, the dead followed by the living.

—Once again, Dingyuan

If A wouldn't give you the key, you and he had no place else to go and could only pace the streets, feeling tormented. You had no choice but to pretend you were going to the movies or taking a stroll in the park or talking about your childhood or about philosophy.

Once when you were waiting for a bus, your passions got the better of you and your intertwined bodies wound up in the staircase of a dark, old apartment building, from which an old man chased you out like a couple of mongrels.

Later you actually fell in love with one of the boys and wanted to live as the sort of married couple you had always imagined. You asked A to let you stay there for a while, and you told your parents you'd been assigned a dorm room. As for the servant couple, who would only rent the place to girls, they mistook you for the spoiled daughter of their old master and were obliged to tolerate the arrangement.

When you passed the place ten years later, a sign nailed to the door proclaimed it to be the branch office of a certain "bubble" political party, which would end up just like one of your love affairs. Another ten years went by, and it suffered a fate far worse than No. 5, Lane 50 of Taishun Street, which had been turned into the northern club office of the original inhabitants, the aborigines. It was hard to tell if anyone still lived there, for the door was nailed shut. Its black fired tiles were swallowed up by a dense cover of flame trees, mangoes, and phoenix trees that spread fast and caught up with other vegetation. The year before, when the street was widened, half of the house was sliced away and became a pit for the neighbors' trash and junk. At the beginning of this year, it was leveled, and a construction fence was erected around it.

When the Qing government took over Taiwan, there was talk in the court about laying waste to it.

Chieko: "The parents I have now love me very much. I don't have any desire to look for my real mother and father.

Perhaps they are even among the Buddhas of the potter's field in Adashimo. Of course, the stones there are quite old."

The soft evening color of spring had spread, like a faint red mist, from Nishiyama across half the sky.

Gion was wall-to-wall people, all of them heading toward Yasaka Shrine. Several Japanese tourists stood outside the Yichiriki Teahouse at the corner of Hanami kōji, waiting to see the geishas. Several years earlier, you and your daughter had sat in the Colorado Café across the street, waiting to observe the geishas through a large window. Curtains covered Yichiriki's windows the year round, but across the yard, as you could see, there was a wide-open, deserted, silent, and austere entryway, like a stage before the performance begins.

You got swept up in the crowd. Little stalls lined the streets from the shrine to Maruyama Park, some selling food, others toys. It had a New Year's atmosphere, just like your childhood. The crowd stopped at the square with the tall weeping cherry trees; though there were daily news reports on the status of the cherry blossoms, people came every day anyway. Where else could they go at this time of year? The same was true at the shops, which laid red carpets under each cherry tree and set up lit torches at intervals along the way. Every once in a while, something would catch on fire, sending sparks crackling, which caused the frightened, yet excited pedestrians to push and shove and yell. Groups of street performers not normally seen appeared at the edge of the square. They may have been foreign students; one played a violin, another, in tails, performed a sword-swallowing routine. There was also a tall blonde dressed like a Greek goddess who played the harp, her snow-white arms bared for all to see and her blue eyes seemingly frozen over with a thin layer of ice. A TV company shone a floodlight on the big weeping cherries, for the sole purpose of illustrating yet again that it was too cold this year for the flowers to bloom.

I was at St. Mark's Square, watching the acrobatic flights of angels and the dancing of the Moors, but, without you, my dear, the loneliness was unbearable.

You walked along, enjoying the sight of drunken people under the trees. One professional with his tie loosened suddenly spoke insolently to his female colleagues, but strangely, instead of being upset, they tolerated him with motherly smiles. The older men drank with abandon, the effects showing in their ruffled appearances. With kerchiefs tied around their foreheads, they began to sing, like your grandfather. One of them saw you amid the chaos, and drunkenly called you Nēsan—Big Sister—again like your grandfather, who would call your grandmother Big Sister after he'd had a bit to drink. What did Grandmother look like when he called her Nēsan? Did she smile foolishly? She was always smiling foolishly in front of your grandfather, but she never forgot to get the servants and your aunts—her daughters-in-law—to roll sticky rice balls and make green Hakka snacks, if it happened to be the Lantern Festival and you had to hang paper on your great-grandfather's tomb the next day. You were disgusted by the cakes, which were green, cold, and sticky and were placed on an alpinia leaf. Everyone knew that the alpinia grew most abundantly in the graveyard, and that the pungent odor was a result of many years' sucking on the marrow of the dead.

Afraid of eating rice cakes tainted with the smell of the dead, you avoided going to the tomb by returning to your parents' home before the fifteenth day of the first lunar month. Years later you would become one of those who forgot you actually had a tomb to visit.

Cantonese prayed to the King of Three Mountains, those from Zhangzhou prayed to the Sage of Zhang, and those from Quanzhou prayed to the Emperor of Life.

On the eve of Misoka, the last day of the month, following customs of the season, you listened quietly and solemnly at Kiyomizu Temple to the monks ringing an ancient bell cast in 1478. On the next day, you made your first temple visit of the year at Heian Shrine, where lingering smoke from the previous day's bonfire was frozen straight. If you remained in the area for another seven days, you would watch the wearisome old White Horse report celestial affairs at Kamigamo Shrine, where spring herbs and seven-herb rice porridge are placed in front of the deity. On the second Sunday of the Flower Festival, the Taikō Flower Viewing Procession at Daigo-ji reenacts the party attended by Toyotomi Hideyoshi at the end of the third year of the Keichō reign, when he appeared for the last time with his wife, Kitano Mandokoro, his concubine, Yodo Jimi, and his official entourage. At the end of the month, the Inari—Harvest God—Festival is held at the Fushimi Inari Grand Shrine, where the eaves are painted vermilion, the columns and beams made of black pine in a contrasting deep green color, and where the sound of drums and flutes is relentless. May is the month for the Aoi—Sunflower—Festival, but you never attended; that is the rainy season. At the end of summer, a thousand lamps are lit for the Baken Buddhist Invocation at the foot of Aiyan Mountain. Then in late September monks from Honnō Temple perform their ritual for hungry ghosts at Ōseki-gawa. At the end of October, a lingering fragrance festival takes place in Tenmangū Temple in Kitano; the twenty-second was A's birthday.

The twenty-second was the Jidai Festival. You followed the crowd and the sounds of drums and flutes to Jingū-do via Gosho, Karasuma-dōri, and Sanjō. Paraders dressed in period costumes, styling themselves after famous individuals in history. An elegant autumn scroll depicting the history and customs of the ancient capital slowly unfurled toward you. There were the late Tokugawa patriots Katsura Kogorō and Sakamoto Ryōma; the famous Edo women Yoshino Dayū and Izumo Okuni; the Momoyama period Hideyori and Oda Nobunaga; Oharame, Katsurame, and

Shizuka Gozen from the Kamakura period; and Murasaki Shikibu and Sei Shonagon of the Fujiwara period. The final scenes were of officials at court in the Enryaku period and the archers under Tanba protecting the move of the Heian Shrine to the new capital.

As for seasonal festivals and holiday celebrations on the island, there were the welcoming of the Emperor of Life on the fifteenth day of the third month; the birthday of the Goddess of the Sea, Mazu, on the twenty-second day of the third month; the City God Festival of Xiahai on the thirteenth day of the fifth month; the Qingshui Patriarch's ascension after obtaining the Dao on the sixth day of the fifth month; the Water God's Festival on the tenth day of the tenth month. . . . The ones you were often forced to attend were the Golden Mother's wedding, her funeral, and other auspicious events. Honestly, her wedding, her funeral, and other auspicious events: if not, how could there have been so many festivals each year? An ugly shelter was erected overnight to block heaven and cover earth at the alley entrance of the Qihui Temple. A huge oil drum was placed in the middle of the road, with a request, written in a third-grader's hand, for vehicles to detour. Then a dozen or more tables were laid out for three consecutive days by the faithful, who, looking quite bored, watched a pornographic version of a Taiwanese street opera or a movie directed by Zhu Yanping. On other days, the custodian and his adherents would engage in the serious business of shamanistic exercises. The site, where organizers of illegal gambling collected and paid out money, was used as a polling station for all sorts of elections; it also served a certain farmers' association in their promotion of medicinal pollens and garlic extracts.

You were confused. Was the local temple any different from the Seiryō-ji, which was put to similar uses in the Japanese neighborhood? Whenever you walked past, there were loud broadcasts of sutra recitations and smoke from paper smoldering in the burner; the custodian, in an undershirt with the logo of X X Golden Lion Troupe, would be sitting with several notorious loafers as they made tea, scratched themselves, and watched videos of the raunchy variety star Zhuge Liang. Otherwise, why would you be willing to sit at the Seiryō-ji for a whole afternoon doing nothing, while you couldn't wait to flee the Temple of Benevolence, which you had to walk by every day?

—Abandoning the ancestors' tombs and the reunion of family clans, they crossed the ocean and traveled in great danger, tossed and roiled at a place where the sky ended and the ocean rose up—

That is how your maternal ancestor was described in the *Zhuluo County Gazette* nearly 300 years ago.

At a time when "Not a single board may enter the water, no goods may cross the border," your ancestor crossed the ocean with nothing but a carrying pole, which is still ensconced in the family shrine. The story of this ancestor had been narrated in different versions, some relating his success, some his failure, depending on later generations' needs when they taught their children a lesson. Your favorite one was presented by Ya'uchimara Tadao: the ancestor was a bandit in his youth, and then grew wealthy in middle age (how similar to present-day success stories).

The bachelor ancestor who carried a pole over his shoulder had once been intent upon becoming a bandit and may well have become one. . . . This thought made you laugh to yourself and brought a smile to your lips.

Enough, you felt that was enough, enough for one night. You could return to the hotel now, whether A was there or not, or even if she came.

An itinerant monk was still standing at the end of the Shijo Bridge; you could not be sure if it was the same one. Along the Kamo-gawa pairs of lovers in tight embrace appeared every five meters, as if following regulations. The temperature had dropped to 2° Celsius.

A large crowd filled the subway entrance of the Hankyū train to Kiyamachi. There was a one-man performance by a foreigner who, still dressed in a short-sleeved T-shirt, was drenched in sweat from singing. It was "Tie a Yellow Ribbon Round the Old Oak Tree," a popular song in your youth. The Japanese who had requested the song was so pleased she began dancing with her girlfriend, a peach genie and a willow spirit. You stopped and joined the crowd. The willows along the Takase-gawa were incredibly beautiful. In your memory, the only comparable scene was the Suzhou described in poems and lyrics, and Master Liu's Canal, which ran past the side gate of your college when you were still a student there.

The song ended and was followed by applause, whistles, and shouts from the young people in the audience. Someone handed the man some money and made a request, another song popular in your youth. It had a slower tempo, as if to let the performer enjoy a break. You liked the song so much you were reluctant to stay for the whole thing, so you slowly walked away.

During the Taiyuan Reign of the Jin Dynasty a fisherman of Wuling once rowed upstream, unmindful of the distance he had gone, when he suddenly came to a grove of peach trees. . . .

This is how it should be: during the Kangxi reign of the Qing dynasty, Guo Xiliu, from Nanjing of Zhangzhou, diverted water from Dapinglin to make a canal for irrigation. He made wooden pipes to channel the water from Qingtan through the Jingmei River and turn it toward Dajianai Fortress after passing Gongguan. From the fifth to the twenty-fifth year of the Qianlong reign it was called Master Liu's Canal.

You needed a good night's sleep, so you passed on the rich, aromatic coffee in the many pretty cafés on Shijō-dōri.

Grabbing hold of the red-latticed door, Chieko watched as her twin sister Naeko walked away. Naeko did not look back. A few delicate snowflakes fell on Chieko's hair and quickly vanished.

The town was as it should be, still silent in sleep. (The End)—The Old Capital.

The plane would depart at ten in the morning, so you left the hotel quite early, when the city and its streets were still in a deep slumber. You turned to look back; the only person seeing you off was the early rising hotel manager. You could not explain to him why you wouldn't wait for the flower festival and even canceled a room you'd originally reserved for the week.

Your instincts told you that A would not come. From the start, you never really believed that she would, isn't that so? She was more like the nightshade trees along the Sansen-dō, more like the melodious whistling of Sakamoto Kyū, more like the many summers of yore, when it was usually you who waited for her at the train station where you'd agreed to meet. The blistering sun shone down on you, but you felt nothing; your heart was young and your veins were tough enough, so you remained odorless even though your front and back were sweat-soaked. Back then there were no five failings of a deity; you were the itinerant monk on the Shijō Bridge, who never moved an inch the year round, your heart motionless as water.

You did not know when it began, but whenever your plane landed on the island with a thump, you would recite to yourself, "The residence of local savages, occupied by sea-going demons, with no system set up by ancient kings." Reciting it as incantation, you would know that somehow it would be easier to tolerate the sticky heat once you stepped outside the airport and entered the chaos, the frenzy.

Predictably, a middle-aged driver of a nine-passenger van solicited you in Japanese and urged you to decide quickly. You guessed that he was pushing both his van and a hotel.

Quietly deciding to play the role of a foreigner, you nodded in agreement and were swept onto the van like a captive. The sign informed you it was a hotel by the train station, where a good friend had once stayed when she'd come from down south to take the college entrance exams.

The hotel ought not to be far from Hon-machi, Book Street. You took out your guidebook about the island nation, which you'd purchased at the Gion Bookstore. It included maps and scenic sites from the colonial period. When he spotted your map as he climbed into the van, the driver pointed enthusiastically, gesturing like a mute to show you the location of the hotel. His expression was that of the "smiling face, friendly" islander described in the guidebook. You smiled and nodded politely, then turned your attention to the van in which you were now a passenger.

No need to rush; you had a week of vacation, and it had just begun.

You woke up from a light sleep, plagued by worries of a fire breaking out. Map in hand, and wearing the lightest clothes in your suitcase, you began your walking tour, obediently following the guidebook suggestions, starting with the observation station of the skyscraper near your hotel.

The skyscraper was listed at 244 meters, the tallest structure in Taiwan, and a close match to the Tokyo Government Office Building.

You had never seen the place where you'd lived for more than three decades from this height or angle. Maybe the gods looked it from such a distance, which for them was neither too far nor too close. It was only from this distance that the houses about which you'd commented a few days earlier in the nine-passenger van, "My god, it's a miracle anything could be that ugly" disappeared. Airplanes landing at Songshan Airport every five minutes floated slowly past the Jiantan hill like eagles. Ah, there's the Taiwan Shrine. Next should be the *chokushi*, the imperial messenger road, which ran past blocks of buildings. There, off to the south, was Taihoku Government House, with the eastern line of the Sansen-dō in plain view. According to the book, Taiwan, with its long summer and coconut trees lining the streets, has the flavor of a South Sea island, and, owing to its beautiful scenery, is called the Little Paris of the East. Extending to the south were #2 Girls High; Shinmachi Church, beneath a canopy of livistona and date palms; the Research Institute of the Taiwan Governor-General's Office; the Medical Specialization Section of Taihoku Imperial University, which Grandfather had attended; University Hospital; the headquarters of the Red Cross (you had to erase the tall office building of a certain political party, which was so disgustingly ugly it ruined the skyline); the clownlike, pitiable Keifuku Gate; the broad avenue at Tōmon-chō, which was called neither Jieshou nor Kaidagelan, and the Taiwan Governor-General's Mansion. You finally had a chance to see the garden in the back.

That was where you'd hung out in high school and wondered what was on the other side of the stone wall that took up so much space. Without having to know it was built in the first year of the new century, you were pleased with its Renaissance flair. Several of you sitting in your school uniforms on the spotless red brick sidewalk in front of the stone wall, for some reason all smiles, mouths open, captured in a photograph. Across the street was the Imperial University Hospital, designed by Kondō Jyurō in the same Renaissance style. Later you saw a similar black-and-white photo in your grandfather's college graduation yearbook: several young men in May Fourth attire sitting on Changde Street. From the *kanji* in the Japanese description on the photo's edge, you guessed this was the street they'd passed most often, the one they'd remember forever.

A coincidence half a century later created a loss of reality for you.

In the future, these could easily become the indelible memories of white oaks for your daughter, so long as you looked down at the city from this angle.

Just as the trumpet starts to play "Sleepy Lagoon" in Woody Allen's movie, when the MRT train slithered among bleak, uneven buildings, you looked down at the city below, and the music that sounded in your mind was Gershwin's "Rhapsody in Blue," so often used as background music for New York City. But you were immediately reminded where you were, for the exclamations around you were coming from people who spoke Japanese and were also holding colonial maps.

You left the building, originally the Railroad Hotel, and saw that the escalator entrance was where you had all come to stand in line once a month for bus passes.

Walking toward Hyo-machi, from a distance you could see the memorial museum for Governor-General Kodama and Chief Civil Administrator Gotō in New Park to the south. The book devoted considerable space to describing this structure, which was the single most typical work from the peak of golden age architecture. It must have been a hundred years since your last visit to the park. Now you learned that there had been a marble statue of Governor-General Kodama in the spot where the flower clock had stood, and where trees were planted following the construction of the 2/28 Peace Memorial, and that Claire Chennault's statue had replaced Gotō Shinpei's, which had been built with donations from Gu Xianrong and Li Chunsheng.

The 2/28 Peace Memorial confused the New Park in your memory. Oh god, who had those olive trees offended this time? Unable to find them, you reluctantly left the grove and went to find the beautiful Spanish-style house, which, you now learned, had been built sixty or more years ago and had served as a broadcasting station. Back when you were picking fallen leaves and daydreaming in the nearby sweet gum grove, it served as offices for the

Central Broadcasting Company, but it now housed the Parks and Streetlight Maintenance Office of the Municipal Bureau of Public Works.

The sweet gum grove was still there, but you suspected that the trees must have been cut and trimmed; such sparse trees could never have provided all of you shelter as you gossiped and dreamed your foolish dreams. You had all looked up to see a clear blue sky serving as a backdrop for temperate-zone leaves that had barely managed to turn a soft yellow. After a while you forgot where you were, and were able to fantasize about where you wanted to be someday, even though most of the places were located at the far corners of the world. Those "abandoning the ancestors' tombs and the reunion of family clans, who crossed the ocean and traveled in great danger, tossed and roiled at a place where the sky ended and the ocean rose up" were not limited to your ethnic group, who had been criticized because their fathers had arrived in Taiwan in 1949.

The guidebook recommended that after leaving the park through the side gate near Sakae-machi, you go to Takase-gawa Bookstore. You recalled the ground floor entrance, which was dark and cold as a fairy cave. The spiral staircase rose along one wall, its grindstone steps worn smooth and cold after so many years. Often the aroma of newly steamed rice cakes seeped through the wall from Three-Six-Nine next door, forcing you to abandon the books. The fairy cave was leveled in 1980, and a new glass curtain building was erected at the site, where it still stood.

The original Bank of Taiwan was a mansard-style wooden building designed by Nomura Ichirō in 1903. By 1934 it had suffered severe termite damage, and it was rebuilt in 1939 into its current form. You and A had enjoyed walking through the area, but strangely, neither of you had ever looked up to study the entire structure, as you did now. Back then you'd agreed that this bank (you couldn't tell how it differed from other banks) would be just like the place where Audrey Hepburn lingered in *Breakfast at Tiffany's* whenever she was feeling blue; all it had to do was replace its windows with glass display cases filled with pretty jewelry and things like that.

The Taiwan Governor-General's Office, completed in 1919, was based on Nagano Uheji's winning design in an open competition. The central tower was lower in the original design, which could be verified with a picture in the book. It did look weird, and was later raised to a height of nine stories, but in your memory it could not have been altered.

On October 31, the Governor-General's Office had organized an advance, exclusive opening for its neighbors. You could not recall if it was required by the school, but you all happily lined up to enter the building, where you bowed and passed on auspicious birthday greetings, after which you were each given a steamed bun in the shape of a peach. You had been so innocent, so naïve, like genteel granddaughters, and it probably wasn't until twenty years later that you understood and had to sigh over an international news report of people wishing Kim Il Song a happy birthday, the smiles on their faces so obviously genuine.

How you envied those girls who had not lined up for a steamed bun (in your memory, there actually were a few in your class), who were neither moved, motivated, nor brainwashed by the patriotic education from those in power. Some were even so shocked by looking at the party flag that they trembled with fear, a reaction that differed radically from yours, for you immediately thought about Lu Haodong, the revolutionary, and Huanghua Hill, and felt hot blood rage inside you. You were all in your teens; how had they managed to do that? How had they saved themselves the trouble of taking a detour in their future enlightenment and growth, as well as in the development of their independent, autonomous personality? It would probably have been easy for a PC writer twenty years later to portray one or two of them as surviving family members of 2/28 victims, or as people whose property had been legally appropriated under the land reform policy, or as those who gained enlightenment after reading magazines such as *Free China* or *Daxue*, purchased at Guling Street. If not, they'd have had an older sister or a boyfriend who had secretly distributed political pamphlets for Kang Ningxiang or Guo Yuxing. But how had your classmates managed to do that? There might have been family members of victims among the few you recalled, girls who were either perfectly clear-headed or indifferent to everything. One of them, after twenty-odd years of no news, contacted you before the mayoral and gubernatorial elections, but before you even had a chance to chat and catch up, she urged you to vote for a certain candidate from a particular party. Another one, whose father ran a sundries shop in Dadaocheng, had studied political science in college and then continued her studies abroad. Her ideas had been strikingly novel during your school years, and you were amazed to learn that she had seriously considered accepting the military education teacher's invitation to join the Nationalist Party and work for the government after returning from study abroad. You suspected she might have preferred to remain undercover or to sign on to the project of systemic reform. But she too invited you to tea just before the election and asked you to support the reelection of her boss, which also amazed you.

—What had those girls who turned down the peach-shaped steamed buns back then been thinking?

After the Governor-General's Office, scenic spots on Hon'in-machi included Taiwan Power and the Governor-General's Library. Standing on Hon'in-machi I-chome, you looked left to Taoyuan Street, where the row of noodle shops had all been torn down, the site now closed off by a construction fence. To your right, said the book, was

Tamsui Hall, which had been the Dengying Academy. In 1898, Gu Xianrong had bought the place and turned it into Taipei New Stage, but that had been bombed out by the Americans toward the end of the war. What stayed in your memory was the Chinese Womens' Anti-Communist Association, but none of you could figure out the function of anything with such a long name. The only exception was: for one of the nursing classes each semester the class would be brought here to make for the benefit of front-line soldiers, no, not uniforms, but cotton balls for dressing wounds. You girls talked and laughed while you turned out cotton balls that were either too big or too small, too tightly or too loosely packed, all twisted or simply dirty, and no soldier would ever have been desperate enough to use one.

Nogi-machi. An all-terrain vehicle was parked outside a big house that was all but engulfed by banyan and sweet gum trees and plastered with militaristic stickers. Like Zhou Zhirou's Spanish-style house the next block over, it hadn't changed a bit over the decades. At unchanged houses like this trees in the yard grew wild (the original owners had mostly planted trees with, yes, a South Seas flavor—coconut, betel palm, mango, banyan), obscuring the tiled roofs and stone walls, thus avoiding attention. There were many like this, all easily named. They sought anonymity because the residents were retired officials of the ancien régime who still occupied official residences. The somewhat more honest and upright among them were humble, careful people who tried to keep their children and grandchildren from troubling shows of arrogance. Still, many of their offspring would arrive home in the middle of the night and lay on the horns of their ATVs and sports cars to get the retired aides-de-camp or aging servants to open the gates for them. Some second-generation children initiated all sorts of stealthy improvements upon their return to Taiwan after schooling abroad. These included adding brick facing to the house in Lane 259, Section 1 of Fuxing South Road, with its fourteen coconut trees, or the property overgrown with Chinese magnolia, nightshade, and camphor in Lane 97, Section 1 of Xinsheng South Road. In the late 1980s, these families acquiesced to the demands of bored third-generation offspring who returned to Taiwan over summer break by cutting down trees and laying concrete for basketball courts, thus creating in these overweight youngsters the illusion that they were future NBA superstars. If you don't believe me, ride the MRT past the official residences along Fuxing South Road and Da'an Road, and you'll get all the proof you'll need.

There were also places that incited public outcries, such as the house whose enormous yard was overgrown with eucalyptus and bauhinias in Lane 135 of Rui'an Street (the house alone was half the size of Heping East Village, which housed several dozen families across the street), as well as the He'an neighborhood house next to Taiwan Normal University High, in Lane 14, Section 3 of Xinyi Road. These houses were likely the residences of presidential political advisors or national policy advisors, for they came equipped with guards and sentry booths. The He'an neighborhood provided a classic contrast: as if by prior agreement, houses in Alley 17 (an odd-numbered alley) were all occupied by high officials—numbers 1, 2, 3, and 4. Separated only by Lane 147, the people who lived in Alley 12 (an even number) were humble citizens of a tumultuous age who had to crowd twenty to thirty families into a single aging illegal structure.

Slogans to incite patriotic sentiment among the humble citizens had once been pasted all over the He'an Neighborhood bulletin board, but in recent years, in response to the new ruler's concept of a community with a common destiny, the slogans, now noticeably gentler, announced cozy activities asking the residents to create a sense of communal identity. . . . You were curious to know how communal living that involved both the humble citizens of even-numbered alleys and the high officials in the odd-numbered alleys was possible, so long as Lane 147, a demarcation between opposing powers, existed, even for a day.

Some of the families had managed to resolve property rights issues and had remodeled their houses in styles that reflected the periods during which their second-generation offspring returned to Taiwan, or their academic majors, or the places where they had lived overseas. There were: a Harvard shoebox house in the Gropius tradition, a Mies-style house in glass and steel, one following I. M. Pei's design when he worked at the Stone & Webster Engineering Company in Boston before becoming a master architect, and a Mier-style house with gigantic glass walls. The limited space and dense population worked against development of designs by Louis Khan and another master, Frank Lloyd Wright, designer of the Imperial Hotel, which, along with the Kuandong Earthquake of 1923, ended the era of Japanese-style architecture; he once said that cities are bases for banks and prostitution, strewn with weedlike skyscrapers.

These remodeled houses were subsequently altered by rental and real estate agencies so drastically that the original concepts were completely obscured. Barred windows, air conditioners, even store signs disfigured the vertical surfaces, while the concrete was so filthy you suspected that addicts' needles must surely be piled up in the stairwells. The rare space that retained traces of its original design was now usurped by motor scooters during the day and vendors of fruit and deep-fried chicken strips in the evenings. Some with a little remaining original flavor could be found in Lane 10, Section 3 of Zhongxiao East Road, which paralleled Ji'nan Road; happily, its simple concrete surface had no mosaic or gaudy veneer tiles. Plants that produced light effects were preserved and clear windows replaced the old ones as boutiques sprouted up along the lane, very much like the row of old apartments on Omote-san-dō in Hara jyuku. There were also simple, ten-story apartment buildings like the one in Lane 97, Section 1 of Xinsheng South Road, where two sweet gum trees rose as high as the building and the design followed the credo of "Brick is humanist," covering the exterior with warm, dark red bricks. On cold days, lights were turned on early. If an apartment building had later gone up in Peyton Place and Allison had had nowhere to go, like you she'd have submitted meekly to marriage. She'd probably be settling accounts under a light like this, or reading a novel and waiting for her daughter to come home after school.

*Two roads diverged in a wood, and I,/I took the one less traveled by,/And that has made all the difference.
—Robert Frost

Seimen-chō, the Japanese pleasure district, according to the colonial map.

Seimon-chō, now Ximen ding, was situated at the site of the long since demolished West Gate. Neighboring streets included Suehiro-machi, Kotobuki-machi, Tsukiji-chō, Shinki-chō, and Wakatake-machi.

The last time you were here might have been right after college graduation, when you took in a movie with your boyfriend, who was on leave from the army. He told you that two different types had come up to ask if he wanted a date during the ten minutes he was waiting for you. One of them, seeing his military uniform, had even assured him, "Hey, silver bar, don't sweat it, there's a colonel downstairs right now," meaning that a low-ranking lieutenant like him had nothing to worry about.

You didn't tell him you were ten minutes late because you had to reject a determined old man who had offered to take you in as a foster daughter, had changed that to having lunch with him, and finally to just his giving you a pair of shoes. Seimon-chō looked so pathetic, no longer the pleasure district of your school days. You saw, for the first time, its decline, its filth, its noise. The snacks in the vendors' stalls were unappetizing. The Bee Gees' "Saturday Night Fever" blasted everywhere. Low-quality, glitzy disco clothes in the store displays underscored the resemblance of the places to aging, heavily powdered prostitutes trying to turn a trick or two. Overcome by sympathy, you decided not to go there again; it was the least you could do for the area.

By reading the kanji in the guidebook, you discovered that the Wanguo Theater, which you'd never entered, had been the Shōnichiza, which had shown only Japanese plays. The Taiwanese theater was located at the site of the current China Cinema; Yoshino kan became Meilidu Cinema after the retrocession, then Guobin Cinema, where you saw *The Godfather* several times. New World Cinema used to be Shinseki kan, and you recalled that it was where your grandparents had seen *Daibosatsutōge* and *Aizenkatsura*. On Katakura-dōri, behind the theater, there were restaurants where sushi, *hatkeni*, *kabayaki*, and *yakitori* were all available. Since you couldn't read the Japanese script in the guidebook, you didn't know if the restaurants had been there before or were there now, but, like the last time you visited the area, you chose not to go see for yourself. Like a regular tourist, worn out by too many new things and sights, you found the brick edgings of a flower bed by a tree and sat down to tour the city on paper.

The tree turned out to be a small-leaf Indian almond, one of many lining the street. Green smoke seemed to rise from the shadows of the trees, which filtered the light extremely well; resembling elms or some temperate-zone species, they actually came from Africa, which was hard to believe. These trees and the dita barks planted on the sidewalks and close to buildings were less than ten years old, whereas the silk cottons had been around for roughly thirty years, and were most commonly seen near junior high school campuses (unless the buildings were old, then yes, there would be banyans, Chinese gum trees in the north, and flame trees in the south, and trees with a South Seas flavor, which you knew by heart—betel palms, mallows, and coconuts). Whoever planted this tree surely hoped that the fast-growing silk cotton trees would help the mass-produced buildings quickly shed their look of newness—small trees, new walls—and would look as if they'd put down roots and been around for a long time. In political terms, wasn't that the reason so many Taiwanese had been employed in Chiang Ching-kuo's administration during that period?

In the forty-eighth year of the Kangxi reign of the Qing Dynasty, the Quanzhou immigrant, Chen Laizhang, was permitted to develop the wilderness of Dajia nabao, and Mengjia gradually grew into a village. . . .

During the Taiyuan Reign of the Jin Dynasty a fisherman of Wuling once rowed upstream, unmindful of the distance he had gone, when he suddenly came to a grove of peach trees in bloom . . . the wild flowers grew beneath them, and fallen petals covered the ground—it made a great impression on the fisherman. . . .

It made a great impression on the fisherman. He went on for a way with the idea of finding out how far the grove extended. It came to an end at the foot of a mountain whence issued the spring that supplied the stream. There was a small opening in the mountain, and it seemed as though light was coming through it. . . .

So you chose to walk back to Seimon Market through Suehiro-machi. The kanji told you that the building always plastered with posters for pornographic movies and replete with homosexual stories had been completed in 1908, and was also designed by Kondō Jyurō. Its octagonal shape was based on the Chinese hexagram, with the idea of warding off evil spirits. The outskirts of the Seimon district had been a cemetery for Taiwanese, a place where wild animals often dashed out and frightened people. So, to fend off the evil spirits, they traveled all the way to the Inari Shrine of Fushimi in Kyoto, where you had watched the Inari Festival in early April, and invited fox spirits over. It was just like a fable. What had attracted you to that fable had to do with the spirits that had ended up here after a period of wandering, just like you. *Their ancestors had fled the disorders of Qin times and, having taken refuge here with wives and children and neighbors, had never ventured out again; consequently they had lost all contact with the outside world. They asked what the present dynasty was, for they had never heard of the Han, let alone the Wei and the Jin.*

Given your complex, even confused state of mind, you decided not to follow the guidebook's suggestion to visit the old sites of Kōkaidō Hall or the Provincial *Yamen*. Nor did you stop at the old sites of the Military Governor's Ya-men, the Governor-General's Mansion, or the police sub-station. The current Police Bureau site also had small-leaf Indian almond trees, which were several stories tall and looked as if they'd put down roots and been there for a long time, although in fact they weren't even ten years old.

Looking south to Kyō-machi, unable to decide whether to go back to the hotel to rest, you saw the familiar round-ed sign, DOUTOR, written in chocolate color on a wheat-yellow background.

Doutor, your secret garden, your little concession, where you drank coffee that had cost about the same as now. Looking around, you found it hard to see how it was any different, for it also had a "droppings lamp," the name you and your daughter had invented. Any Doutor chain with a large enough space would have a similar chandelier hanging from the ceiling; the beehivelike lamp shade was a mosaic of clear and irregular tea-yellow glass. You and she had once seen a news report about the storage tank on an airplane that malfunctioned at an altitude of several thousand feet, sending human waste falling like ice cubes into the bedroom of a small-town Midwest American family. The unknown objects that fell through the roof and awakened the sleeping couple must have looked something like that. You called it a droppings lamp, under which your daughter did her math homework on the central table, her round little face framed by two loose braids, at the age of seven or eight, a period when she was still willing to hold hands with you.

Your eyes were burning—too many smokers.

The hotel clerk still hadn't figured out where you were from and continued to speak to you in heavily accented, all but incomprehensible Japanese. You guessed he was trying to tell you that you got a better rate of exchange for your money at the hotel than at a bank. Turning him down with a smile, you decided to continue being a foreigner.

In the future it would be the Japanese who brought calamities.

After another confirmation of escape routes that included the fire escape outside the window, you felt safe enough to stand by the window and look down at the street, where shops had already turned on their lights, even though the sky to the west of the city was still quite bright. The city's west side had always been like that, due perhaps to the nearby river. In high school, when you girls hadn't felt like going home but needed to talk, you often took the road just beyond the gate, so absorbed you crossed the street without realizing it. When you reached the Patriarch Temple, you would, as if by prior agreement, turn back or walk down a street to the right, feeling that another country lay ahead of you. The river was in sight where the road ended, but you wouldn't go there. Later, when you came across the phrase "Numerous thefts in broad daylight," you settled on the idea that it must concern the river's pier, to which you had never gone, without even checking the actual meaning of the phrase.

Numerous thefts in broad daylight.

Wondering about the progress of the cherry blossoms, you turned on the TV in your room and easily found *NHK News*, whose familiar tone and unintelligible language were hypnotic. You'd missed the square with the weeping cherries at Maruyama Park.

No news of the cherry blossoms, nor of a plane crash anywhere. You fell asleep fully dressed, not even remembering to remove your contact lenses.

In the third lunar month, Chinese roses spread their vines, magnolias write on the sky, amalanchiers explode with color, weeping willows fall on the water like duckweed, begonias sleep, and hydrangeas fall.

On the third day of your holiday in this southern nation, you rose early, feeling an urge to blend in. And so, following a crowd of people heading to work and to school, you roamed around Hon-machi, where only a third of the bookstores were still open for business. You couldn't recall where the O-mei Restaurant or Maxim's had been, nor could you remember what had originally occupied the St. Mary's and KFC sites. So you retreated to the teahouse on an upper floor of the Mitsukoshi Department Store in the concession, where you had your Western-style set breakfast and picked up the morning paper, which you put aside after reading the first few pages; numerous thefts in broad daylight.

Taking out your colonial map, you contemplated the day's schedule.

The First Zhongzheng Branch of the Police Bureau had been an examination hall in the Qing dynasty, where the topic for the free-verse poem for the Xiucai exam had been "tap water and telephones." In 1895, when Japan colonized Taiwan, it became the Second Infantry Regiment's Field Hospital. After the Army Medical Chief, Mori Rintarō, whose rank was equivalent to colonel, landed at Aodi in the company of the Crown Prince, Kitashiragawa no miya, he was stationed here. Mori's army journal would later be published by Iwanami Bookstore, under the pseudonym of Mori Ogai.

You followed Mori Ogai's daily strolling routine, hoping that the old governor, who had occupied No. 5, still lived there. You didn't know who lived in No. 1, whose owner, like your grandfather, had survived in the South Pacific and returned to plant breadfruit trees, described by Darwin as "especially eye-catching, with their broad, smooth, deeply lined leaves," which now completely covered the beautiful tiled roof. You wondered if your grandfather, who had studied and interned around here, had seen this place while strolling in the area and vowed to build an identical home in the future. A giant breadfruit tree in the northeastern corner of your grandfather's house shaded an entire lotus pond, an orchid shed, and grapevine trellises. Only the plum tree and the generations of dogs that guarded the side entrance did not fall under the breadfruit tree's shade. When your grandfather was off seeing patients, you picked the large leaves and tied them together with grass stalks to make boots, which you wore to ward off leeches as you entered the pond to catch fish. You never ate the breadfruit, though the neighbors took some home to put in their pork soup.

Of course your grandfather might have vowed to imitate yet another place, No. 5 of Xuzhou Road, at the far end of the school. At his house there was an identical entryway for bicycles, a reception room up front, and a study on one side, where he saw his patients. The hallway connected to the living quarters and a nursery. Toward the rear were a dining room, the kitchen, the maid's room, and the bathroom. A typical Showa-era house of mixed Japanese and Western styles.

Again following the routes of Mori Ogai and your grandfather, you crossed the eastern line of the Sansenō. A filthy old bus too impatient to wait out the red light took up half the pedestrian crossing. Its sign read DANHAI. You rapped on the door and the driver opened it to let you on.

Taishō-machi. To the left was Zhao'an Market, Zhao'an Hamlet. The people of Zhao'an, Zhangzhou, made a living fishing—

Mitsuhashi-machi. The gunite exterior of the Renaissance-style bank was filthy. It had taken the place of a small community park with lush, fragrant grass and pretty flowers. The vibrant greenery had been an essential sight when you looked out at the street scene from three of your favorite coffee shops (CAT, Roundtable, Dream Café), all of which were now gone.

Miyamae-chō. That southern Min–style, red brick restaurant—strange, what had been there before? . . . Whatever happened to the Taiwan Cement Building, for which you had little emotion and few memories, but whose existence had been so familiar? . . . Foreign workers and Filipina maids congregated outside St. Christopher's Church.

Maruyama-machi. The bus traveled over the Keelung River on the Meiji Bridge that was to said to imitate either the Niju Bridge at the Imperial Residence or the Uji Bridge—in the twelfth year of the Taishō era, while visiting the Taiwan Shrine, the Crown Prince had praised the Meiji Bridge with the words, "Pretty scene, unending green field, flights of egrets, lovely sight"—A gust of fetid wind; *they looked for the spots he had noticed, but they lost their way and could no longer find the route.*

If not for the fire caused by a Japanese fighter plane shot down toward the end of the war, the ruined Taiwan Shrine would have been a lot like the Yasaka Shrine, which you visited often. In Governor-General Nogi's time, the Imperial Council decided, on advisement, to build the shrine in Taipei, Taiwan's control center. Tainan and Keelung had both been considered. The reason for the final decision was: if the ancient city of Taipei was to be considered the site of the imperial residence, then the Keelung River would be the equivalent of the Kamo-gawa and Jiantan Hill would be Higashi-yama, making the geographical location of the Taipei Basin a simulacrum of Kyoto.

You did not know which route the bus would take, the Qili Coast and Xialaobie in the foothills, or Dadu Road after a left turn at Wang Family Temple.

As if drunk, the driver kept passing other vehicles and laying on his horn, something that hadn't changed in decades; that, it seemed, was the sole job requirement for this company. You watched him as he pocketed fares. In urging passengers to board quickly, he helpfully waved off their attempts to put money into the fare box, offering to do it for them so they could quickly find a seat. He'd toss the coins noisily into the box, keeping the bills curled up and hidden in the palm of his hand. Then when he came to a red light, he'd touch his nose and scratch himself before wedging the money inside his sock. In your youth, you'd have exposed him, even at the risk of being beaten up. But now you simply looked outside at the Guandu Plain, which had been bought up by conglomerates of self-employed farmers. People who stole a fish hook were punished, while people who stole from the country became high officials; when the thieves came, you welcomed the thieves, and when the thieves left, you welcomed the officials, the so-called loyal subjects of the Great Qing.

You were hoping that the bus would take the Dadu Route, for the guidebook said that the hundred-year-old nightshade trees on the western line of the Sansen-dō had all been transplanted to Dadu Road.

The bus raced past the entrance to Dadu Road without turning; alongside the broad field were enormous signs advertising large showrooms for Toyota, Subaru, and Chrysler, just like small-town America.

The bus flew past the Guandu Temple Pass, a place you hadn't visited for a very long time.

The bus driver pocketed three passengers' fares; numerous thieves in broad daylight. You were puzzled by sights along the hundred-year-old highway, which itself resembled a redistricted area in a new town or city. Could the eucalyptus trees along the highway also have been transplanted to Dadu Road? The Tamsui MTR Line's cement wall blocked out the mangroves and the river. Whether it was an official from the central or a local government, from the ruling party or the opposition, everyone vied to see who loved this island more. It was indeed no easy feat to love this island *that* much.

The bus traveled at a maddening speed; the closer it got to your destination, the harder it was to recognize the route. Although you were seized by shock and doubts, it never occurred to you to ask for help from Mister Driver, who was too busy pocketing bus fares. You were like a real foreigner, certain that others would not understand your question.

In your flurried and flustered state, your gaze fell upon some Chinese hibiscus outside the window—there beyond the screw pine grove and the Chinese hibiscus was the ocean—so you decided to get off at the next stop.

It turned out to be Youchekou, where, in 1939, the Japanese Shrine was completed.

You started walking back alongside the short bend in the river, where you girls had enjoyed watching people fish, watching the tides rise and ebb, watching the mist rise and fall in the Guanyin Mountains, gazing at the stars, watching fishing boats enter and leave port, and feeling the urge to go out to sea with them. Occasionally, when one of A's male friends had some money from a tutoring job or had been paid by a magazine for photos, he invited the two of you to Banyan Gardens, where you ordered a bottle of beer and a plate of stir-fried little shellfish, and talked about the national shame of the nearby Dutch garrison, called the Red Hair building, until you choked on your own words.

The price of coffee in Banyan Gardens had spiked. After silently calculating the exchange rate, you realized it was more expensive than in any other country (except for the Blue Mountain coffee in the Imperial Hotel, designed by Frank Lloyd Wright), but you needed to sit a while to put your colonial map in order.

It was so cold outside that you were the only person sitting beneath the tall banyan tree. The wooden floor at your feet was raised above the river, like the Kamo-gawa cooling bed in the summer.

The scene before you, the spot where the river meets the ocean, was the same as that you had seen at the age of sixteen. How could it compare with what had been seen by the sixteen-year-old young man in 1939? You were curious about that sixteen-year-old young man's feelings, as someone who had witnessed the daily construction and eventual completion of the shrine, and about his feelings when he saw, while leaving high school each day, senior Japanese officials entering and leaving the golf course. Maybe he felt that great men should all be like that. Otherwise, many years later, when he became the head of state, how would he manage to ignore criticism and find his own enjoyment there?

Walking along the riverbank, you believed that the sixteen-year-old Iwasato Masao had also enjoyed after-school strolls here. The houses with tiled roofs covered by Chinese hibiscus had been official property and concessions during the Qing dynasty, then became administrative offices and official dormitories once the Japanese took over. Again, because great men should all be like that.

To your surprise, you actually found the lane directly opposite Lane 11. With a quickening heartbeat, you started up the stairs, but were blocked by an iron gate. Afraid that your memory might be faulty, you returned to Zhong-zheng Road and walked up the alley by Fuyou Temple, made a left at Chongjian Street, crossed someone's front yard, and arrived at a small path midway up the hill, where you saw the red brick building below. But again you were blocked, this time by a gray wall. Had it possibly been designated a historical site and moved away from you? The coptis tree was still there, and under it sat a sixteen-year-old white skeleton gazing out to sea, which did not surprise you at all.

You were forced to follow the little path that stuck in your memory toward Qingshui yan, Clear Water Cliff. The noonday sun shone down on the river, the glare so bright you had to look away. "The ambience of Nagasaki, the scenery of Kagoshima," is how the Japanese described the ancient city before you, which must have been during Iwasato Masao's youth.

This was the first time you saw no incense smoke rising from the burner; the Clear Water Patriarch Temple was undergoing a renovation. The scaffold blocked the front view, with old workers straddling the roof ridge. You felt sorry for the temple, now imprisoned, for the broad, open view from its yard in days past was now obstructed by ugly apartment buildings on either side, allowing only a glimpse of rippling water through a narrow opening. You had already decided not to visit the area around Mackay Hospital, Zhengli Street, and Dingpu, fearful of getting lost and not knowing how to get back.

Ducking under the scaffold, you entered the temple of the silent, black-faced patriarch, flanked by the masters of the Xiao family and Western Qin. You prayed to him and drew a fortune-telling lot. It was number 46, a good draw on your first try. "The appearance of things has not changed," it read. "The mountains and rivers are the same now as they were in ancient times. If you desire to know what is on your mind, flowing water will bring good news."

How could he be so sanguine?

You headed down the stairs. There were few visitors at the ferry landing. Pretending to be a tourist and mingling with them, you did not know where to go now. Maybe take the ferry over to Baliben, on the far side. Schools of flying fish the size and brightness of gold coins broke the surface of the river and sailed into the air, a sight you desperately missed. In the end, you decided to take another ferry and go upstream, like the ancestors, the Spaniards, and the Dutch, to Dadaocheng. The guidebook informed you that your tour would be complete once you visited Dadaocheng.

As you kept an eye out for the arrival of the ferry, you felt like Koxinga of 300 years before, who climbed a tower to look west to the Pescadores Islands and wondered, "Has the grain barge arrived yet?"

The barge you were waiting for was called Mahāsattva, the great bodhisattva, but it would not take you across. Worried that you might be considering suicide, since you had been pacing the landing too long, the seasoned owner of a Taiwanese sausage stand, who let buyers win sausage in a game of roulette, struck up a conversation. You told him you were waiting for the Mahāsattva Ferry, only to be told that business was so bad it had stopped running quite some time ago.

Didn't someone say he would never be a buddha until hell was empty?

Left with no alternative, you returned to the market by Fuyou Temple to wait for the bus. Now that the morning market was over, the swept-up fish blood and scales baked in the sun, emitting a scent of wronged ghosts. You imagined that the more than 200-year-old Fuyou Temple across the street, crowded with the roiling, noisy fish ghosts, would ignore you. . . . For a brief moment, you could just about recapture the sensual feeling of being sixteen. The sun poured down like hot water, and you, overdressed, were drenched in sweat; but you waited, with all your heart and mind, for something impervious to all poisons.

*A land with no master; an island with no chance encounter.

You opted for an express bus, expecting it to take Dadu Road, for you were determined to see the old nightshade trees that had sheltered you girls all those nights when you were sixteen and seventeen and had never once laughed after listening to all the silly things you said to them. If those old trees were still there, then many other things would still be around. It did not matter whether or not you saw them, such as A, such as the Old Moriyoshi Tofu shop by Seiryō-ji, such as the white oaks imprinted on the heart of Thoreau before his death.

The bus passed Dadu Road, driven by yet another drunk driver similarly focused on pocketing bus fares. Given that there were no bus stops or stoplights on Dadu Road, at that speed, if the bus had had wings it would have soon been airborne. You sped along, spotting old trees that looked like injured veterans, the ends of their amputated limbs wrapped in straw, as if bandaged. The guidebook said they were transplanted in the third year of the Heisei era, but why did they show no signs of putting down roots and sticking around? Except for a very few that had small clusters of green leaves, most had turned into specimens and models, like the skeleton under the coptis tree by Red Tower.

Upon discovering that you had witnessed his thefts, the driver slammed on the brakes over and over, maybe to eliminate you by flinging you out of your front seat and knocking you unconscious—on warm April days when the sun was out, snowy white moneses appeared at east-facing corners of the ancient city; eleucine crept up on roadsides. In May, before the rainy season, the lemony yellow oenothera would bloom in profusion; the Chinese fern would open up in dark cool cracks in walls and fences, whether someone was there to appreciate them or not. The month of June saw the purple spiked loosestrife, while American radix flowers could be seen all over vacant lots, and yellow chrysanthemums like ragweed covered hillsides along roads in Osaka. Mounting the stage in July were the calystegias, which were in fact impomoea, which could be easily seen on the sandy beach with pandanas and Chinese hibiscuses—the driver failed to knock you out, and you stumbled off the bus at Nissin-chō near Taihei-chō.

You ended up leaving the colonial map on the bus. The bus was long gone. After a brief inventory, you discovered you were also missing the hat that made you look very much like a foreigner, which was no big deal, since it was actually an out-of-season DAKS fisherman's hat bought at the Takeda-shi in Nishiki-shi.

The streets all had the appearance of municipal redevelopment, except for the bridge in the distance that arched brightly into the sky. It must have been the Taipei Bridge over the Tamsui River. You walked along, following the landmark map in your head, to Dihua Street, where you had shopped for all kinds of things for the three major holidays of the year.

The red brick Western-style building on Ganzhou Street had been leveled, in spite of its having housed the Planning Committee for Recovering the Mainland, and a rehab center for opium addicts during the Japanese occupation. So you were forced to enter from Lane 49, one side of which was taken up by food stalls packed with diners who looked up from their four-herb soup or oyster pancakes to stare at you. The looks in their eyes were of indifference mixed with curiosity, sort of like yours when you sized up girls clad in Chanel suits at Doutor. But you were not holding a map and your clothes were rather ordinary, so why were they "shocked to see the fisherman?" Mustering the courage, you fled past them, like double-time on a parade ground, toward Cisheng Temple, where, again, many eyes looked up at you from the stalls lining its wide and open courtyard. So you had to pretend to be interested in the temple, but, god, you hated the idea of going in, because it was so unimaginably ugly. A huge yellow acrylic sign with red lettering gave the temple the appearance of a trade shop, yet you felt sorry for its life of misfortune: over the past hundred years, it had first escaped to Eiraku-chō from the armed fighting in Mengjia, and then been moved here after city replanning. The dedication gave the date as DRAGON BOAT FESTIVAL OF THE SIXTH YEAR OF THE TONGZHI REIGN on stone pillars encircled by iron bars as if for fear they would be stolen.

You retreated to Taihei-chō, to the Dadaocheng Record Store, now closed, likely turned into a residence for cats or ghosts. The First Theater had become the ten-story Da'an Bank (cities are bases for banks and prostitution, strewn with weedlike skyscrapers, Frank Lloyd Wright said). You backtracked to North Street, where yellow rays of the afternoon sun slanted into shops whose owners sat like mannequins; the goods they were selling, too, were imitations—farming implements, leavened rice buns, lanterns, spirit money, vegetable seeds—making them look a lot like museums of sorts. Someone was brushing a big old British sheepdog, a live one, in front of the Tiger Mark Instrument Rental Shop. No. 321 was in total ruin, completely absorbed by demonic kidney ferns and ficus. The section of Lane 342 beyond the arched walkway was completely deserted, the walls, like the one at No. 358, covered with slogans cursing the new mayor: WE'LL LET THE PLACE FALL APART BEFORE FALLING IN LINE FOR PRESERVATION.

Returning to familiar Central Avenue, you tried your best not to be distracted by goods under the walkway eaves (except for buying half a catty of dried scallions and jelly figs in Kamo-gawa Shop—Oh no, has even Guo Yimei, next door, been moved to Dadu Road?). Concentrating on appreciating the baroque or modernist design on the front of each shop, you tried to transform the street scene into the painting *Picture of Disaster Relief on South Street* done by Guo Xuehu sixty-odd years ago. You found the main branch of the Ganyuan Herbal Medicine Shop in the painting, and it turned out to be the Ganyuan Shop where you had made frequent purchases of ginseng roots and bitter-peeled tangerines. Images of ginseng were carved around the ox-eye window openings on the third floor; blooming wayfaring plants, ferns, and tree saplings grew out of cracks in the wall. Xinjiyi, at No. 88, across the street, had Corinthian columns with acanthas leaves on the second floor, but its resplendent baroque flavor was not enough to keep its owners around; the new owner was the vibrant sparrow banyan spreading out from the cracks in the walls.

Similarly embracing your impression of the turn-of-the-century painting *Small Food Vendors in Eiraku Market* by Tateishi Tetsuomi, you walked toward Minato-machi from the alley across from the Xiahai Temple of the City God, but since the sacred ground of the 2/28 Incident was now occupied by Black Beauty Restaurant, you could not pay your respects.

You walked past what had once been called Liuguan Street, imagining how the feet of the spoiled sons of Lin Benyuan of Banqiao never touched the ground, since they were installed in sedan chairs whenever they left their house. At the corner of Guide Street, Inagakei Tōbei from Hyōgo County had once run People's Home and the Inari-kō Charity School to give the poor, colonized children a free education. The place was now the location of the Co-op Bank (city, bank, prostitution). You continued on through the forest, and where it ended at a source of water, there was an empty warehouselike building. In the 1920s, the Culture Association led by Lin Xiantang and Jiang Weishui held forums here every Saturday. Now tic-tac-toe games had been drawn in chalk on the gray cement walls by children, one of whom, impatient with his opponent, had written, "The Zhuang family has a tagalong." The ground under the walkway eaves had been trampled cold and smooth by the children's bare feet.

Feeling a powerful urge to go barefoot, you walked by the onetime residence of Li Linqiu, following the aroma of tea. The structure that managed to rise to the same height as the ugly apartment building next door was the baroque-style mansion of tea tycoon Chen Tianlai, a must-see place for Japanese aristocrats visiting Taiwan, who referred to it as "a typical Taiwanese residence." From the second-floor balcony it had been easy to watch the sunset and the forest of ships' masts on the Tamsui River. But now you'd have to level the apartment buildings across the way and demolish the River Expressway and levees before you could appreciate why Chen Tianlai had lavished so much money on his precious house. The aging Governor-General had a pair of ancient eyes. Chen Shoushan, his most prosperous descendant, had retired. Could he have been as sanguine as the black-faced patriarch, who said, "The appearance of things has not changed; the mountains and rivers are the same now as they were in ancient times"?

When you walked out of Jian-chang/Qian-qiu/Gui-de Street, on one side was the River Expressway, where dump trucks and the Tonglian buses raced noisily along. Not far from where you stood was a kindergarten that had been the residence of Gu Xianrong. If you turned around and followed Minsheng West Road, you would arrive at Bolero Coffee Shop and Jiangshan Pavilion. In your grandfather's album of black-and-white photos was a group photo of his class, a couple of dozen men in Japanese yukata. In one of the lower corners was written: "Taken at Jiangshan Pavilion on such-and-such date in such-and-such year of the Showa reign." At first glance, you couldn't be sure, but you had the distinct impression that Jiangshan Pavilion was a pleasure house, and you were embarrassed that someone as stern as your grandfather would have frequented a pleasure house and, like everyone else in the photo, not have been able to hide the smile on his face, looking as if all great men should be like that.

Jiangshan pavilion was run by Wu Jiangshan from Jinjiang County in Quanzhou. The Four-tiered Ryōtei, built in the sixth year of the Taishō era, with the same materials as those used for the Taiwan Governor-General's Office and Museum, was now the locale of the Jiangshan Shrimp Fishing Farm.

During the Taiyuan Reign of the Jin Dynasty a fisherman of Wuling once rowed upstream, unmindful of the distance he had gone, when he suddenly came to a grove of peach trees in bloom . . . the wild flowers grew beneath them, and fallen petals covered the ground—it made a great impression on the fisherman. He went on for a way. . . .

But where would you be when you walked past the small sluice gate after risking your life to cross Huanhe Road (the dump trucks, as usual, showed no sign of slowing down or braking when they came to a red light)?

There was a small opening in the mountain, and it seemed as though light was coming through it. The fisherman left his boat and entered the cave, which at first was extremely narrow, barely admitting his body; after a few dozen steps it suddenly opened out onto a broad and level plain . . . it turned out to be the Dadaocheng Pier for the Mahāsattva Ferry. You were hoping to use the toilet in the tiny pier office, but you didn't see even the shadow of a dog, let alone a person. So you headed toward the riverbank.

This riverbank had no *rich fields and pretty ponds.* No *mulberry, bamboo, and other trees grew there,* no *criss-cross paths skirting the fields,* no *sounds of cocks crowing and dogs barking,* but where were you? The moon obscured the ferry landing while the tower and balconies were lost in the fog. The slanting sun shone down on the rippling surface of the river, so blindingly bright you could not keep your eyes open, so you stayed clear of the river and walked toward a spot where there were mulberry and bamboo, afraid you'd see a corpse floating on the river.

The spot where there were mulberry and bamboo was actually taken up by Chinese hibiscuses and banyan trees, under which were a basketball court on the east side and a skating rink on the west; they hadn't decided what to do with the place. Alongside the basketball court was a small temple covered in white tiles commonly used for public toilets. Not knowing which deity or ghost was installed inside, you kept a respectful distance from both. Even though there was indeed a public toilet on the other side of the wall by the temple, or so the sign said, you stayed away, uninterested in the possibility of rescuing a victim of an immoral act, whatever that might be: an old man raping a young girl or sodomizing a little boy, a middle-aged woman seducing a young man, or what have you. So you walked toward the place in the distance where *men and women were coming and going about their work in the fields. The clothes they wore were like those of ordinary people. Old men and boys were carefree and happy.* Actually, most of them were sitting under the tree on rickety rattan chairs either they or someone else had discarded. They were waving fans, making tea, picking teeth, digging between toes, and listening to plays whose characters you did not know, while caterpillars slithered down along tiny threads from the Chinese hibiscuses overhead. That was the drawback of Chinese hibiscuses, caterpillars and spiders often hung from them at various heights, so no wonder they gave the impression they were filthy.

When they caught sight of the fisherman, even though they didn't ask you where you came from, you wondered how they could tell you were a foreigner, as you reflected that you'd lost your colonial map and had no red letter tattooed on your face. Many years ago, you'd taken your then young daughter to the site of Da'an Park before the old structures were demolished and the residents relocated, with the intention of telling her you'd grown up in this neighborhood. You'd barely entered the village when pairs of eyes the same age as your father's came at you, showing surprise and fear, and they asked you where you came from. You didn't think you looked all that different from other young village women, children in hand, and had no idea how a single glance could have marked you an outsider. You told them the truth. It turned out that there had been a massive protest against the demolition and relocation, and that the villagers had thought you were a reporter or a rubbernecker. After clearing things up, they began to complain to you, but *as he was about to go away, the people said, "There's no need to mention our existence to outsiders."*

But you and the men and women under the tree spoke different languages, so, afraid they'd be able to tell who you were, you shambled off. The bare, unpaved ground had probably just been submerged under water that had spilled over the riverbank, and you sank a couple of inches. The slightly odorous, potent, marshlike ground was covered by tiny ball-like crab droppings. As expected, you heard the men and women behind say something, but you ignored them, preferring to head toward the sunny basketball court where a few youngsters were having a pick-up game, not caring if she *was invited to go to their house, where* she would be *served wine while they killed* someone *for a feast.* You weren't surprised. The blindingly bright sun's rays were saturated in moisture. Wasn't there a movie scene where a group of people who are neither vicious nor benign join forces and kill an intruder, or a stray dog, one afternoon out of sheer boredom? Then they yawned and continued waving fans, making tea, picking teeth, digging between toes, and listening to plays whose characters you didn't know, while caterpillars slithered down along tiny threads overhead.

Their ancestors had fled the disorders of Qin times and, having taken refuge here with wives and children and neighbors, had never ventured out again; consequently they had lost all contact with the outside world. They asked what the present ruling dynasty was, for they had never heard of the Han, let alone the Wei and the Jin. . . .

A helicopter hovered in the air, probably searching for a corpse floating in the river; an old man on a motor scooter that belched dark smoke came toward you, an old woman seated behind him, then passed by, probably on their way to identify the body after being notified of the drowning; a pack of wild dogs was now under the Chinese hibiscuses, all looking up at you, neither barking nor wagging their tails, and that included a puppy that, normally not on its guard, was looking at you coldly; the high-pitched sounds of a funeral song came to you softly from the far side of the river; someone was burning leaves and grass, giving off a smell that had hung in the air ever since humans had learned to use fire; the young basketball players had vanished, leaving an orange ball bouncing on the cement all by itself; near the overpass, the gray wall that kept getting taller, like a prison wall, was clean and unmarked, no graffiti, nothing!

What is this place? . . . You began to wail.

. . .

A shimmering ocean, a beautiful island, the essential site of our sage kings and wise elders' destiny.

December 1996

NOTES

ix Chaoyang Liao, "Catastrophe and hope: two literary examples from Taiwan," *Inter-Asia Cultural Studies* 3, no. 1
(2002): 64. This essay, while a bit heavy going in its theo-
retical formulation, is likely the most rewarding study of
the novella in English.

1 San Mao (1943–91), a writer best known for her travel essays on the Sahara.

3 Zhang Guixing (b. 1956), a novelist born in Indonesia but
educated in Taiwan.

14 Pai Hsien-yung (b. 1938), considered a master stylist, wrote of
the melancholy of Taiwan's dispossessed mainland refugees.

20 Should be "fifteenth-century."

25 KTV (Karaoke TV), private karaoke rooms that were popular in Taiwan.

28 Chiang Kai-shek's grandson, Jiang Xiaowu.

35 This line is inspired by 1 Corinthians 4 and Hebrews 11 of
the New Testament, in which faith overcomes adversity.

46 Paris 1842.

46 Karl Marx. All citations are from the online translation (www.marxists.org/archive/marx/works/1844/manu-scripts/preface.htm).

65 Adam Smith, *An Inquiry into the Nature and Causes of the Wealth of Nations, Book One* (1776).

65 Jean Baptiste Say, *Traité d'économie politique* (1803).

74 Li Yuancu.

75 Hao Bocun.

89 Apparently to France, since she is referred to later as his "little French girlfriend."

95 Diane Ackerman, *A Natural History of the Senses* (1990), 14.

101 Ackerman, 61.

104 Ackerman, 60.

104 Longquan, the city in the previous line, was the name of a famous sword (Dragon Wellspring) in ancient times. The lines of verse come from a Jin dynasty (third to fifth centuries) "Music Bureau" poem, "Dulu pian."

113 1857.

114 From a poem by Cui Hao of the Tang.

117 Southeast Asia, as opposed to East Asia, as known in the West.

125 The Daoguang Emperor, 1821–51.

131 1972.

135 This and all subsequent citations of Kawabata Yosanari's novel *Koto* are from J. Martin Holman's 1987 English translation, *The Old Capital*.

141 Last line not in the English translation.

143 From *A Comprehensive History of Taiwan* (*Taiwan tongshi*).

143 The Kangxi Emperor, 1662–1723.

143 Shen Baozhen, the last emperor's tutor, promoted making the island a province.

143 The Qing official who signed the island away to the Japanese.

151 Takeshi Kaneshiro is a movie star born in Taipei to a Japanese father and a Taiwanese mother. He stars in Chinese-language feature films.

155 Qiong Yao (b. 1938), an author of popular romances.

174 Named after the founder of the Republic of China, Sun Zhongshan (Sun Yat-sen).

174 From Tao Yuanming, "The Peach Blossom Spring," English translation in John Minford and Joseph. S. M. Lau, eds., *Classical Chinese Literature: An Anthology of Translations, Volume I: From Antiquity to the Tang Dynasty* (New York: Columbia University Press, 2000). Excerpts here and below are taken from pp. 515–517.

179 One of the new political parties, such as the New Party, which had short life spans.

183 Authors, respectively, of *The Tale of Genji* and *The Pillow Book of Sei Shonagon*.

183 A Quanzhou, Fujian deity.

189 There is conflicting evidence regarding the construction and location of these no longer extant statues.

189 Memorializing the February 28, 1947 incident that led to the imposition of martial law.

192 Anti-KMT dissidents.

194 Promoted by then President Lee Teng-hui.

206 Former ROC President Lee Teng-hui's Japanese name.

209 1932, Heisei being the reign title of the current Japanese emperor, Akihito. The transplanting was carried out by the mayor of Taipei.

211 1867.